DON'T YOU KNOW
I LOVE YOU

DON'T YOU KNOW I LOVE YOU

— A NOVEL —

LAURA BOGART

DZANC
BOOKS

5220 Dexter Ann Arbor Rd.
Ann Arbor, MI 48103
www.dzancbooks.org

First Edition: March 2020
Cover design by Matthew Revert
Interior design by Michelle Dotter
ISBN: 978-1-950539-13-0

This is a work of fiction. Characters and names appearing in this work are a product of the author's imagination, and any similarity to real persons, living or dead, is coincidental and not intended by the author.

Printed in the United States of America

10   9   8   7   6   5   4   3   2   1

For my mother

CHAPTER ONE

WHEN ANGELINA FELT HER BONE snap, she thought of home. She was driving down Sixteenth Street, that narrow road bridging Silver Spring and Washington, D.C., when the Infiniti SUV rocketed past a stop sign and smashed into the passenger side of her Honda Accord.

Angelina's left hand shattered against the wheel: ring and pinkie fingers, bent at ninety-degree angles. Her wrist was a sausage casing, as thick and purpled as the ones her father used to jab with a fork while they sizzled in oil. Whenever she remembered him, her mouth filled with the coppery sharpness of blood. This time, she'd bitten her tongue.

Angelina had never been in an accident before. She thought it'd be louder. Her mind was like the air around a tuning fork. The starts of thoughts—*what the fuck just happened; who the fuck just hit her; where the fuck was her insurance card*—were sucked into the ripple and dispersed. Her right hand still held the CD she'd planned to pop in. The passenger window cracked like a spiderweb; moonlight winked in the glass strewn over Angelina's knuckles.

Gingerly, trying to keep her wrist straight, she raised the heel of her hand off the wheel. Her purse spilled on the passenger floor; her graphite pencils were safe in their pouch, but her wallet sprawled open and her phone mocked her, half hidden under the seat.

Angelina looked into the rearview mirror, instinctively checking for any damage to her face. At the moment of impact, her temple knocked against the door, but there was no bruising. Normally, her skin was fair; now, she was a bloodless shade of pale. When she was in a mood to be kind to herself, she'd say that her features had the sleepy sharpness of a Modigliani woman: heavy-lidded and heavy-lipped, a long nose that tilted slightly to the left. At least it wasn't her father's "Eye-talian" nose; hers was too small and straight.

The passenger door had been crushed inward like a beer can stomped on a curb. If anyone had been riding with her, they'd be dead.

Scorched rubber choked the loamy smell out of the air. She had wrecked near a temple, alongside the little garden adjacent to the synagogue. Whenever she drove by in daylight, she saw children crouched down with their mothers, digging.

"Are you okay?"

The girl in the Infiniti hadn't bothered to open her door. She'd rolled her window down—not even halfway, just a quarter. Angelina glanced at the Infiniti's crumpled bumper; its headlights burned through the cracked glass like tea lights in a jack-o-lantern. Then she looked back up at the girl's face: a smear of blue eyes and lunar-pale skin, heavy curls from-the-box red.

Her car had been knocked out of alignment. Angelina nudged her shoulder against the door and popped it open.

"You ran the stop sign!" Angelina shouted.

The girl didn't say anything back.

"I said you ran the stop sign!"

The passing cars moved fast enough to rattle her Accord. Angelina's pulse beat a tattoo inside her skull; she couldn't hear the shouts and the footfalls approaching. She stared at the girl in the Infiniti, who looked back only once—her face inscrutable, save a slight widening of her eyes—before lowering her forehead to the wheel.

"It's broken."

A man's voice came from her bad side. Before she even saw him, she felt his fingers on her forearm; they pulled the pain out of her wrist as if sucking venom from a snakebite and consolidated it into five even points. Angelina expected him to say he was a doctor, or that he'd been a medic in the war. Or even that help was on the way. All he said was, "It's broken."

She looked into his milky blue eyes and spoke in a voice that startled her: "Please, don't let go."

Sirens howled, and the old man released his grip. He was gone, replaced by a petite woman in a taffy-pink hoodie and matching lipstick. The woman had the heart-shaped face and exquisitely overripe features of a silent film starlet. She talked so fast, so loud that Angelina couldn't understand her until she squinted toward her lips. "Hit you," the woman mouthed, over and over until Angelina finally heard, "I saw her." Angelina turned away, toward the windshield; the passenger side had splintered, but the driver's side was whole.

"You got anything to write on?"

Angelina nodded toward the backseat. There was always a sketchbook and a trash bag filled with wire and strips of old T-shirts; also a few dozen coffee cups, and the receipts that Angelina had thrown out of her purse. She planted her left boot on the pavement. She couldn't help but notice the woman's green flip-flops. There was only a half-inch of dirty rubber between her pedicured feet and the broken glass.

"Oh no, honey, no," the woman said. "You need to sit back and let them help you."

She flattened her manicured hand against Angelina's chest. Angelina couldn't recall the last time she'd been touched with such sudden intimacy. She'd never really had a girlfriend or friends who felt familiar enough for an unprompted hug or stroke of the arm. Angelina clasped her right hand around the woman's wrist; she took deep, shuddering breaths against the woman's palm. The woman smelled of coconut lotion and hairspray, and Angelina wanted to ball that sticky sweetness into something she could hold in her mouth. The woman cooed over her: she was going to be okay, thank God she was wearing a seatbelt, thank God she hadn't hit her head. Angelina asked the woman for her name. The woman just said "It's okay" again before gently pulling her wrist loose and going for Angelina's sketchbook.

"You've got a lot of naked people in here," the woman said, thumbing toward a blank page. Her expression was bemused. "You're a good drawer."

"Thank you," Angelina said. "It was my major." She didn't know why she mentioned that, knew the woman probably hadn't heard her, and probably didn't care—but her teeth chattered, and the dry clacking sound, the staccato of molar on molar, made her feel sick. Better to talk, for once in her life. Wasn't that what all her teachers said? What her mother always said? *You're always so quiet.*

As the woman wrote everything down, she narrated exactly what she'd seen: "She didn't even stop and look both ways like you're supposed to—she was texting, that's against the law you know—she just went ahead like there wasn't no sign." Angelina kept nodding and saying, "Okay," because as soon as the woman stopped talking, she'd become acutely aware of how hungry and cold she was. Her left wrist was an anvil struck by an unrelenting hammer.

"You take that girl to court, you call me," the woman said, putting the book on Angelina's lap.

The cop cars came before the ambulance. The first cruiser spooned Angelina's Accord; the second blocked off the Infiniti. There were two cops, a younger, stockier guy and a taller guy who might've been a bit older—he had a hitch in his step, as if his left hip was haunted by the kind of ache coaxed out by a flush of humidity or a sudden chill. The kind of ache that she'd hold, now, in her wrist. Angelina watched the taller cop walk toward her, then realize that he'd left the driver's side open and rush back to shut it. The stockier cop leaned into the Infiniti's window.

"I have a witness," she told her officer. He had the kind of burnt umber hair that might've been a louder, more carroty red in his youth. He was clearly middle-aged; still, he had freckles, tiny smatterings and the large ones that would invite a mother or a lover to make a game of tracing constellations between his cheeks.

"I have her name in here."

The book slid out of her hand and hit the pavement. She hinged forward to pick it up because if she could pick it up, she was still strong and capable. The officer beat her to it. He chuckled mildly as he looked down at her sketchbook. She'd let some pixieish vixen from her "Theories of Line" class Sharpie "This Machine Kills Fascists" across the top.

"Can we call anyone to meet you at the hospital?" he asked. "Maybe Mom and Dad?"

"I'm twenty-one years old," she said.

"You're never too old to call Mom and Dad," the cop replied. He tried to make it sound jokey, as if it were cute, somehow, that she was trying to be independent.

Her phone was filled with numbers she should've deleted: girls who were never going to text her back and an international array of takeout places. The Indian woman always said her phone number as if it was her name.

At 11 p.m. on a weeknight, her mother's voice would be a tiny rabbit caught in a snare. She'd yell out "Jack." Wordless mumbling would crowd the line like a storm cloud thickening in the sky. A decision would be rendered: they'd ask where they could find her, or they'd tell her she was on her own. If her father got on, she might as well hang up. He'd only remind her that she'd wanted it this way. An insurance card and forwarding her mail—that's all she'd asked for when she'd walked out.

The first thing her father would ask, if he talked to the cop, would be whether it was her fault. She couldn't have that—not when it really *wasn't* her fault.

Him and Her: that's how she'd always stored them. Never as Mom and Dad, and certainly never as Home.

In the hospital, her whole arm quaked as she tried to keep her broken wrist upright. The woman behind the ER desk told her to elevate it above her heart. When Angelina asked her if she was a nurse—she wore scrubs and scowled authoritatively down at a clipboard—she snapped no, she was the intake clerk, "but you can't work here without learning a thing or two." A break, at least, got Angelina into a private exam room: She didn't have to clench in the pain, or hold a taut focus on keeping her hand above her heart as children coughed around her or the man with an ice pack at his temple moaned a series of low, indecipherable curses.

The room was small enough that she could decipher each of the various faces on the tatty pain scale poster tacked up opposite the exam table. Old-school smiley faces—or at least one and two were old-school smiley faces. Three, four, and five were in escalating calibrations of annoyance, smiles dropped, eyes narrowing. Six, seven, and eight veered right into agony, with squiggles of mouths and x's for eyes. Nine and ten reminded her, in their own loopy way, of Munch's *The Scream*, with their circle mouths howling a silent agony. When she was a kid, *The Scream* was her favorite painting; she supposed she could say that was before she really knew anything about art, or that she was just another suburban punkling who saw the postcard at a Greetings and Readings and thought liking it above the Monet or Degas made her smarter. But really, she was drawn to its wildness, the way it made her own inner ache feel profound.

Angelina exhaled in slow, stuttering breaths as she lowered her forearm to rest on the pillow of her chest. Her mother used to call them her *bosoms*; only she'd say it like "buzz-ooms" and exaggerate the "ooms" just to tease her: "Oh honey, be grateful you have them." Over the years, Angelina had frowned at herself in the mirror and thought, "*Ugh*, milkmaid;" smiled at herself in the mirror and thought, "*Sexy* milkmaid." She'd counted down the minutes until their end-of-day release from underwire and Lycra; she'd savored their soft sway, the way the weight of them balanced her wide, spoon-shaped hips and fleshy thighs. They made her body feel warm and sturdy, never more so than now: They were a nest plucked from straw and tufts of loose cotton, perfect for the wounded bird of her wrist.

Angelina's pulse quickened. Her father was in the hallway, yelling for her. With each boom of her heart, Angelina exhaled. *This is not my fault.*

"*Cara* fuckin' *mia.*"

He opened the door so hard the room shook. Her father had the bow-legged lumber of a bear. When she was a little girl, he'd endeavored to teach her a few words of Italian. She'd sit on his lap and study the shapes his mouth made: *il pad-ri-no, mad-re, gra-zie, cu-or-e.* She wanted him to teach her all her favorite animals: *le-on-e, lu-po,* and *or-so.* The bear: the wild black whorls of his chest hair, the wiry black hair on his head, the scratchy black of his moustache and goatee. She'd playfully slap her palm against his chest and yell, *or-so, or-so, or-so* until he'd start snuffling and growling. He'd toss his head back and roar, and the sound rolled clear through his body into hers like a wave that caught her from below, pushing her up so high, so fast that her head rang and her stomach flipped with a delicious dizziness that made her feel terrifyingly small yet also infinite. She'd lean forward to nip and growl at his face; he'd tease her by lolling his neck side to side, always just out of reach. Then, finally, he'd give in. He'd level his face with hers and let her roar.

He hadn't changed much since then, at least physically: a high forehead and a blunt jaw, deep-set cinder eyes and a lean blade of a mouth. Grey hair threaded through his moustache, bristled at his temples. His wrinkles and sun-leathered patches of skin didn't make him look older, only sharper, like some totem carved from unyielding stone.

They caught each other eye to eye. His gaze said, *Goddamn, girl, I bet that hurts.* Hers said, *Don't make this harder than it has to be. Please.*

Her mother slid past her father as if edging through subway doors about to close. Mother moved on the balls of her feet, which always made her seem small, even though she had a tall, sporty Katharine Hepburn kind of body—only a bit curvier, more languid. Her face, though, belonged to one of the heroines in those screwball comedies that she watched on the classic movie network. Narrow chin, a bud of a nose; sloe eyes, now glassy with tears; cheekbones like fluted edges smoothed along a pale clay bowl. She gasped out her greatest hits: "Oh honey," and "Oh no, no, no, oh God."

Her hands were long-fingered, deft as they gathered the hair that fell over Angelina's face and tucked it behind her ears. *I didn't wash my hair this morning*, Angelina thought. *And I won't be able to for a while.* When she hadn't washed it for a few days, her hair went from a deep blue-black to oil-slick and limp like a wilted stem. Mother's hair was white-blonde and spun-candy soft. A small pink curler bobbed above her shoulder. Absently, Angelina reached up to free it. Mother slipped her fingers through Angelina's; her wedding ring was a crescent of cold in the purring warmth of her palm.

The officer came in, shook her father's hand and started to talk to him about the damage to the car. Angelina couldn't hear much over Mother, but she did catch the word "totaled."

"How bad does it hurt?" Mother asked.

"You mean, am I the braindead shiny happy smiley face?" Angelina said, nodding toward the poster. "Or am I the screaming, 'pay attention to me or I'll burn this place down' face?"

"See, that's good," Mother said. "You're funny. You're still funny. They say that's a good sign."

The nurse who pushed a wheelchair into the room had one of those plump, boxy bodies with curiously small feet. If Angelina were observing her in a grocery store, arching up on her toes to reach the packaged oatmeal, she'd have taken a moment, pulled out her sketchbook in the dry goods aisle, and sketched her, sweet and loose, in a variation of that pose—only with her back arched in triumph, both arms extended over her head, and her other leg kicked out mid can-can. That kind of happy musing was over now. After the nurse locked the wheels, she offered Angelina her arm to steady herself as she scooted off the exam table.

"Is she going to need surgery?" her mother asked.

"That's only if the bone comes out of the skin," her father replied. He looked at Mother with a pitying kind of tenderness.

"The x-ray helps us to determine that," the nurse said. Angelina detected a fine crackle of bemusement in her tone, like her father had no iota how wrong he was. Then she thought, *Oh God, he could be wrong. I could need surgery.*

Waves of pain oscillated through her body as she lowered herself into the wheelchair. She hadn't been sure how to hold her wrist and it dinged the arm of the chair. Her mother cried out, "Oh, oh, oh," and her father yelled, "Goddamn it." The officer winced.

The hallway was like the inside of a fluorescent tube: endlessly long and numbingly bright. Her mother walked at the nurse's side, asking if the x-ray would hurt, if the technician could "accidentally, of course, make the break worse." Her father and the officer followed behind. She could hear her father asking what the accident scene had looked like, but she couldn't catch the officer's response over the warble of someone being paged for a code blue. As they rounded the corner toward the x-ray room, Angelina saw the girl who'd hit her strapped to a gurney outside of the heavy gray door.

The girl's red hair spilled over the pillow, listless. On her back, she seemed tall; her body occupied that vague space between muscle and chunk. Her feet were bare, with the knobby toes painted a coral blue. A hot tongue lashed through Angelina's insides. She felt scraped raw and singed with anger. Then the girl looked at Angelina. As her eyes moved from her bruised, bent wrist up to her face, they got wider and glossier; she closed them to let the tears fall.

Her father must've noticed her noticing the girl. He put his hand on her right shoulder. He didn't press down; just the weight of his palm was enough to get her attention. He mouthed the word, "Her?" Angelina stared at the girl's un-bruised, un-blemished face. Not a scratch on her. Angelina nodded.

The x-ray room was a dingier version of the medical bay on the spaceship in *Aliens*. The machine looked like a metal fang poised above a long table covered in crinkly white paper. An arsenal of levers rose from the console against the back wall. She expected the licorice-whip body of the Xenomorph queen to come gnashing out of the machinery.

"Mom, I need you to step outside," the nurse said.

Mother clucked her tongue, as if the gross absurdity of the sound would reverse the decision.

Once she left, a slim man with hairless hands but five days' worth of stubble entered the room. He told Angelina that it was okay to scream if she had to, "I'm used to it." As he flattened her wrist against the tabletop and turned it in stop-motion increments, everything inside Angelina—her blood and breath, the tiny orbits of her cells—halted. She'd known sharp pain, and she'd known dull pain, but she'd never met them together. This pain was an iron fist in a velvet glove, a muffled knock that broke the door off its hinges.

Angelina was startled by the sound of crying. She touched her face with her right hand: dry. Her father's voice filled the hallway: "You *look* when you turn!" Then a female voice, likely belonging to some nurse or aide, yelled out, "Sir, sir!" Angelina knew what came next: her mother abandoning her post outside of the x-ray room, racing toward the voices, her father backing off just before security was called. Wasn't this what she'd asked for, in calling them? The tall bear, *l'orso*, reared back on his hind legs, throat opened in a savage bellow that might, for the first time in a long time, find the object of its wrath in someone else.

CHAPTER TWO

CORVIN'S COFFEE DIDN'T LAY HER off outright; they cut her hours until she was as good as gone. One four-hour shift a week barely covered the cost of a metro fare to and from the hospital, where an orthopedist in their community clinic did her follow-up x-ray and told her she could bank on eight weeks in the cast. He offered to write her a prescription for an in-class note-taker or a week off work. "There's got to be *some* perks to this, right?"

"Not for us poors," Angelina said. "But thank you for trying a joke. I feel moderately more human now."

He did, at least, give her a script for a refill of Oxycodone. Those little white pills were moth wings that ferried her to sleep every night. Without them, she'd be up past sunrise, cutting and pasting her resume into online applications (after she'd already uploaded said resume) and watching YouTube clips of medical procedures: fibroid removals and congested sinus cavities pushed open with balloons inflated at the ends of catheters. The videos had an oddly cathartic allure—terrible violence done to the body to do the body good. She Googled "ways to remove a cast yourself" in between applying for mindless printmaking gigs she was overqualified for and secretarial jobs she knew she'd eventually get fired from, a kindly but exasperated boss explaining that she "just wasn't a people person."

There was no hope for unemployment since, technically, she still had a job. By the end of her first week, she decided to apply for food stamps. Armed with copies of her birth certificate, pay stubs, and tax records, she arrived at the social services office with its dingy industrial exterior, hard rows of soiled brick and smeared metal beams. The offices inside were a honeycomb of acid-washed walls and fluorescent lights, chairs with battered, stained (with God knows what) fabric, and tiny desks strewn with manila files. The air smelled of coffee breath and lemon Lysol wipes.

The woman who reviewed her materials asked how she'd broken her wrist. She should've said she'd tripped on a curb or fallen while walking a friend's dog. Hindsight came quickly, in the amount of time it took her to walk to the bathroom, close herself in a stall, and punch her cast against the door as hard as she could. (Why waste her good hand when she craved a sound loud enough to swallow her anger.) "So, you'll be getting some kind of settlement, then?" the woman asked, folding her manicured hands over Angelina's paperwork.

Once those French-tipped fingers steepled over her W-9s, Angelina knew she was done for. Without public assistance or a job, she had no choice but to move back into her parents' house.

She got back to her apartment as sunset flushed the sky. As she drove past, she saw a gaggle of teenagers, maybe five of them, standing in a circle near the dumpster. She rode slowly, rolled her window down as one of the taller boys chucked something into the center of the circle. From the back, he might've been playing dice or even jacks (if people actually played jacks), but Angelina knew better: His movements were crisp and assured in the way that cruelty without consequence can be. The smiles of the boys around him confirmed it before she heard the dog cry.

She slammed the rental car into park. As she stepped out of the car, she slid the handles of her cloth grocery bag over her cast. The bag was filled with cheap eats, cans of soup and beans and two glass bottles of ginger beer. It dangled loosely off her left arm, so she could grab anything she might need to throw or to break off into a weapon. Anything hard and heavy. Anything that could draw blood.

Her stomach flattened into an iron sheet. She slammed her cast down on the trunk of the car, screamed, "Stop it!" with a force that pulped her throat. The boys turned to her with their faces ranging from *what the fuck* to *who is this bitch* to *oh shit*. They were so young. Their features were blunt and unformed, waiting for the fingers of some unseen sculptor to pinch and smooth them sharper and more distinct. Some of the boys still had rocks in their hands. Angelina looked at the dog, crouched on her belly, her eyes dazed with pain.

"Big men, picking on an innocent animal."

The dog sensed her cue. She was a big dog, a black and tan Shepherd mix with sweet dark eyes and a graying muzzle. As she heaved herself up, her hip cracked. Angelina didn't look down at her; she needed to keep her eyes on the tallest boy, the ringleader. The dog leaned against Angelina's legs, pressed her tender hip into the heat of Angelina's bare skin.

"Why don't you throw your little dick pebbles at someone who can fight back?"

The tall boy smirked, and she felt the press of male bodies surrounding her. A cold flicker of fear cut through her, but that flicker was swallowed by the hiss that sizzled at the back of her skull, made her body thrum. The tallest boy called her a fat cunt under his breath. She pulled a bottle of ginger beer from the bag and broke it against the trunk of her car.

This sound startled the boys into backing up. Except for the tall boy, he had to hang tough. He might have been an older teen, all Adam's apple and blond fuzzy scruff patching his chin. She watched his eyes move from the jagged edges of the bottle to the liquid dripping down the trunk, and then back to the bottle. His nostrils flared slightly. Still, his posture, the general feel of his body, seemed defensive and confused—as if he knew only how to stand firm. He may have been strong, but even if he was, he didn't know how to throw a punch. People who knew carried themselves differently.

The ginger beer dripped and fizzed down the trunk, along Angelina's leg and the dog's fur. The dog licked Angelina's calf in furtive slurps. The compounded stickiness made her want to rocket through her skin. She stepped closer to the tall boy, holding the jagged edge flush with his throat. His eyes flashed *crazy bitch*—his fear was a tiny flame leaping on a wick. She remembered the late-night movies she'd mainlined on her laptop until her father's footfalls passed her door: *Switchblade Sisters, Foxy Brown, Kill Bill,* volumes one and two. How the knife-wielding women moved so taut and controlled—and yet with a sense of play, a dance in how they bobbed on the balls of their feet, dipped their shoulders low, ready to surge forward.

"Go away. Now. Or I'm going to spit in your throat after I open it."

The tall boy spat on the ground, inches from her feet. She did not look down. Did not look anywhere except his eyes. He shook his head, muttered, "Fuck this, fuck *you*," and turned to leave with his buddies. Long after they'd become specks against the setting sun, Angelina stood there holding the bottle, wishing she could feel their most tender parts crushed by her kick, her fist. That wish was a long snake body that whipped out and pulled back, again and again. Then the dog wagged her tail; it thumped softly along the backs of Angelina's knees, fanning a private breeze. The dog's gift to her, sweet and cool.

"That seems a bit premature, don't you think," Angelina said. "For all you know, doggo, I'm no better than those assholes."

Still, she walked toward her apartment, making soft kisses of "come here." The dog followed her, lingered on her doorstep while she got the pitcher of water, the steel wool, and the roll of paper towels so she could clean off the car. The dog sat on the grassy patch of front yard, leaning on her sore haunch and panting. Angelina wet the paper towels before setting the pitcher in front of the dog, who drank in deep, unreserved gulps. When the dog lifted her head, Angelina marveled at the wolfish elegance of her profile. Her fur was mostly white, with a broad brown patch along her back. She had wide-set hips, a narrow waist, and a wide, densely furry chest; if she'd been human, hers would've been an Old Hollywood body. Her eyes were warm and dark, lined with fine black fur that gave her otherwise graying face the feeling of a femininity that was both brassy and sad.

"You should have a movie star name," Angelina said. "Like Marilyn, but not Marilyn because that also doubles as a PTA chairwoman name."

The dog snuffled about the concrete. Her snout lingered over the stickily drying patches of ginger beer before she decided all that good taste had already been spent. When she looked up at Angelina, her mouth opened in a loose, mild pant that seemed bemused and expectant, as if she were truly waiting on her name.

"I don't think you're a Mia or a Gia—those are little girl names. How about Francesca? No, that sounds like a nun. Sophia? Valentina?"

The dog responded with low, affable grumbles, sounds of contemplation. When Angelina suggested Valentina, the dog flattened her ears and belched.

"Okay, I'm going to take that as a sign. Valentina it is."

Angelina didn't even try to tell herself that she'd take the dog to a shelter or contact some rescue group. She knew, as soon as Valentina showed that she was already quite at home—submitting to a bath her first evening, patiently enduring Angelina's one-handed fumbling with the baby shampoo and the shower nozzle, only losing patience as Angelina attempted to pat her dry with a towel and then shaking herself with a rapturous vigor; lifting herself onto Angelina's full-sized bed and settling contently along the left side, the side where nobody ever slept, so unblemished by other bodies that Angelina had never even washed the pillow cover; and gently pawing at Angelina when she had to go outside—that she would keep her. Valentina had been somebody's pet once. Just as she'd been somebody's daughter.

Valentina's paws moved in her sleep, the toes twitching in rhythmic precision as if pressing on piano keys. Every day, Angelina learned something new about the dog. That she didn't howl in unison with police sirens, but she did flick her ears back in annoyance at those goofy viral videos of other dogs yipping to Christmas carols or "Single Ladies." That she grumbled along affably, a kind of running commentary, Angelina imagined, about the smell of the rice and beans

Angelina prepared for lunch and dinner, or a gentle admonition to relax and take a break after yet another job search engine crashed just before she could save her search history. That, when she was deeply at ease, she slept on her back with her paws splayed limply in the air. When Angelina read that dogs who were "comfortable and secure in their environments" slept that way, her chest and neck flooded with warmth—and that warmth, for once, was pride.

Angelina spoke in a low, can't-wake-the-baby tone when she talked to Hunter, the insurance rep who was assigned to her "accident." He didn't sound much older than she was; his voice was bright and muscular with confidence. If she'd known him in school, he'd have been one of those nice-guy jocks who'd make a valiant attempt at working on a group project—nodding, somewhat reverently, as she pulled together the outline by herself, and making a great show of carrying the materials into the classroom. He might even ask her where she was from, and when she said "Baltimore," ask her, in complete earnestness, if it was, "you know, like *The Wire*."

On this call, Hunter asked for her "occupation" and she said, "Trying to grow a lotus in the mud." The Oxy had left her system and her cells were steel traps. The only thing soothing her was the gentle heft of Valentina's warm body pressed against hers.

"I studied art and I don't even think I can paint now, not really," she said.

"So, we'll put your occupation as artist," he said.

His voice ebbed on in the heavy warble. She scanned the walls of her apartment, where she'd hung pieces from her senior thesis show: models from life drawing class in stiff-necked Victorian get-ups, assuming stiff-necked Victorian poses as they sat atop packing crates on empty stages with a banner reading SIDESHOW hanging behind them. She'd given the women antlers and the men fox tails. She'd tacked them up (hopefully? arrogantly?) beside framed prints of Kahlo's *Self-Portrait with Thorn Necklace*, *The Two Fridas*, and *Self-Portrait with Cropped Hair*. But there was no dialogue between the works, only a series of hiccups and belches.

"So, I talked to your dad just because his name is on the policy. He told me that he'll be handling the financial negotiations for the settlement. Said he wants to give you the time to recover. I assume that's okay?"

The real question sheathed in his tone, in that ever-so-tentative but definitely palpable lilting of his voice on "okay," was, "So, is he always like this?" And *always like this* was talking over whoever he was talking to, filling the air with words and the space between words with heat, that humid sky-rumbling sense that he was only waiting for you to stop talking so he could start again—because whatever he had to say mattered. You were standing in air that made you feel slightly nauseous with its thickness, waiting for the constant booming. Or maybe there was no question in Hunter's tone; maybe she was just imagining it. Maybe her father had come across like any other Italian father of a certain kind of old school: a bit overbearing, sure, a bit loud, but fundamentally loving.

Of course her father wanted to handle the negotiations. Of course he wanted to be Michael Corleone as the door swung shut (or maybe Vito Corleone moving over the rooftops with a leonine assuredness after he shoots Don Fanucci). Of course she was nothing in her own pain.

"I mean, I'll have input as well. After all, this happened to *me*."

She tried to put some conviction in her voice, to hold it as long as she could, like taking a swallow of ice water and letting it linger as she stepped outside into a scorcher. Her father would be calling. Any moment now, which turned out to be almost immediately after she'd hung up with Hunter. Valentina put her head on Angelina's lap and whimpered in sympathy.

"We have to talk strategy," he said. "This could be good for you, bad as it is. I told the guy you were in too much pain to work. We need a settlement that could cover a month or two of lost wages—at least. I even said you might have to move back home over it."

"I don't think it'll take that long," she said. *It can't take that long.*

"If you take anything now, you're low-balling yourself. You don't know what kind of medical bills you're going to have."

"I thought insurance covered most of it."

He sighed. His *I'm trying to be patient with you* sigh. "Most of it. Not all of it. And you need to think about quality-of-life expenses."

"My quality of life—"

"I know you want to live on your own. Believe it or not, I respect that. I do. But we need to string them along, let them think we could honest to God take them to court. No half measures, honey. I'm going to get you all that I can."

At the dinner table, he'd always joked that he made a blood sport out of negotiation. Down payments were "lower than a snake doing the limbo" and yearly bonuses were "higher than my Uncle Tony on payday." He'd laughed and mussed her hair when she said she didn't understand. "Good," he'd said. "And I wish I could kick the world's ass, so you'd never have to."

Mother reached over and playfully swatted him on the cheek. "Hey, buster, please say *butt*. You're not the one who gets calls from the principal."

He'd looked at Mother in a way that Angelina wouldn't understand until she'd started watching old movies where an actor's eyes had to evoke everything the censors didn't allow. "Well, then, you tell him he can sit on it and spin." Then they'd started laughing so hard that she had to take a drink of lemonade and he had to set down his fork. Angelina hadn't even cared that she didn't share in their secret, she'd just loved sitting in their glow.

"I'm not some kid anymore," she said.

"You're my kid. Always."

Angelina felt a vise close around her left hand, and she heard the voice of the slim young doctor who'd bound her wrist, ring, and pinkie fingers in padding and plaster: "It'll be snug." Her middle finger, at least, was free.

"You know what I mean."

"If this wasn't a possibly life-changing amount of money, I wouldn't be so involved. But it really is. And you need someone who can be a Grade A asshole to wrangle it for you."

"I can be a Grade A asshole."

"You've never dealt with attorneys and insurance people. You can be stubborn and sarcastic—or you can be set."

"Do you really want me to come back?"

"It'd probably make your mother happy."

He always told her that he could beat her at her own game (her game was, apparently, being stubborn and sarcastic). The only one he couldn't beat was the only one he never knew about: the quiet game. She'd invented it as a child. She'd start herself with a score of one hundred and deduct twenty-five points each time she could hear her own footsteps.

There was something exhilarating about seeing how high she could arch on her tiptoes (admittedly, not too high; she was built like her father, brutal and squat). Days she retained her hundred points were thrilling. She'd never won anything in her life, except a best attendance trophy from the softball league that her father made her join when she was in the third grade, the one he'd tossed in the trash before they even got in the car. "Best attendance is what they give people with no talent."

She begged off their phone call by saying she had to puke. Then, suddenly, she did. The excuse came into her mind and her belly obeyed. As she bent over the toilet, she pulled her own hair back hard enough to coax tears. Valentina followed her into the bathroom, yipping and crying. The dog forced herself into the narrow space between shower and toilet to lick up Angelina's tears and the spit trailing down her chin.

The blood came roiling to Angelina's face, not from the exertion of throwing up—from pure anger. Her body had betrayed her will, chosen dumb instinct over rational fact. She was grown now. There was nothing he could do to her. Not like before. Not since that day in the kitchen. *If you put your hands on me again, I will kill you.* She'd dreamt those words before she ever said them. She still dreamt them now. She'd wake up numb to everything but the hot engine of her heart.

CHAPTER THREE

SHE FINALLY MADE THAT CALL—THE call asking to come, not home, but "back"—when she was broke. Not "guess I'll have to eat beans 'til payday" broke; not even selling clothes she'd actually miss to the thrift store so she could buy the goddamn beans broke. This was contacting the blood bank only to hear that they don't take plasma from people with broken bones (and snapping "I know" at the receptionist when he said, good-naturedly, "You should be healing, honey"). This was sell-all-the-furniture-to-pay-the-rent broke. She'd only had the cast for one week, and already she was a failure.

She used the last bits of her loan money to take Valentina to the vet clinic at the local shelter. Valentina was, mercifully, already spayed, and since Angelina had rescued her from the street, she got a steep discount—all vaccinations and registrations, a nametag and microchip, glucosamine chews for Valentina's arthritic hip, and a big bag of food for one hundred and fifty dollars.

Valentina, shaking and whimpering, flattened herself on the exam table. Her cries turned Angelina's bones into tuning forks. Angelina could only make a loose fist of her right hand and sweep her knuckles along the top of Valentina's head, a figure eight between her left ear and her right ear. This was Valentina's favorite touch, the one that had soothed her on those first nights in Angelina's apartment, when she'd wake up not remembering exactly where she was. Angelina would sleep flat on her back, on the floor; Valentina—now occupied with an object to sniff, to lick, to paw and nudge—would stop pacing. She would circle once, and then lie down on Angelina's left side, with her head on Angelina's shoulder. Her breath was soft and clammy in a sweet, dry way, like a familiar hand sweeping its gently callused palm over Angelina's face.

The vet cooed to Valentina as he inserted a thermometer into her rear. Valentina looked at Angelina as if she had the power to make this terrible thing stop. Angelina's eyes bloomed with tears. She didn't cry when her wrist and fingers had been broken or set. She did not cry when the Oxy waned and she emerged back into her drab, directionless life. But this, this did it.

"You're doing really well with her," the vet said.

"I don't know that I can keep my apartment." Angelina didn't know why she spoke so suddenly, so abruptly. Something, maybe, about the antiseptic bluntness of the exam room, and the glass jar with an enlarged, pickled Frankenstein's monster of a heart floating in formaldehyde atop the filing cabinet, next to a placard for some heartworm medicine Angelina couldn't afford.

"I'm sorry to hear that," the vet said. "We do have fosters that take on older cases, but she's very content with you."

"I want to keep her," Angelina said.

Giacomo at least likes dogs, she thought.

After that vet appointment, when she got back to the home that would not be her home soon, she texted her mother and asked if they could talk sometime tomorrow. A second later, her mother texted back: "Looking forward to it!" Angelina chucked her phone on the carpet, not against the wall, since she sure as hell couldn't afford to replace it.

Marie hadn't expected Jack to be so excited about Angelina's lone condition for coming home: that the dog came with her.

Angelina's words were tiny fists, pummeling forward without caution where they landed, as if moving harder and faster were victory enough. "No, Mom, I mean it, this dog is my responsibility now and I have to honor that." Marie's whole abdomen constricted, as if preemptively wringing her out before the fight to come—and not just the fight between Angelina and Jack, but the fight between her and Jack, where she'd introduce the subject with a strategic gentleness that made the idea appear mild and palpable yet still bright enough to catch his eye. Persuading him of something that didn't seem innately logical or practical (that was his word of choice, "practical," as in, "Honey, you know it's not practical") made her think of twisting balloon animals, carefully arranging her words and looping her ideas through each other in frenetic sequences of curlicues that eventually took the right shape (or, ultimately, the wrong one)—in this case, the shape of a dog.

But the night before Angelina's arrival, Marie sat at the dining room table, watching him pace from the front hallway to the kitchen, from the kitchen to the dining room, and then into the living room— searching for the best place to put Valentina's bed. She asked him if maybe they could go out to dinner before they went to the pet store. He rattled off an absent "Yeah, sure, you pick" before resuming his hum— *Valentina bambina*, the goofy little two-word song on his lips for two days, ever since Marie had told him Angelina needed to come home, and she had a dog, a big dog that she rescued from a group of kids, a dog she was taking responsibility for, and wasn't that what they wanted for her, especially at this stage of her life: a sense of responsibility?

She'd first broached the subject in the dining room. Before she could even read his face, she felt herself fade out of her body, move up to flutter about the overhead lamp, banging under the white-frosted glass like a moth that had just been swatted. She heard her own words to Angelina ring inside her head: *I'll try my best, but it's such a big ask.* Slowly, he'd sat back in his seat, and slowly, he'd smiled, this smile she'd seen in those few photographs of him as a little boy in a cowboy costume, pointing his plastic six-shooter at the lens.

He stood in the kitchen now, determining where Valentina Bambina's food dish and water bowl should go. Marie tried to imagine such a large, wolfish beast in her space and all she came up with was a memory of her own mother sitting on the sofa hooked to an oxygen cart, telling her how to decorate the house so Jack would like it: dark, solid colors for furniture; plain white walls; a glass tea cart in the dining room that lent the feel of quiet hominess (though it was never clean, always somehow smudged, and she only touched it to dust it).

Still, she had managed a few touches just for herself: the coral accent wall in the dining room, which he had resisted, until she reminded him that he'd promised, and even then she had to give up her lilac bedroom. The coffee and end tables in the living room had a subtle curve to their edges, reminding her of the tables one of her former housemates—a nursing student so new to town that she baked "house cookies" on Friday nights and spoke emotionally about where she was when Kurt Cobain died—brought for the living room. She called them "Japanese style," said she'd inherited them from her GI grandfather. When the girl moved into a group house full of other nurses, Marie was surprised by how much she missed the sight of her in her Minnie Mouse scrubs, singing "Come as You Are" while she mixed chocolate chips into a bowl of dough.

Normally, Jack moved through the house with a mild obliviousness, attuned only to the location of the remote and the setting of the thermostat. The last time he'd paid such attention was when he endeavored to babyproof the house—putting covers on every electrical socket and safety latches on every cabinet, and checking for catches or cracks in the floors. "Jackie, she's still in the womb," Marie would say. He rubbed Marie's back and her feet, his hands intuitively finding the stiffest, most swollen parts of her body and pushing that pain so deep inside her that she could hardly feel it. He would sit in the rocking chair with Angelina crooning silly little songs. Seeing him this way again, if only for a dog, made Marie feel that old sweet ache.

"We could go to the TGI Friday's," she said, figuring that the promise of steak might tempt him away from measuring a space for the dog bed along her accent wall.

He did not look up or give her so much as an "uh-huh." Finally, Marie said that the dog would likely sleep downstairs with Angelina, so he might as well put the dog bed against the wall opposite the sofa bed that Angelina would be using. Jack gave her a clipped little nod, told her (in his you-ate-the-last-ice-cream-bar voice) that he would meet her at the car, and they'd better hurry since the pet store closed at nine. When they arrived at the Friday's, he told their server, a tiny girl with bad skin, that they needed to be out quickly so they could get to the pet store because his daughter (*his* daughter) had rescued a dog: "She didn't go to a pound or anything, she actually *rescued* the dog from this group of asshole kids. She has a cast on her left arm, so she literally fought them off one-handed."

The server said, "You must be, like, so proud. I mean, I just feel like, we need so many more strong women in this world who are just willing to fight back against all the bullies and the jerks."

"Yes, that's my Angelina," Marie said. She took a long, prim sip of her unsweetened iced tea.

After the server left, Jack talked about how things would be different this time. Having the dog would give her a greater sense of responsibility. Now, she'd "have actual sympathy for how hard it is to be responsible for somebody." As he talked, his hands moved in elegant half-loops, curling upward and rushing down as if conducting some unseen orchestra. Every so often, his fingers would glide above Marie's plate, and she picked up her fork just so they'd sweep against hers.

Angelina parallel parked the rental car right beside her parents' driveway. Their house was on that thin line between city and country. The lawns were clipped but the pavement was cracked. The fissures made such rich, dark lines. When she was in high school, Angelina used to lay vellum and newsprint over the concrete and rub over it with charcoal to catch the textures in relief. She did this everywhere she'd ever lived. Collecting textures. Sometimes, she'd paint the pocked textures in a patch of acne, or she'd conjure a particularly jagged line for a swivel of hip or a strand of hair. Her hands moved without her; she simply hummed inside the symphony of their motion. She became the glide and pause, the scratching stroke and the smoothing erasure.

Valentina endured this first long car ride with relative calm. She didn't paw or nip at the bed sheet Angelina had stretched over the backseat; she sat up at the window, ears perked and eyes wide, watching the highway. As they approached the house, though, she began to yip and whine. The noise shocked Angelina into cutting the wheel too sharply, scraping against the curb.

"You have good instincts, girl," Angelina said.

Everything about the neighborhood pinched her with regret. When the houses were first snapped up by young GIs and their hometown brides, they must've seemed tidily cheerful in their uniformity, like a busload of kindergarteners just starting school. Aging owners and steel mill closings and new buyers who got conned by their contractors finally differentiated them, left them in various stages of battering: wind-stripped siding and mossy chimneys, front stoops beginning to detach from the sidewalk, gutters sighing low with the weight of rain.

Her parents' house stood as a lone sentinel of vigorous up-keep: the white paneling power-washed pristine and the red shutters replaced at least biannually, the eternally clean gutters and the roof her father inspected for rot after every snowstorm. He got discounts on the materials, but he did the work himself on almost everything, except his pride and joy, the driveway.

That had been his project throughout her senior year of high school: pricing and interviewing contractors, reviewing the materials, and standing outside to "supervise" the workers while her mother distracted their actual boss with coffee and chat. He told the crew, often and loudly, that he was a foreman himself; he knew how these jobs went. Of course, they were much larger jobs. His firm was one of the largest in the state, "branching out all across the Mid-Atlantic" that was, really, a satellite office in Delaware. The noise kept Angelina from sleeping in on the few Saturdays when she didn't have to work the early shift at Starbucks. Still, she was grateful for anything that took her father's attentions.

That concrete was still unblemished, just like the day it'd been laid down. Part of her wanted Valentina to squat over it, to let loose a torrent of righteous piss. But Valentina merely sniffed it, saved her prolonged, after-the-car-ride peeing for the lawn. Still, even this gesture, insignificant as it was—*dogs pee on that lawn all the time*—made Angelina tighten and clench. *This is temporary.* As if to solidify this, she teased out the syllables inside her mind: *temp-or-ar-y. Or was it tem-por-ar-y?* Either way, it wouldn't be long.

Her father answered the door wearing sneakers and jeans, not the rubber-soled slippers and sweatpants usually reserved for weekends. Valentina approached him with her tail at half-mast, swinging slowly. He offered his hand to Valentina's damp, snuffling nose. The three of them stood on the porch for an everlasting while or a finger-snap, Angelina couldn't tell. Finally, Valentina licked his knuckles. Her tongue darted in quick little laps at first; then her tail rose up, wagged in salute, and she began to lick his palm, up his wrist, as if his skin was raw nectar.

"You must taste something good, pretty girl," he said.

Whenever Angelina's mother was trying to smooth away the debris of some "disagreement," as she called them, she described a man who crooned Sinatra as he changed diapers, who carried his five-year-old Supergirl on his shoulders when they went trick-or-treating through miles of neighborhoods because "you go a few blocks north, and they've got the good stuff. Baby Ruths for my baby girl." This man was a shadowboxer on the walls of Angelina's memory. He moved with an easy, intuitive gracefulness, but he was gone as soon as light left the room. She saw him emerge again in the mild, nimble way he rubbed between Valentina's ears, around the back of her skull, and then down her muzzle, under her throat. Valentina gave a contented little grunt to his, "So you like that, huh?"

Mother materialized beside her, stage-whispering that Father had been looking forward to Valentina's debut. She took Angelina's face in her lotioned hands; her skin smelled light and vaguely peachy. Mother was bare-mouthed, no trace of the lipstick that left trails of greasy pink or soft red over Angelina's cheeks, which, years ago, provoked her into paroxysms of girlish indignation. Angelina couldn't remember the last time her mother held her face like that, kissed her cheeks with a brightness, an eagerness, that so humbled her she forgot her joke about Fredo and Michael Corleone. All she could say, under those kisses, was a shyly mumbled "Okay."

The house burned with an antiseptic odor of lemon cleanser. Nothing much had changed since Angelina moved out: a living room furnished in tasteful neutrals, celery-green sofa and matching love seat, a recliner in royal blue next to a rectangular coffee table, and, of course, matching end table. The dining room had a lone accent wall—not in a full-bodied red, something vivid that would've betrayed a hint of the actress her mother had been, the artist strangled in suburbia. It was fucking coral. It demanded kudos for being slightly bolder than pink. Never mind that it didn't have the stones to go for scarlet.

"It's so good to have you home," Mother said. "Even if it's not forever, I'm glad to have my girl around."

Angelina looked down the narrow hallway toward the kitchen and saw a large rubber mat in purple beneath a stand holding two metal bowls. Her father said, "Come on, honey, you must be thirsty after the drive," and it took her a blink or two to realize he was still talking to Valentina. He tapped gently on the dog's back, between her shoulder blades, to prompt her to the kitchen. Angelina watched him as he took in Valentina's subtle limp, that slight hitch; he frowned softly, shook his head as if he was assessing how to remedy this pain.

"She's had that since I found her," Angelina said. "The vet said I could get these chews for it. Glucosamine, I think."

"We'll get her the chews," her father said. "I saw something on the news about arthritis in animals. They were using lasers to help this cat. I could care less about cats, but if we need to, we can look into the lasers." Valentina made a soft snuffling sound, and he laughed. "Yeah, I bet you gave some cats some Hell back in your day. Look at the size of you." He ruffled her ears and ushered her over to the water dish. Then he laughed, honest-to-God laughed, when she slopped water all over the floor.

He hadn't laughed when Angelina spilled water, and milk, and soda, on the floor. The water he'd given her a pass on, he said, because of how small she was. But with the milk and the soda, she should have known better.

Angelina set her suitcase down. Only then did her father notice the load she carried, two duffel bags and the easel tucked under her arm.

"You're going to hurt yourself again, carrying all that crap."

"It's fine," she said. "It's all I have."

Still he lifted the duffel bags off her shoulder. The relief came instantly, the sweet throb of a muscle unclenching. She raised her arm and let him take the easel. He smiled in a sweetly hesitant way, as if he felt guilty for his gratitude at having a simple, tangible task, a purpose, however momentary, however much she was in pain. She nodded at him because she'd have felt the same way. She did feel that way, a little, even though her purpose—for now, only in this instance—was to be burdened.

Her father had set up the basement bedroom with a Spartan quality that pleased her: the same old off-white walls and dust-colored sofa bed. The treadmill against the back wall had a broken hinge; the back end wouldn't lift up, so he'd draped holey old sheets over it. There was a hanging clothes rack next to an oversized oak desk, which still bore a giant computer monitor that probably hadn't worked since before Angelina was born. He'd hung some of the framed prints from her old bedroom, including the Kahlos that she'd had to leave behind, above the sofa bed, on the wall between the laundry room and her sleeping quarters.

"This lady sure had a weird thing for monkeys," he said.

Valentina paced the room, sniffing everything with great fervor. She made a study of the dog bed that was catty-corner to the sofa bed.

"Purple is your ma's favorite color. Or at least it was," her father said to the dog. "They didn't have purple at the stores we went to. But I guess dogs are colorblind, so what does it matter anyway?"

Valentina licked and nuzzled the bed, circling around once, twice, three times before laying down, then getting up again to lean against Angelina's hip.

"Yes, girl, I can see you have a bed," Angelina said.

"You should do some paintings of Valentina. She's a very smart dog. You can tell it from her eyes."

"I guess people would buy that," Angelina said.

"You say that like it's a bad thing."

What could she tell him? That she hadn't really made anything that wasn't for a grade? Still life with fruit. Still life with cow skull and roses. Figure drawings, a kaleidoscope of nudes directed by life drawing professors to turn a certain way to show their back muscles, to bend or flex so the students in a circle of easels could squint at the proportions of thighs, the appropriate length of elbows. Abstractions that weren't sparked by self or soul, but in-class challenges to "play with color and form."

Sure, she had her senior thesis show, but *everyone* had a senior thesis show. She'd shared the gallery with a girl who made large replicas of bird nests from sticks oh-so-elegantly bundled, and then painted in luxurious umber reds, coral blues, and edge-of-sunrise yellows. The interior of each nest was treated with prints of black and white photographs that had been thinly shredded and affixed to the sticks, arranged loosely in their original images. In the reddish nest, the girl, just a child in jelly sandals, sat, unsmiling, on the lap of a large man who shared her mouth and the haughtiness of her jaw. The girl and her boyfriend smiled up from a rumpled bed in the nest of blue. The girl, alone, nude, confronting the camera with her fists on her hips: the proud, solitary center of the yellow nest.

No wonder everyone who passed through the gallery stopped and ah'ed and oh my'd over the nests—they were innovations, especially compared to Angelina's Kahlo derivatives. In her artist's statement, the girl wrote that this conception came to her in a dream, which did make Angelina cluck her tongue in rhythm with *well, la dee da* in her head; still, dream or not, it was evidence of a vision. Angelina was, her professors said, a master technician, but they said it in ways that suggested getting all the angles right and making the proportions sing gave a piece its bones, but no heart.

She could start painting Valentina, then use that portfolio to snag commissions, portraits of other people's pets, their kids, and their spouses. It would be so easy and would only get easier; it would become that groove in the carpet from bedroom to bathroom and back again, trod every day while half asleep.

"I guess money is never a bad thing," she said.

"No guessing to it," he said. He called the dog to him, smoothed his hands around her muzzle and back around her ears. Valentina's tail wagged robustly, starting a breeze. "You could be a helicopter dog," he said. "Take off and fly all over the city. That'd be fun. You gotta take a crap when you're over Madison Avenue? Bombs away, baby."

"Helicopter propellers go around in circles, not side to side."

Her father didn't look at her; he massaged Valentina's neck, moving her head side to side, as if leading her in a gentle dance. His fingers circling her soft, white-furred throat.

"Helicopter dog, helicopter dog," he half-sang, half-laughed. "Dropping deuces on douches."

Angelina said she'd been convinced he'd be pissed that she'd taken in a stray, especially considering that she had no money. His smile was a bright piece of pottery, shattered and reassembled; carefully so, but the cracks still showed.

"I like that she's so big. Got a big bark, too, I'll bet. Very protective."

Angelina made a noncommittal little clucking sound, continued to unpack. Her shirts swayed like hanged men on the portable clothes rack. She started to refold her skirts when he piped up again. "There's a storage bin from Ikea. It looks like a bookshelf, but it's got these baskets where you can put your stuff. It's compact, so you could probably take it with you wherever you go."

"I don't see it," she said. She shook her right hand, but the cramps wouldn't loosen.

"Like I said, I haven't set it up yet."

A gray skirt slipped out of her fingers to the floor. She wanted to lie down and ice both of her wrists until the numbness beat through her body like a wing. Oblivion, however slight, was preferable to the dull stubbed-toe stinging she felt now. She thought of the crickets she'd killed in her old apartment, and how they sang the loudest right before that final blow with *History of Renaissance Art, Volume One.*

Her father picked the skirt up and folded it. She hadn't ever considered him handling, let alone folding, women's clothing.

"Still hurts a lot, I guess?"

"It starts throbbing and I feel like it'll never stop."

"I worry about arthritis," he said. "That's what pisses me off, because it isn't just that it'll bother you now. You'll suffer from it down the road."

Her father stopped in front of her lone Munch, *The Scream,* which he'd hung on the wall opposite the bathroom (Angelina had to admit that was a pretty great placement for it). He looked up at the thumbprint whorl of a figure, head in hands, mouth open in an everlasting howl. "I feel you, buddy," he said. "I get it."

Jack could tell Angelina had the common sense to be grateful for the chance to come home. Especially given how vicious she'd been before she left. Now, there was no eye-rolling, just a polite "No thank you, but I appreciate it" for Marie's offer to carve her meat for her. She pinched the fork between her free left fingers and sawed as best she could with the steak knife in her right hand. Something about the awkwardness and the pointlessness of the gesture made his throat tighten. It reminded him of his next-door neighbor growing up, a retarded girl whose mother would doll her up in party dresses.

"Well, look at this," he said. "Everyone at the dinner table. It's Thanksgiving in June."

Marie at least indulged him with a "That's funny." Even if she didn't laugh. Angelina fussed over Valentina, who stuck her snout over the edge of the table, her nostrils fluting at the scent of roast. Snapping the fingers of her right hand, Angelina tried to lead Valentina away and put her in a sit. The dog was too smart for that. She knew what was up. And she must've been hungry. Angelina said she'd bathed and brushed the dog, clipped all the mats out of her fur, and afterward, Valentina had been "not quite SPCA commercial skinny, but pretty damn close."

Jack could see where the dog had already put on a bit of weight; her ribs were in silhouette against her skin, not too pronounced. Growing up, he had known a spaghetti and ground chuck diet—and never enough of it. His stomach felt carbonated, always rippling and fizzing. Sometimes he ate pork sausage—only if the butcher was feeling either sweet on, or sorry for, his mother, a seamstress who dressed like a widow. Buns and long braids. Dark dresses that fell to the middles of her calves. She was tall and straight. She moved with a kind of cold, queenly dignity he could glimpse, every so often, in his daughter.

Some little prick from the neighborhood, Paulie Mack—who thought he was hot shit because his father was a foreman—said something about Amish pussy smelling like manure when Jack was in earshot. Jack used Paulie Mack's head to make a drum roll echo on the concrete. That was the day he was discovered, so to speak, by the guys who worked out of Mangiano's Deli. Guys who wore suit jackets that cost more than the rent.

"Here baby," he said. He cut a hunk of roast and held it up, kissing and calling, "Valentina bambina." Angelina yelled "*Dad*," started to complain that the roast was too rich for the dog's stomach. Valentina came to him, though. He simply raised the meat over her head, and she dropped into a sit. He lowered his hand to let her take the food. She was so quick and gentle.

"She must have been somebody's pet once," he said. "Anyone who could have abandoned her has ice water in his veins."

Angelina called Valentina back over to her, snapping her fingers so that Valentina would lie at her feet.

"I don't know, maybe she wasn't abandoned," Angelina said. "Maybe she escaped."

When he was almost thirty, an age that seemed like ruin to him when he was as young as she was now, his boss's boss's boss was put away.

If he weren't living through it, he'd have found it funny. He'd always regarded his particular line of work as recession-proof. He was told there was a job, a straight job, waiting for him in Baltimore. His thank-you for years of good work.

Fucking Baltimore. The only thing it had to recommend it was that it was Marie's hometown. When he'd come to Marie's apartment, drunker than he'd meant to be, drunk enough to tell her that he'd been transferred, she'd looked at him for an everlasting twenty minutes and finally said, "I haven't been back home in a while."

He drove down the turnpike, biting his lip until he tasted blood. Marie made him pull over at a rest stop to get ice. He didn't even get out. He sat with his hands draped over the wheel, watching cars streak by in the direction that had once led home. Marie came back with a soda cup full of ice and some napkins. She pressed the thin paper against his mouth in tiny gestures made precious by their hesitancy, as if this, and not the way she'd looked up at him, with her hair in her eyes and his cock in her mouth, made her truly his wife.

As he merged onto the Baltimore-Washington Parkway, she told him about how her father used to take her out for "Daddy and Marie dates" to a restaurant that housed the world's largest ball of string, just so they see how much that ball of string had grown. Marie said he should take her to that restaurant once they "got settled."

He couldn't remember, now, if he'd ever taken her there, although he supposed he'd remember seeing the world's largest ball of string. He'd spent so much time taking Marie to restaurants that were fussy—not fancy, or classy—because the only places in Baltimore that were safe were for the tourists or the gays.

Those first few months, the whole first year in Baltimore, really, he was moving through molasses. Every time he asked his boss for extra hours or to sit in on a developers' meeting, every time he mowed the lawn or painted a shingle, every time he'd gone with Marie to the Babies-R-Us and nodded when she said that this stroller or that crib had been well reviewed in some maternity magazine, he blinked through a darkness that should've been breakable but wouldn't yield to chisel or fist.

"How long do you think it's going to take?" Angelina asked. "For the settlement, I mean."

"Hard to say. Geico has the police report, and their girl got a reckless driving ticket."

Geico had already made an offer. A lousy one. One that would cover the cost of the car, which, he had to admit, was a real fucking junker. They threw in $3K for "pain and suffering." He'd rejected it outright. He wanted to give his daughter enough to start a real life.

"She better damn sight get a ton of points," Angelina said.

"That we can agree on," he said.

Angelina set her knife down and picked up the toucan-shaped saltshaker, part of a porcelain set Marie had since before he first met her: a parrot pepper shaker and a rhino creamer, a sugar jar lion and a teapot hippo. As she cradled the toucan in her palm, the slightest smile twitched across her lips. When she was a child, she'd begged for "the animals" to grace the table on her birthdays, or days when she got A's on her tests. Sometimes, Marie would just surprise her with them. He'd walk in the front door and hear Marie in the dining room: "It's a just because day!"

Marie had always been the kind of woman he could show off with pride: soft eyes that could seem haunted and happy in the same look. He hadn't known that he loved her until he first saw her old tenth-floor walk-up. She might have shared it with three other girls, but the décor was all Marie: ceramic cats and fan-shaped music boxes where geishas danced on tiny wires. She had a closet full of kimonos and a Charlie Brown Christmas tree. Something about the unapologetic uselessness of her pretty, precious things cracked him open, slid its long fingers around his heart.

He'd felt that way after Angelina was born, though she'd never believe it.

Once Angelina asked to be excused, followed by the jangling of Valentina's tag down the stairs, Marie sighed, "I just wish she had a proper room."

Their house was supposed to look like all the others in the court. Marie called it a cul-de-sac; he called a spade a spade). Jack had chatted with the builders, finagled a higher ceiling in the dining room and a few extra square feet in both bedrooms. He'd made damn sure the basement was insulated with polystyrene foam boards *and* that it was carpeted. The apartment he'd shared with Ma had concrete floors, the kind of cold that bit through socks.

"The basement is a proper room," he said.

"The washer and dryer are there," Marie said.

"Well, yes," he said, smiling. "You put washers and dryers in rooms."

Marie laughed his favorite laugh: a soft half-hmm, half-ha that promised other, deeper-throated things.

"And you walked barefoot in the blizzard, uphill both ways."

"Don't forget the broken glass," he said. "From when all those dogsleds loaded with Chianti wrecked."

"How long will it take, do you think, to get the settlement?" Marie picked up the toucan, circled her thumb over the beak.

"Even when I get it, honey, it'll still take a while for that amount to clear her bank account." He knew what answer she wanted. One that would let her imagine she'd have all the time she needed to knit things up with Angie.

"She was asking, well, she just wondered whether maybe it might not be a bad idea to consult with a lawyer. Not to hire them or anything, necessarily, but to just see if they had any advice."

"She thinks I can't take care of this?"

Angelina had been so much easier before she reached the double digits. When she was eight, nine years old, she used to ask him questions about everything—and they weren't little kid questions, either; they were actually smart. What made a car engine work? Why was the moon so far away? If a dog got lost in the woods, would the foxes and wolves just take him in, since they were all related?

"That isn't how she meant it," Marie said. She picked up the toucan, rolled it between her fingers. "I shouldn't have mentioned anything. She's tired. She thought she was helping."

"She needs to worry less about this favor I'm doing for her and more about how she can help herself."

"I'm just saying, she can't snap her fingers and boom, there's a job.

She's broke and she's scared. Maybe you don't remember what that feels like, but I do."

He brushed her fingers off the toucan. He'd been at the desk for a while, but his hands were always a little stiff from power-sawing and swinging hammers—and all the things he'd done before he power-sawed and swung hammers.

The feel of the toucan in his palm, warm and smooth, was a small pleasure. But Marie looked at him like he might snap its beak between his fingers. Like he'd do it on purpose.

He let his boss at the construction firm, Eleanor Crostini, bitch about the phone a few times before bringing up the idea of an assistant. Their last secretary, a Black woman named Rosemary, had retired three months ago, and they'd never gotten around to replacing her. She'd been one of those on-the-job-for-twenty-years, made-as-much-as-the-boss (because she was sort of the boss) assistants. Pumping her salary back into the firm had been a small boon.

Though the company branch they worked for was huge, the trailer they worked out of was tiny: an office, a kitchenette, and a bathroom. His desk faced Crostini's.

The engineer before her, a quiet guy named Larry Patterson, would sometimes bring Jack with him to those meetings—"Since you'll be supervising the men on the ground in implementing the plans, anyway." Patterson had the anxious uncertainty of a man who'd never played with boys his age. He'd tried to pass that uncertainty off as flexibility, even magnanimousness. Jack saw through him, and he knew it. He deferred to Jack's considerable experience.

"You ever think about getting anyone to help you? Like an assistant?" he asked Crostini.

"There's a draft of a Craig's List ad on my laptop at home, but I haven't had the time to finish it."

For all the ways she could annoy the ever-loving hell out of him, he had to admit that Crostini was good at what she did. Her specs were flawless. She didn't let the architects or executive engineers ride her. He supposed she'd be a pretty good business mentor for Angelina. Angelina might even like her, enough that working a job with a future looked a little more attractive.

"My kid came home yesterday, but she's been looking for a job for a while. And she has a dog now. I told you how she saved the dog from those psycho kids, right?"

"You did," she said. "She sounds like a brave girl."

"I suppose she'd need to be to work here, huh?"

Crostini gave one of those laughs that turned into sighs. "We could start her out at twelve dollars an hour and see how it goes."

"I haven't even asked you yet."

"Call it intuition. And desperation."

"Fifteen," he said. "And she can start tomorrow."

"Twelve fifty," she said. "And we'd have to come up with a list of tasks for her before she comes in."

"Thirteen," he said. "And we can start her on the phones right away."

She didn't say *sure thing*, or even *fine*. She just nodded.

He'd push the insurance company for twenty thousand. They'd likely settle for fifteen. Maybe seventeen thousand. If he managed it soon enough, he'd even get to tell Angie that this could be strictly a summer job. Very part-time. Maybe she could go on to graduate school. Study something useful. Maybe nursing: he remembered some news reports about a hiring shortage of nurses. Or even social work. The one social work supervisor who'd lived on their block drove a Subaru four-door.

Of course, whenever he tried to tell Angelina this—which, hey, he wouldn't have said anything if she hadn't turned that one Thanksgiving dinner into a goddamn pageant of her announcing her major—she pretended the phone line was cutting out. "Fine," he'd say into her protests of static. "You think it's cute to be broke? You go on ahead."

He knew what his daughter thought of him. Overbearing asshole. He wanted to tell her that he didn't want her to feel like her life was something to flail against. Not that she would believe him.

CHAPTER FOUR

THE DOG WATCHED PRAYERFULLY AS Marie ate her yogurt and toast. Marie sat at the dining room table, wondering whether to give or not to give. Jack had already begun to spoil her with food. Angelina didn't like it at all. Buttered rolls, peanut butter straight from the spoon, and lunchmeat (of course, he didn't have to live with that smell, once she'd digested all she could and let the rest rip in a few terrible farts). The two of them courted that dog: Jack handfed her, speaking so sweetly to her; he told her she'd had a hard life on the streets, and goddamn it, she deserved some peanut butter. From the window, Marie would watch him walk her up the street and back before he left for work; he held the leash so gingerly, moved so easily with her, as if he'd been walking her for years and they'd bonded over the comfort of routine.

When Angelina woke, she made a big production of feeding her the "proper breakfast" of dry kibble. The showiness of her gestures— opening the kibble bag and measuring the exact right amount, and then lowering the bowl slowly to the floor—reminded Marie of how, on walks, tiny Angelina would bend down to pick flowers and hold them up in chubby fists: "Mama, for you!" Sometimes an errant purple pansy or a pale-yellow lily growing in front of a mailbox; most often a dandelion, because "they look like the sun!" Jack laughed at her, gently at first, for putting the dandelions in mason jars—"Why on earth, Marie, are you wasting a good glass on some weeds"—and then his expression would soften with pity and a kind of mild contempt, like the center of a sweet fruit beginning to rot. He started buying bouquets at the gas station on his way home from work; he'd walk into the kitchen carrying Angelina on his shoulders, the bouquet clenches in her tiny fists. "I'm bringing you real flowers," she'd say, carefully annunciating the words, as if she'd been taught to say them and wanted to say them clearly, brightly, even if she didn't entirely understand why she had to say them at all.

Marie imagined, for a moment, that the dog was looking at her with a sort of casual, bemused curiosity, her eyes brightly asking, "And who are you, exactly?"

She still had a few hours before her shift at Belle's Beauty Boutique, and about forty-five minutes or so before Angelina would wake up. Marie regarded the dog's phantom question with a sigh. "I don't know," she said. "I just don't know."

The day promised to be lovely and crisp, more spring-like than the sludge into summer. On the summer days, she usually drove to the mall early and lapped the ground floor before her shift. Sometimes she'd go even on her days off: When the faces in her Zumba Fest streaming video seemed simultaneously too young and too stale and familiar, she'd go mall walking just to see new people, to catch fresh wisps of conversation. She frankly preferred mall walking to walking outdoors, even in nice weather—nobody new, nothing fresh in this neighborhood. She couldn't remember the last time she'd walked outside. But maybe a dog would make it new. People would come up to pet a dog. They'd make small talk. Oh, how Marie missed small talk. Valentina fairly danced with excitement when Marie clipped on the leash.

The dog was strong and willful, wanting to see and smell everything. Valentina found a wonderland in the squat boxes of white houses, the chain-link fences and sidewalks the color of old eggshells. Marie didn't have the same easy rhythm walking the dog that Jack did, or even Angelina, one-handed. Valentina pulled four steps ahead, straining her collar. The dog panted and rasped, twisting and bucking her neck. The tiny heart of her nametag jangled like a tinselly laugh. Marie felt the sting of her heart and lungs working harder than they had in ages. Not in the blissful exertion of movement, but in an escalating dread: The back of her head started humming, a high and ugly droning on and on as she realized that it was too hard to hold on to the leash; she couldn't hold on to the leash; she was going to let go of the leash.

One of the neighbors, an older man in a black T-shirt that said VIETNAM POWs NEVER FORGOTTEN gave a long, low whistle that Marie realized was for Valentina. He called out, "That's a big dog for a tiny lady!"

In the time it took for Marie to smile and nod, Valentina caught sight of a rabbit. She tugged clean of her collar and bolted up the street. The old man tried to open the latch to his fence, but his swollen fingers fumbled. Marie ran after the dog; muscles that had gone long unused, certainly untested by the benign mildness of Zumba Fest, were snapped and stretched rudely awake. Her whole body felt sharp and tart, like the saltwater sting of fresh tears. Sweat lashed into her vision; the dog became a whir of fur. And then, miraculously, the dog slowed down. Her back leg stuttered; she began to limp toward the curb. Marie screamed "Valentina!" and the dog dropped flat to the pavement. She was panting hard, her sides swelling and retracting almost in staccato. Terror and exhaustion: Marie knew what she'd find in the dog's eyes.

Marie hadn't thought of herself as old and stiff. She thought she exercised. She stood on her feet all day at work. Yet her lower back slowly, persistently, announced its intention to ache, fiercely and for a long time, as she knelt beside Valentina. Their breathing was aligned, hot and ragged. The dog would not let Marie slip on the collar, even after several iterations of "That's a good girl" and "It's okay." Marie slid her fingers under Valentina's throat, gently scratching until the dog raised her head. "Silly, silly girl," Marie said. "Never fall for that trick, it's the oldest one in the book."

The mall where Marie worked was built the year Angelina was born, and it hadn't changed much since. Two floors stretched out ever-long, connected by several escalators and one elevator, bookended by a J.C. Penney's and a Sears. The tiling was gold and green, covered in the black shoe scuffs, calcified wads of gum and candy, and the streaks of soda puddles that couldn't be power-waxed away. There was a penny fountain on the bottom floor, in front of the Easy Spirit and Dairy Queen. Marie had tossed many a penny in herself, always the same wish.

Jack's company had actually built the mall, and he never let her forget it if he was home when she was leaving for a shift. "I built that place," he'd laugh. "With my own two hands." The mall had been Jack's first big project with the new company, and he'd taken such pride in his work. More than he'd expected, she thought. They were still house poor then. With every payday, every other week, they ordered a new piece of furniture—a loveseat, a sofa; tables for the kitchen, the dining room, the bedside; a box spring, and, soon enough, a crib—and Jack would devote those weeks in between to "christening the new goods." His hands so rough, but his fingers buffed smooth, his tongue deft and tireless. His was such a strong body, though not strong in that blunt, careless way that assumed strength alone was enough to impress—an intelligent strength that knew when to smother and when to release. Marie had had orgasms before Jack, but those were little flutters of the gut. He cracked caverns inside her.

It was almost perfect, would have been perfect if they'd gotten that starter apartment in the city, maybe something in Charles Village. But he'd thought the suburbs would be a natural start for their lives as a family—and, sure enough, within months of their arrival in Baltimore, she was pregnant and he was right.

She took the job at Belle's Beauty Boutique when Angelina went to college and was surprised when her four-year anniversary passed. "Seems like I've been here forever, but also only for a minute," she told the shift manager, who'd brought in cupcakes topped with tiny candle fours.

That shift manager had moved up from Atlanta so her husband could take some job at "the D.C. firm." She talked fast and wore tight clothes (which she had the body for) and wore highlights upon highlights in her already blonde hair, which gave her the bright, airy look of a dandelion. For years, Marie had always worked on that manager's shifts, even if she had to swap out with one of the other girls.

Still, Marie declined her invitations to "come up to the house for some wine and whining" or to join her for Pilates class; if she'd come home tipsy, or, worse, had to ask Jack to come pick her up—well, he wouldn't have liked that. The shift manager had moved back to Atlanta last month, and Marie ached with an old loneliness, the kind she'd felt when she first moved here. At least she knew what to do now. She eased into that loneliness like lowering a bruised body into a hot bath, settling into the hurt.

Now, she mostly talked with the customers. Though her coworkers were nice enough, they were mostly college girls; they'd smile, say hello, and ask for help with the register or whether a particular lipstick was matte or creamy. When she wasn't helping someone, she was tidying her station or restocking the hair gels. Being useful.

Above each station were posters of models' faces—a cultural rainbow of girls who still had all the same features, which were not unlike Marie's features: large eyes with a sleepy slant, a thin-bridged nose with upturned tip, and a slightly over-plump mouth—made up to look sultry in smoky-eye, cheery in coral blush and pink lipstick, or a girl-next-door in a "no makeup" look that drew attention to how polished and precise it was. Their teeth were airbrushed into pearly oblivion. When she got really bored, she'd stare at the posters and wonder where those models were now. She didn't see their faces in the copies of *Vogue* and *Elle* she browsed in the bookstores or the supermarket checkouts. They'd likely ended up just like her.

Marie talked companionably with the woman in her makeup chair about Angelina's return home. The woman clucked with sympathy and said that must be so hard: "Must seem like she just left the nest and now she's back."

"Oh, it'll just be for a little while," Marie said. "I'm just so glad I'm able to be there for her. She's in so much pain."

"Mind if I observe?"

This was Janet, a new coworker of only two months. Janet had a small face with features so raw and broad they seemed almost unformed—a bud of a face steamed open after a hot rain. If Marie were (oh God, like twenty) years younger, she and Janet would've become the kind of girlfriends who got so close so fast that they fell a bit in love with each other. Marie had reached the age of "tasteful" over "daring," the years of Capri pants and ballet flats. Janet was young enough to pull off a pink and green paisley scarf, navy-blue tube dress, and orange sandals. She could hide away in the break room to yell at soon-to-be ex-girlfriends on her cell phone and still seem passionate, not pathetic.

Marie showed Janet how to treat the girl's skin with tea tree oil. Then she swept a light brushing of powder over the girl's face, followed by a peachy blush that muted the scars while brightening the girl's eyes. Marie used a purple eyeliner pencil (which she'd toss in the girl's makeup bag, free of charge) to draw a faint half oval on the lash line.

Janet wrote for a beauty blog and was into theatrical makeup and costuming. She soaked up Marie's Manhattan stories: coming so close to being cast as the understudy for Stella Kowalski in an off-Broadway production of *Streetcar* that she'd been fitted with that signature torn slip dress; nibbling cold cream from a jar when the makeup artist turned his back to attend to one of the other girls, during a catalog shoot her agent had gotten her last-minute, because rent won out over groceries every time.

As a child, Angelina cut out her old catalog spreads—mostly evening wear and swimsuits, since she was always (according to her agent) "one of those versatile blondes who could go from aristocratic bitch to fun-loving and beachy"—and glued them on a poster board for show-and-tell. She'd even taken that poster board home and tucked it at the back of her closet, protected behind her art supplies. Marie would see it whenever she hung up the laundry—until one otherwise unremarkable day after Angelina's thirteenth birthday. Gone. Just an indent in the carpet and a black streak on the wall.

After Marie finished with her customer, she and Janet went to Starbucks. When Marie used to badmouth Baltimore to her Manhattan friends, she'd said it was "the kind of place where people are more interested in where you went to high school than what you're doing with your life now." Here she was, standing outside the Starbucks that had, when it first opened, made the cover of the little community paper tossed on their doorstep every week. When she'd read that cover, she'd felt a little flutter of actual excitement. *Someplace new.*

"So, I'm totally going to do an article on 'beauty hacks under five dollars from a former model,'" Janet said. "I want to interview you, obviously. You really give your clients confidence, and I just feel like that's what beauty should be about. Not this body-shaming shit."

"I wasn't much of a model," Marie said. "I mean, I did a few things. Nothing really special."

"But I mean, just the fact that you tried," Janet said. "That's more than most people ever do."

Janet asked for Marie's New York stories the way that Angelina, as a girl, begged for lullabies. Just as Marie would launch into "Somewhere Over the Rainbow" (the only song she ever hit perfectly on key) over and over until Angie fell asleep, she would tell Janet about driving to Manhattan in her father's brown sedan and selling the car, right on the street, to some Russian man who looked like a tattooed Santa Claus. That got her two weeks' rent for a motel room and money for headshots. She'd brought a duffel bag and a Walkman, and she listened to her father's cassettes as she walked to diners and cattle calls, his beloved Buffy Sainte-Marie, Karen Carpenter, and Nancy Sinatra. Women with voices like spun glass.

Janet's phone began to vibrate inside her purse. She looked at the screen and frowned. She'd broken up with her girlfriend of seven months, a pampered pharmacy student named Ali. Their parting was supposedly mutual—though it was a bit more mutual for Ali. Janet thrust her phone into Marie's hand. "You have to hold this so I don't hate-text her back," she said. "I'm already disgusted with myself for giving so much time and agony to someone who writes *u r* instead of *you are.*"

"My daughter always texts in full sentences," Marie said. "She uses semicolons and everything."

When Angelina was a teenager, Marie always offered to drive her to the mall, to the movies. Marie told her there was no harm in walking through the stores, in seeing who was around, maybe trying to make friends. There weren't just packs of kids; whenever Marie had stopped at the Pizza Hut in the food court to pick up their standard Friday night to-go order—one Meat and Pepper Supreme (Jack's favorite) and one mushroom, with mozzarella sticks and a side Caesar salad—she saw smaller groups of girls, or girls walking on their own, each of them wearing a tenderly hopeful expression as if tonight would be the night that something beautiful would happen.

Angelina met all her suggestions with a glass-cutting contempt: "You seriously think I go to the mall?"

So many times, Jack started up the stairs to "talk to her," until Marie coaxed him back to the couch. Angelina had forgotten that. Or maybe she was never aware of all those nights Marie spent next to a man who'd been talked out of it, but not talked down.

"She's home, isn't she?" Janet asked.

"Yes, but I worry, you know. The only people she really knows here are me and her dad, and well, we're old."

"First of all, you're not old," Janet replied. She demolished the whipped cream, unloading the mushy, milkshakey part in straw-fulls. "I'd like to slow down and meet new people. I've barely been home."

"Mr. Paulson still up to his antics?" Marie asked.

Mr. Paulson was Janet's next-door neighbor; Janet described him as "averse to his bipolar medication and basic hygiene."

"I don't even want to think about it," Janet said. "Anyway, I've been all me, me, me. How is your daughter doing?"

"Sick of me already, I suspect," Marie replied.

Angelina hadn't even been home a week and she was already a phantom, a mug of coffee dumped out in the sink. Marie would see her sketchbook on the coffee table and think maybe they'd cross paths; she'd sit in the living room for an hour, pretending to watch television. Finally, she'd have to get up and make Jack's dinner.

"She's in her twenties now; a little shame about living at home is healthy," he'd say, sloppy Joe mix staining his lips.

Marie's phone vibrated in her apron. Jack had called. Four times.

She excused herself to call him back, standing outside of the children's barbershop just a few stores down and watching a small dark-haired girl in a bouncing kiddie ride shaped like a space shuttle. The girl seemed hesitant at first, as if she was unsure that her weight could move anything forward. Then she looked intently at her chubby fists, which clutched at a fake lever that wouldn't get her anywhere.

Her lips hadn't formed around the "o" in hello before Jack started describing some job he'd gotten Angelina: part-time assistant on his latest construction site.

"I know what you're thinking, but she and I won't have to interact much. She'll mostly be working for Crostini."

"You mean that woman you don't like?"

"A job is a job, Marie."

He said her name like it was part of an order a clerk had read back to him wrong. She was smart enough not to push him, but nothing good could come of him *informing* Angelina of where she was going to work. They'd had their nastiest spats whenever he told her what her best interests were (even if he was right; *especially* if he was right).

When Marie walked back to the Starbucks, Janet asked her if everything was okay. She'd just started to tell Janet about the assistant job when she heard her daughter's voice at the front counter, asking if the manager had seen her resume yet.

"Have you been on our website? We have the applications on—"

"Yes, I have. I've applied online. And I haven't heard anything. That's why I'm here, now, to talk to an actual human being."

Angelina wore clothes that Marie bought her for assorted birthdays and Christmases: flats with a flared skirt and Oxford shirt, all black. (Marie *had* given her more than one colored shirt.) She rested her hands on the counter, and her cast came down with a hard bang. Marie imagined Angelina's hand inside the plaster: as swollen and flushed as a baby's face as she cried herself to sleep.

Janet was already up and at the counter, her hand on Angelina's shoulder.

"Do I know you?" Angelina jerked free. She stared at Janet, her eyes taut slits of rage. Janet gave a little flutter of a laugh; still, she lowered her hand to her waist and discreetly shook out her fingers, as if they'd been singed on the stove.

Marie stood up. She mustered her best easy-breezy voice, and called out, "Oh Angie, honey, hi! You should join us. Get yourself a coffee."

Angelina looked over, her face forming a quick rictus of surprise and dismay—not just dismay, but disdain, as if she were the night guard who'd caught Marie sneaking into the community pool after hours.

"We're on break for another couple of minutes," Janet said. "Come, sit." The man in line behind them nudged forward, started giving his order. Janet turned to him: "Come on, dude. Seriously."

"Yeah, I'm not done yet," Angelina said. She made a show of staring at the menu before finally drawling out an order for a large latte with whole milk. Marie watched Janet, who seemed to take this in with a kind of cautious bemusement. When Angelina fumbled, one-handed, to get her wallet out of her purse, Janet lifted her hand as if to help, and then, apparently, thought better of it. Angelina rooted through her wallet, held it upside down over the counter. Nothing tumbled out. She mumbled to herself, "Well, fuck me."

Janet blinked at the line snaking out of the door; then she turned toward Marie, her face blanched with anxiety. But Marie was already at the counter, handing the barista a five-dollar bill and telling him to put the change in the tip jar. There wouldn't be much change left, she knew that, but at least she'd slid a thin needle into the swollen balloon of the room, letting the pressure out.

"You are the best," Janet said. She put her hand on Marie's arm, her fingers folding over that nook inside the elbow. Her touch was soft yet insistent; it reminded Marie of the first drops of rain just after the sky goes gray.

Angelina was the tar-dark cloud. She picked up a chair with her good hand and set it away from the one bearing Marie's jacket. Janet must've noticed, because she gave Marie's arm a conciliatory little squeeze. Most likely, Janet had been that girl who got more Valentines than anyone else in the class. Every parent-teacher conference Marie ever sat through began with the teacher gingerly explaining that while Angelina was "exceptionally bright" (or "advanced beyond her peers," or, more mildly, "well above average"), she "lacked certain social skills" (or "needed to come out of her shell," or, more bluntly, "could use some help making friends").

Angelina opened a packet of sugar with her teeth, sending a flurry of white granules across the table.

"Oh no, let me do that," Janet said as she sat down. She picked up two of the other packets and opened them in a gesture that was ginger yet assured. When she passed them to Angelina, their fingers touched, and Angelina's eyes took on a kind of delighted confusion.

"I'm sorry I snapped at you," Angelina said.

"I shouldn't have been so familiar with you," Janet said. "I saw a girl with Marie's eyes and mouth and I just wasn't thinking, since I've gotten chummy with your mom. She's so sweet."

Marie set Angelina's coffee down in front of her. Angelina looked at her as if she was unfamiliar. Not a mean or sarcastic side-eye, but the probing stare that Marie had encountered in the rare lady casting director—not exactly cold, just without passion or excitement, trying to determine if she could fit the one-sentence character description.

"Are you in pain today?" Marie asked.

"It's mostly itchy. I'd actually prefer it to be achier. The itching is so annoying."

"I've heard about people bending wire hangers and sticking them down the opening of the cast," Janet said.

"I've been wrapping a cloth around the end of the wire hanger," Angelina said. "It's the only thing that takes the edge off."

Marie imagined Angelina's sore, papery skin snagging on the unclean edge of the hanger. "Oh no," she said. "Angie, please, that's gross."

"I can imagine it's this sort of exquisite feeling," Janet said. "Like, ache and relief all at once."

"Yes," Angelina said, her voice getting soft with a kind of reverence. "That's it. That's the perfect way to describe it."

"I hope it feels better, that you get, like, a more permanent relief soon." Janet said.

Angelina cleared her throat sharply. "I'll feel more relieved when I can find a job." Back to her old self.

"Don't even worry about it," Janet said brightly. "It seems like—"

"They have all the positions filled," Marie said.

Janet squinted quizzically, and Marie tried her best *no, really, don't say anything, please* look. A stupid move. Janet may not have known that look, but Angelina sure did.

"Mom, what's going on?"

"Did you see a help wanted sign?" Marie asked. "Seems to me that they aren't hiring if they don't have the sign up. I really haven't seen any up this year. It's the economy, you know. It's all hard." If only she'd been this good in any of those tiny rooms that were always somehow too cold, in front of those professionally unimpressed people who never seemed to feel it.

Angelina stared listlessly at her cup. Marie wondered if she might be defeated enough to take the "good news" with the spirit of its intention. She picked up Angelina's latte, watched her daughter's eyes to see if a coal had been stoked, and, finding the same dullness, took a sip. Not a deep sip; she was careful to keep her lips tight, to drink in mostly air. But Angelina was tuned toward Janet, her hips and shoulders tilted in a subtle lean.

"Well, it doesn't have to be all bad," Marie said. "Dad says there's an opening at his job. Part-time clerical work. Very, very easy. And it would be under the woman who's the big boss."

"On what planet is that a good idea?"

Angelina's voice cracked on the second syllable in *planet*, a fissure of rage. That anger rumbled through Angelina's eyes, stilled only when Janet gently interrupted: "Don't they always say the best time to look for a job is when you have a job?"

"I guess they do," Angelina replied tightly.

"It's temporary. Very temporary," Marie said, trying to keep a little music in her voice. Maybe she'd overplayed something or underplayed it. She shouldn't have said anything to Janet. Jack was trying. He really was.

CHAPTER FIVE

ANGELINA HAD THOUGHT HER FATHER'S office would be fancier, certainly bigger than one of those trailers for overflow students at the middle school. Giant computer monitors sat on tiny desks facing windowless walls. There was no attempt at art, just motivational posters—pictures of sunrises and eagles with phrases like "With TEAMWORK everyone WINS" or "GOALS are the difference between TRY and TRIUMPH" underneath. These posters weren't framed, not even laminated. They were just tacked around willy-nilly: in the bathroom, eye-level with the toilet; above the kitchen sink, beside a coffee-splattered sheet of OSHA numbers for reporting unsafe working conditions; half hidden by an iron maiden of a filing cabinet. They didn't tamp down the tongues of wallpaper that licked up in odd places.

Angelina felt some invisible hand wrap its fingers around her neck, press its palm into her throat. In the café, at least there had been abundant people-watching, and she'd been able to get her art on the walls. She had made a little money—very little—but the money wasn't the most satisfying part. She watched the customers glance up from their mugs and absorb her pieces, if only for a moment; she imagined a half grin or a slightly tilted head not in reaction to a daydream or something the person on the other side of the table said, but in temporary rapture over her play with lines or her choice of colors. And maybe she wasn't just imagining. If—no, *when*—she had a gallery show, then she would know, absolutely, that people were thinking about her work.

Her mind left the temple-white walls of her dream gallery and returned to the trailer. She sat down at her father's desk, picked up his nameplate: J. Moltisanti.

He'd framed her old drawings, even the ones she'd given to him as a middle schooler trying to (gently) sass him: a male lion sunning himself on a construction beam, a gorilla in a mobster's pinstripe suit.

"So, you must be Angelina."

Her father said Ms. Crostini was tall, but Angelina hadn't been expecting the boss lady—who came in wearing Keds, not the high heels she'd soon pull out of her cloth Whole Foods bag—to be as tall as he was. After years of life drawing, Angelina could read bodies. Like many tall women, Ms. Crostini was toned in a mild, almost apologetic way, a body that said, "I want to be healthy, but I won't take up any more space than I have to." This coltish vulnerability played quickly across her face before she cleared it with a cough.

"You must be his kid," she said. "I thought, for a second—"

"You'll get another hour or so of peace," Angelina said.

Her voice opened with a conspiratorial warmth. Perhaps that's why she was spared a compensatory "but, no, really, your dad, he's a heck of a guy" speech.

Angelina looked at Ms. Crostini's lavender skirt suit, her pearlescent pantyhose, and her heather gray heels, at her plum-colored lipstick and the pinkish opals of her nails—all that work for a place where it wouldn't be appreciated.

"The last woman we had in here had a great phone voice, and she was very adept at small details," Ms. Crostini said.

"Sounds like I have some big shoes to fill."

"Yes," Ms. Crostini said. "But the coffee she made, it was always lukewarm even when it was hot, you know? I like it strong, very strong. Very hot. Loads of sugar and just a tiny bit of half-and-half."

"I get to be, like, one of those *Mad Men* secretaries, but for a woman?"

Ms. Crostini laughed, loud and warm and slightly musical. It was not a laugh for the sake of politeness—that lilt at the end told Angelina that she'd said something truly amusing. "Well, unfortunately, we won't have rows of other secretaries in angora sweaters typing away, but we have a lot of the same old-fashioned attitudes."

She said the line about the other secretaries in angora sweaters so casually, no wink in her tone—still, Angelina wondered if her father had said something. If he'd added another word onto his description of her as "artistic." How could he have known the evening of delicious dreams she'd had after the college career fair? He couldn't have. Rows of women in pinstriped suits, pantsuits and skirt suits that simultaneously announced their curves and gave them a Spartan martial appeal; women with severe hair, slicked back or in tight, uncompromising ponytails, and red lips, poised for battle—battle over what, Angelina didn't know, because her fantasy never got much further than these women walking, languidly, but with a warrior's alertness and purpose, down a long hallway full of glass doors. She was lonely. It didn't take much.

Angelina's big projects, for now at least, would be logging the invoices and typing up notes from the developer meetings. Ms. Crostini steered her through a maze of passwords and voicemail codes, call transfer protocols, and email away messages. She named the vendors that were "prickly" and the ones that would need follow-up calls to their follow-up calls. She schooled Angelina in Outlook and Excel. Angelina's head swelled like a steam kettle on a slow burn. Then her breast grazed Angelina's arm, just above the cast. It was armored in suit jacket and crisp blouse, but it emitted a dry, pleasant heat that spiraled the length of Angelina's arm and settled, balm-like, over the break in her wrist.

"By the time you're done, you'll probably be able to collect that sweet settlement your dad says you're due for," Ms. Crostini said, nodding toward the cast.

Angelina wasn't sure if her tight smile betrayed some unfortunate knowledge about her father's negotiating abilities.

"What if he, like, asks me to do something?"

Ms. Crostini looked down at her jacket; the button hung limp on its thread and, with a quick grunt, she tugged it loose. She opened her desk drawer and tossed the button inside, with countless others. Then she stared up at Angelina, pursing her mouth.

"I get what you're saying. He is a senior member of the team, so if he asks you to do something work-related, then of course you do it. But if he asks you to, say, go mow the lawn during your lunch hour, then no."

"Yeah, okay. No. I can do that."

"*No* is the most beautiful word you'll ever learn," Ms. Crostini said.

"That should be on one of those motivational posters. They should have a cheetah springing out of a leafy clearing, teeth bared."

"No, that would be me without my coffee."

Ms. Crostini lifted the mug from her desk, a thick red mug with some insignia in gold—probably her school symbol. And she was probably the kind of Phi Beta Something Something student who got a new school mug every year. Angelina hadn't even put in a forwarding address with the post office or her college. Her diploma was going to molder on the front porch of her old apartment.

"Your dad tells me you majored in art," Ms. Crostini said over the rush of water from the kitchenette sink.

Angelina nodded, but Ms. Crostini was staring down into some caked-in crud at the bottom of the mug. Ms. Crostini asked her what she did—"like, draw, paint, make clay pots"—while vigorously scrubbing out the mug with a brown paper towel. Angelina's answer disappeared when Ms. Crostini tossed the towel in the trashcan and it hit the edge with a wet slapping sound.

Mercifully, her father started the day offsite. Angelina took her first break outside; she sat on a small plastic bench attached to a small plastic table outside and watched men move heavy rows of piping from one truck to another. Sunlight winked off the metal, and the men shifted their hands along the shafts, wincing at the heat that ate through their gloves.

Angelina did a few loose gesture drawings of the men loading the trucks—easy exercises that took her mind off leash. This was what her father called "work work": grueling and tangible, nothing as feeble as moving around numbers or words. And yet, when she told them that she was majoring in art (and she'd insist to herself that she'd told them only because they'd asked, and only because of the joint she'd smoked in the car before Thanksgiving dinner, but, really, she told the truth because she'd made a choice and she was fuck-it-all proud of that), her father shook his head in that slow, tight way, as if his disappointment was threaded into the fibers of his muscles.

But her mother was the one to let her fork hit her plate, to say aloud, and loudly, in a voice that thrummed with an unfamiliar anger: "Come on, Angie, don't mess up your life." *This* she would get angry over; *this* would gall her, when so many times she'd closed the door or turned up the TV on the shouts and the thumps, when she'd tend to cuts and blisters with another variation on her greatest hit, "That's just how he is." Angelina made a show of jawing an overcooked piece of turkey skin before finally replying, "Just because you never made it to Broadway doesn't mean I don't get to do what makes me happy."

Vultures circled the remains of that dinner. He wanted to hit her; she could sense his arm, taut as a roll of wet twine. She could imagine the relief he'd feel if he could just let his hand crack her cheek—like some fractured part of him would snap back whole. But he wouldn't hit her. Hadn't in years. Still, later on, she cried in the car. Not hard. Just a little.

Angelina studied the men's hands moving so quickly, so effortlessly, as if their fingers and the knobs of their wrists were impervious. Her mind roamed to the ghostly blue of x-ray film. Watching them, she saw their joints sing open with every motion: vertebrae spreading and patella hinging to let them bend. Sure, she'd studied anatomy for life drawing, but she couldn't divine the real architecture of the body until she'd seen her own x-ray. Her ring and pinkie fingers, two snapped pieces of chalk; her hand, just a globe of bones tilting away from her cracked wrist, like it'd been blasted out of orbit.

Pieces of a skeleton emerged over a course of pages: a clavicle, a spine, that spidery cage from wrist bones to fingertips. Inside each bone, she wrote the names of a building material she'd saved in Excel: adobe and brick, cellulose and glass wool, urethane foam and polyvinyl chloride, cinder block and wire rope.

Most of the men were around her age. Straight-up Dundalk guys, they drowned each syllable in a nasal thickness and gelled their close-cropped hair into lustrous brown shells (even if they were natural blonds). They'd greeted her with a nod and a "hey" after the perfunctory "So, you're Jack's kid? He's a good guy. Knows a lot." She searched their words for a stowaway hole, a way she could cross over to the world they lived in, where her father was a good guy who knew a lot.

"Your dad is always saying how talented you are."

Angelina felt the man settle beside her with a weary affability before she even looked at him. Hector. He was short and balding. The bulb-nosed bluntness of his features pleased her, made her think of him as open, honest—even though her father had ranted about him: "He's a 'Jesus is my new high' type. A twelve-stepper who forgot about the 'anonymous' in the title. Talks all the goddamn time. Distracts the other guys, like work is a time to make friends."

Angelina shifted. "He said I was talented, huh?"

"He used to show us those drawings you done. Very imaginative stuff."

Her father had asked her for drawings of "the great Italian sculptures," but Angelina had no interests in cold hulks of men. She'd loved the bristle of fur and the glassy dampness of animal eyes. She'd loved the gradations of shadow that sank into the valleys of clothing folds. She'd wanted to give him what she'd loved.

"Imaginative is one word for it," she said.

"His word exactly, hon. He said you get the artistic side from your mom."

The most Angelina had ever heard him say about her mother's acting was an occasional remark about how some actress in one of those crime or doctor shows they watched before the 11 o'clock news "couldn't hold a candle" to her.

"Well, I think it's just terrific that you haven't let this get in your way," Hector said, nodding toward her cast. "You could be a medical illustrator."

"Yeah, I suppose so."

There were so many things she could be whenever she uploaded her resume and "high-resolution JPEGS of work samples that suit client needs"—but they were all, in the end, the very same thing. Right now, that thing was nothing. None of her samples suited client needs, and even though she was trapped and desperate, she took a kind of pride in it. That pride was a tiny fist in a burlap sack, punching, punching, punching until it scraped its knuckles raw.

Hector told her about his son in Los Angeles, who was "artistic, too" and did "hairstyling" for the movies. "He does what you might call 'independent pictures.' Maybe you've heard of some of them?"

Hector named a few movies Angelina hadn't heard of, and one she'd wanted to see because she had a crush on the lead actress. She started to ask if his son had ever mentioned that actress when her father's car rumbled up. He walked out of the car with an unexpected ease; she supposed she'd thought he skulked around the office like Yosemite Sam. She'd come to know his bad days by the way he'd close the front door, and so many days had been bad days. Now, his step was brisk.

As he walked toward the trailer, he waved toward all the guys, whistled to get their attention. He held two white paper bags that were splotched greasy on their bottoms.

"This is my girl," he called. "Angelina. She just started today."

A ripple of palms, dusty and flushed, greeted her.

"Nice to be the boss's kid, eh?" Hector said.

"I thought Eleanor, er, Ms. Crostini was, technically."

"Technically what?" her father asked.

"The person I report to," she said.

"She called me from the road, you know. Said she appreciated my suggestion for bringing you on."

He nodded toward Hector, who stood up. Then he tossed the bags on the table and sat down beside her. He was sweating and red and the heat of his flank against hers radiated through her skirt. Her skin felt dry and taut, like she'd lain out in the sun for too long. She closed her sketchbook, pushed it to the edge of the table.

"I got lunch. Since it's your first day and all," he said. "I got the Italian cold cuts with hots because you always liked the hots." He cleared his throat. "I figured you hadn't gone vegetarian or anything while you were at school. Or at least your mother didn't say you had."

"Actually, I went to a dandelion-based diet," she said. "Vegetables have nerves so I only eat weeds."

He smiled at her the way he would when she was a small child who could please him with A's on spelling quizzes and perfect recitations—down to the swollen Brando inflections—of the "make him an offer he can't refuse" monologue. He'd taught her that speech well before she could watch the movie, laughed and clapped and called her mother into the room, every time.

And now they were going to have lunch together, and it was going to be normal, even happy. Her father rummaged through the bags, flattened and smoothed the napkins with a fussiness that made her feel as if some necklace or heirloom ring she'd lost years ago had been returned to her. Though she dearly loved it once, she'd become so accustomed to its absence that the sight of it brought the realization that, at some point, she'd simply stopped missing it.

CHAPTER SIX

HER INBOX WAS A CATALOG of rejection. She sent her slides—still lifes and portraits rendered photo-realistically, impressionistically, in savage expressionism and perfect cubism; in all the styles she'd had to learn through all her years of schooling—to agencies in D.C. and New York, and, just for the hell of it, San Francisco, because she'd always wanted to live someplace warm. The rejections they sent her (when said rejections came in written form and not just a void) said that her work didn't "exemplify brand standards" or "lacked provocativeness and the sense of play that distinguishes us as a thought leader in creative solutions across industries." This latter type of rejection, surprisingly, stung her; she could laugh at that corporatese, but she suspected the inference that she lacked vision could be true.

She was not Robert Mapplethorpe, showing photographs of a bullwhip up his asshole in a New York loft, or Frida Kahlo, fucking Trotsky and Josephine Baker while painting the savage poetry of her body. She wasn't O'Keeffe in the desert or Patti Smith scrawling reams of poetry in the Chelsea Hotel. She was lying on a sofa bed in her parents' basement, watching the ceiling tremble under their footsteps. She couldn't even get her work in the crappy café in the basement of a converted rowhome on Preston Street that also housed, on the top floors, a vendor of essential oils and a psychic who didn't replace her neon window sign even though the *p* and the *s* had long since burned out.

This was one of the last places she tried, after she'd been waitlisted or outright denied at the spaces where she would've actually wanted her work to be shown. The New York galleries, sure, she expected them to pass her over (though, of course, there was a tiny wire of hope humming in some tin chamber of her heart). The Baltimore venues—waterfront galleries and coffee shops whose websites featured that typewriter font that Angelina knew to be played-out and pretentious but still loved for its retro preciousness—surprised her. Then again, there were so many talented and industrious people in the same zip code—and they all had their own styles and visions.

Ms. Crostini felt the need to "be a good, or at least decent-ish, mentor to another young woman," so, in the mornings, before the guys arrived (and in between her harried bites of muffin or Danish), she gave advice about "connecting with other people who are doing what you want to be doing." Angelina said thank you, made a show of taking notes. The only person she could think of who was doing what she wanted to be doing (different art, but same principle) was someone she was thinking of a lot anyway: Janet. Who she was trying to think of as *that girl Janet*—that girl with the crushed diamond eyes and the long, confident fingers, a smile that seemed kind, but like it could, in a moment, betray some sharp thought—and not Mother's coworker Janet, because any image of Mother, however peripheral, turned the incandescence of that feeling instantly lukewarm.

Still, Angelina was forced to ask her mother if Janet meant what she said when she said that she'd be open to hanging out, and, if she did mean what she'd said then, "Could you maybe give me her number, or give her mine, or whatever." Mother looked like she just opened a birthday present—not a construction-paper bookmark or a clay mug, but something she wanted. That evening, she came down to the basement with a plastic grocery bag to shield Angelina's cast in the shower and an unused perfume tester strip with a cell phone number written on it.

"You know I'm going to tell you to be yourself," Mother said. "But, you know, spend some time asking her about her. Don't just be 'goal oriented.'"

Angelina scouted out Janet online, looking for the articles she'd written about fashion and makeup and, yes, for evidence of a girlfriend. But for more than that—more than just a pretty lady laying claim by kissing Janet's cheek in an artful selfie—she looked for the essays and the costumes. *City Paper* had reviewed a burlesque show that Janet was involved in; the author devoted two full paragraphs to how Janet's costumes "perfectly wed theme and character (sometimes much better than the performers wearing them) in beautifully assembled pieces that, I have to admit, I wish I had hanging in my closet." Janet was also interviewed for a longer feature about the burlesque scene in Baltimore. She described herself as "still that little girl who petitioned her local library to start carrying *Vogue*," talked about her creative process ("I do a little freewriting about the character I'm designing for, and once I think I understand them, I start sketching and I do a list along each sketch of materials and practical ideas for constructing the piece"), and waxed philosophical about the feminism of burlesque ("It's about women of all shapes, ages, and orientations taking full ownership of their bodies and presentation; it's about as awesomely 'f-word' as you can get"). And the costumes were everything the reviewer said they were. They endowed girls whose bodies were aggressively ordinary, not unlike Angelina's, with an essence that was mythic and delicious.

Angelina drafted a lengthy text explaining that she badly wanted her own place, and that she wanted her own work to pay for that place, but that she was sad and scared that this would never happen and needed someone to talk to and help her figure out how to be moderately successfully and less lonely. She immediately deleted it (and checked and double checked to make sure she deleted it instead of somehow accidentally hitting "send"). She wrote another text, this time asking if they could "meet up and do that networking thing everyone online says is so important," and thought on it a minute before deleting that one too. Finally, she sent a short message asking if Janet wanted to "get together sometime soon."

Within minutes, her phone pinged and that digital Christmas package of an envelope appeared onscreen. It could be her father with some update about the epic struggle against the insurance company, or her mother asking if she could get eggs on the way home from work. But it was Janet, asking what she was up to on Thursday.

Angelina wrote back: "Well, I have an x-ray appointment."

Janet, within seconds: "I've never hung out with a girl while she was getting x-rayed."

And so, half an hour before Angelina's appointment, Janet's '05 Volkswagen Beetle (in a perfect daisy yellow) appeared in front of her parents' house. Janet made fast friends with Valentina, cooing and scratching her in that sweet spot behind her right ear. Angelina asked if Janet had pets, and Janet said no, though she sure had a lot of friends with cats. Janet marveled at how soft Valentina's fur was and how bright her eyes were. Angelina had no idea why her Valentina voice for her comeback—"The better to see you with, my dear"—sounded like Don Corleone, but Janet laughed.

"So, you have the whole day?" she asked.

Janet haloed her blue eyes with shimmery gold shadow. She wore the faintest bit of mascara—not enough to melt in the heat, just enough to tangle her lashes.

"I have the whole day," Angelina said.

Eleanor had given her the whole day off, though she'd only asked for a few hours. Angelina caught herself looking behind Eleanor as she said it. Her father frowned into his ledger; then, with his eyes closed, he rolled his neck from shoulder to shoulder. He only acknowledged her after the third pop. "Remember, you have pain and suffering," he said. "You're losing wages." He didn't open his eyes.

At the orthopedist's office, Angelina and Janet rode the elevator to the fifth floor and emerged into a waiting room awash in coral green, filled with children on their parents' laps, young guys on crutches, and a few older women sitting next to their dumpy husbands. The walls were covered with framed advertisements for the hospital system. The faces of elderly and adolescent models grinned under quippy copy about "dem bones, dem bones, dem strong bones."

"Thanks for coming with me," Angelina said. "It would suck to be here alone."

"It sucks to be anywhere alone," Janet said.

Angelina started to say that she was pretty sure the bathroom was a good place to be alone. Then she remembered those acting exercises Mother showed her to help her with her "people skills": drawing her mouth into a soft, contemplative pucker and thinking of something that genuinely interested her. This last part was the most important, Mother had said, "Because you can't fake it in the eyes." This was back in the middle school years, the years when playground taunts of "fat girl" and "weirdo" were answered with lunchboxes swung into sides of heads.

So Mother endeavored to teach Angelina "how to look like you care about what people say, or at least like you're not annoyed by it." Angelina would watch her mother's face become a moth on a window, illuminated through a casual drabness, these bland, transactional expressions assuming a kind of unforced prettiness. This was before Angelina made a connection between the doors Mother closed and the TVs she turned up and the smothering of her screams; this was when all she knew was that Mother didn't wield the belt. And even now, when Mother was the sound of the lock clicking and the sitcom laugh track, Angelina couldn't help but feel grateful that she could offer Janet that give-a-little-to-get-along smile—because maybe they could do more than get along.

The orthopedist, a wiry-haired woman whose glasses eclipsed her tiny face, hmmed and sighed at the x-ray; she said Angelina was healing "okay" and sent her on her way with an appointment to come back in another five weeks, whereupon she'd "probably, depending on what the scan looks like," be liberated from her cast. Nodding gravely seemed appropriate. Her body had always been a liminal concern, something she was only aware of in extremis: a broken nose, a broken bone. The occasional orgasm.

"What does 'okay' even mean?" Angelina asked Janet as they walked to the car.

"I think 'okay' means you don't have the instant healing powers of Wolverine, but you're probably not going to need surgery," Janet said.

"You read comics?"

"No, but that nineties cartoon version of X-Men was on YouTube for a while, and I felt this intense empathy for Jean Grey, so I guess I had a transferred attraction to cartoon Wolvie."

"She had all this power," Angelina said. "And she never knew it, until it was too late."

Janet clucked her tongue, said, "You know it, sister," and turned the key in the ignition. Angelina rested her cast against the glass. Subtle vibrations hummed through the plaster, licked her weary bone.

"I just want this off of me," she said. "Patience is not a virtue of mine."

"But you're an artist, right? That's all about patience, and punishment, really."

"It doesn't feel like patience, though. My whole process—or, like, whatever you want to call it—is either me having that kid-on-Christmas-morning feeling, or me standing there telling me to go fuck myself."

"All of that time stuck in my room really prepared me to wait for the muse," Janet said. "I wasn't grounded, I was in art ninja training."

On the drive back to Janet's place, she talked at length about her past. She came from one of the Southern Maryland counties "where people forgot that the Confederates lost" and her mother had found Jesus "in a house, in a mouse, in a box, in a fox, in everything except me." She moved out at seventeen and only returned on the Thanksgivings when she was low on grocery money. "Christmases, I have to be, like, nuclear-level broke, so that I can appreciate the meager amounts I get when I pawn the hideous porcelain Madonnas and gold crosses she gives me. Although every so often, she gets me a sweater or a set of pearl earrings I can't bear to sell."

"How do you make it through the church services? Stoned?"

"Tried that, got too paranoid. Now I just lose myself in my head."

"So, you chant to yourself, like 'ooooooooom'?"

Janet laughed. "No. I just imagine I'm watching an actress I love in clothes I designed just for her. Or being named the *New York Times*'s new fashion and beauty columnist."

"The *Baltimore City Paper* sure seemed to like you," Angelina said.

"You Googled me. That's sweet."

Janet spoke with such nonchalance; still, her hands jittered on the wheel. She accidentally struck the left turn signal. Angelina wasn't sure what face to put on now—should she laugh to put Janet at ease? Maybe praise something specific from one of Janet's articles? Or would a kind remark about her general body of work seem less stalkerish? She squinted at the buildings as they flashed past, thin and gray like the edges of palette knives.

"My mom said you had some articles online, so I checked them out," she offered. "I really liked the one where you talk about the history of eyeliner and how thicker eyeliner was this sign of, like, 'don't-give-a-fuck female liberation.'"

"I had to really fight my editor on using the f-word."

"It was right, I think."

"I Googled you, too," Janet said.

"So then you know I was recently elected secretary of the Society of Lady Mercenaries."

Angelina rolled the smooth-glazed ball of a joke toward Janet because there really wasn't anything of her to find online, and she couldn't bear to hear Janet say that aloud, even in jest. Janet picked up the ball and gently lobbed it back: "Keep this up and next election, you could be president."

Then came a silence of radio murmur and the soft thud of wheel over pothole. Angelina didn't know if she should keep trying to massage the joke, even if she accidentally choked it to death, or just sit. Mercifully, Janet remarked that she had seen a few of Angelina's drawings on the student work section of a professor's website—still lifes with cow skulls and flowers, nude models—and she really liked what she saw. She'd like to see Angelina's "other work."

"So would I," Angelina said.

Janet slowed the car as they approached a block of row houses in various states of hominess: bougainvillea trained along metal railings; pots of rosemary and basil and mint standing at attention on wooden fences that had been painted pink, purple, or blue (or a combination of the three); pinwheel flamingos and weathervane ravens stuck in unruly bushes.

"I'm on the top floor of that one," Janet said.

She pointed to the lone unadorned house on the corner: plain brick and a rain-battered railing, cracked shutters over scraggly front bushes. Windows opened their maws for AC units that clicked on and off, humming in discord.

Angelina started to tell Janet that her landlord needed to get cages for those units. The ground floor made easy pickings, and that roof wouldn't be too difficult to scale. Instead, she tried a playful ribbing.

"How can you live in a row house and not know how to parallel park?"

Janet laughed, said to wait and see, wait and see. She turned the corner behind the house and pulled onto a parking pad of cracked cement slabs. The slabs lifted away from each other like the sides of a wishbone. Janet kept pulling in and backing out, Tetris-ing her Beetle ever so slightly away from the only other car on the pad: an'03 Chevy Cavalier that could've been lifted from the set of some post-apocalyptic thriller. The doors were pocked and dented, and the right side mirror was attached with a band of slightly mildewed duct tape.

"Of course *he* has to be home," Janet muttered. She jerked the parking brake so fast that Angelina lurched forward.

"Who's home?" Angelina asked.

"The evil Mr. Paulson."

They opened the back door and pressed through a narrow hallway cluttered with a rusted bicycle, flattened basketballs, and tatty green crates stuffed with men's clothing—soiled white sweaters and pants in garish paisleys, flip-flops with broken thongs.

"That's all his shit. I swear, he's turned this place into a sty, and yet he'll bang on my wall when I like, have music on my computer—not even a stereo, just my dinky little laptop."

Flakes of dry white wood came loose in Angelina's palm as she pushed herself along the banister up to Janet's third-floor apartment. There were only two apartments on the narrow floor, E and F. A curlicue of craft-store ivy coiled around F's domino-sized doorbell, and Angelina knew it was Janet's before Janet even turned the key.

"The walls are thin, then?"

The hardwood floor had been scarred by furniture legs and broken glass, punctured and gouged by boot heels and bottle caps. Though her flimsy work flats couldn't have furthered that damage, Angelina followed Janet's lead and slipped her shoes beside a hall mat that must've come from the November first clearance sale at Party City: a rhinestoned skull on black rubber.

"My décor is essentially an eighties prom on Halloween," Janet said. "I'm compensating for my tortured girlhood of L.L. Bean turtlenecks and yellow wallpaper—and I mean that in both the literal and literary incarnations."

Angelina padded into a kitchen with a pink Formica countertop and doorless cabinets that had been lined with blue fleur-de-lis wallpaper. Janet pulled two stemless wine glasses from a bottom shelf before rooting through her freezer for an ice tray and a bottle of ginger ale. The dining room table was some cheap Ikea number that Janet had spray-painted white before hot-gluing fake ivy around the legs and up the corners.

"If I had my own place, I'd like it to be like this," Angelina said. "It has character."

Janet led her out of the kitchen and into the living room. The furniture had either been carefully curated from Saturday yard sales in the more manicured parts of town or snatched up from a Craig's List curb dump. The crown of the living room was a Victorian sofa set with cushions the color of devil's food cake. A black steamer trunk served as a coffee table, and the side table was an ionic pillar made from heavy plastic.

"You mean it *is* a character. A faded starlet of the silent film era, grown fat and addled on champagne and pills."

"No. I mean, I don't know. If your apartment were a person, I'd want to get to know them. They seem cool."

"I guess you sort of are getting to know my 'apartment-as-a-person' right now," Janet said. She flashed an L-is-for-loser sign on her forehead. "I mean, fuck it. *I* like my things, even if Ali didn't. Oh God, she *hated* my place. Well, I guess still actively *hates* my place. I just don't have to be around her active hatred of my place anymore. Thank *God.*"

Janet slid her socks off and tossed them toward the back of the apartment, near an open doorway. Angelina could only imagine what that bedroom looked like.

"We always had to go back to her place, which is, like, okay, it's much *technically* nicer. It *is* a condo in the Harbor, but it was so sanitary and dickless."

Though she'd drawn her legs up on the sofa yogi style (a gesture that Angelina's knees, as rigid as a Ken doll's, couldn't emulate), Janet's back arched with a feline assertiveness. She was clearly reliving one of her and her ex's oldest, most constant fights. In this retelling, she landed those long fists between the ribs that Ali dodged the first go 'round. And yet, in the subtle dampening of her voice, in the quick downcurl of her mouth, there was the lingering love that rued the punch.

"Sanitary and dickless," Angelina said. "I can imagine that apartment. Black granite countertops and inlaid lighting. One of those ridiculous showerheads—no, I'm sorry, *shower panels*—with the massage settings—"

"Oh honey, you don't need to be coy. They're totally masturbation settings," Janet said.

Janet raised her left hand for a high five and Angelina, unconsciously, returned it with her cast.

"I love that we're both so awkward," Janet said. "I knew we'd get along just from how your mom describes you. 'Angelina is my odd duck,' that's what she says."

"Does my mom know that you're—"

"Gay? Sure."

"Does my mom know that I'm—"

"She sure was keen to get us together."

"Does that, like, strike you as weird at all?"

"If by weird, you mean sweet."

A sudden thump shook the wall. Three more thumps followed in succession, each one blunter, nastier than the one before. Unexpected noise turned Angelina's heart into a fat rabbit pinched under a wire fence.

"Oh Christ, it's *him*," Janet groaned.

"It's a terrible thing, to dread coming home," said Angelina.

Another bang forced the framed pictures on Janet's wall askew, and Angelina to her feet. She stared at the pictures—photos of Janet and her friends (unless one of them was Ali?) all done up as old Hollywood stars for Halloween. Janet was Marilyn Monroe in full *Seven Year Itch* mode. The Hepburns flanking her, Audrey and Kate, wore their fall jackets, but Janet went unarmored against the chill in her white dress and sequined sandals. Her bra was padded, but not cartoonishly so: just enough.

Before she was even aware why—something to do with Janet's eyes in that photograph, a little soused, a little sad even under all that glitter—Angelina's cast swung against the wall with a velocity that quaked the whole apartment. Must've sent aftershocks through Mr. Paulson's unit, too, because the bang that volleyed back was sharper, more concentrated—a broom handle bang.

"Shit," Janet said. Her voice was a pair of soft hands thrown up against a haymaker.

Angelina's father had taken her to the basement and taught her to hit. He'd offer his open hands to her tiny fists. His palms were nests of bone. Then he'd pinion her wrists between his fingers, tilt and twist her arms to show her how to rotate her arm for a proper punch.

Angelina's wrist twitched and sang through the plaster. But she banged back until Mr. Paulson started knocking on Janet's door.

Angelina swung the door open and stood face to face with Mr. Paulson, an emaciated man with beetle-shell eyes and witch's broom hair. His face had been carved out of rotted wood, all mottled edges and hard lines etched around his cheeks and mouth.

"People are *sleeping*," he hissed.

He jabbed the broom handle toward Angelina, but Angelina swatted it away with her cast. The crack of wood on plaster must've shocked Mr. Paulson, because he swayed backward. Angelina could only imagine that Mr. Paulson—a ragdoll stuffed with burned fuses—had felt that sound in the flesh, *on* his flesh, at least once.

"No, *people* are *talking* at *reasonable* volume. Psychotic assholes are banging on walls."

Angelina's feet spread along the hard floor; her right shoulder dropped low (but not too low), hips pivoted to generate force; chin down and eyes ahead. She raised the cast in front of her belly, held it a few inches away so she could strike out easily or maneuver it for a block.

"You don't live here. Who are you?"

"I'm the bitch who makes you leave her alone."

Angelina kept her eyes trained on Mr. Paulson; she'd learned, early on, to never be seduced by anything peripheral. Yet she was aware of Janet standing up, moving behind her.

"I pay rent. I don't have to deal with this shit from some fat dyke who doesn't even live here."

"She's not fat."

Janet's indignant cry was enough to distract Mr. Paulson. Angelina knocked the broomstick out of his hands. It fell away with the lightness of a matchstick.

Angelina felt Janet's breath against her collarbone before she felt the gentle tug at her elbow. Janet released her torrent of threats—that the next time there was banging on the walls and yelling in the hallways, *she'd* call the cops, which she should have done *months* ago.

Janet closed the door and danced a victory lap around Angelina; she pumped her fists and whistled, every so often stopping to cry out, "I love you. I love you. I love you." Angelina stared at the blank space where her opponent's eyes had been. Then Janet touched the small of her back, led her back to the kitchen.

To celebrate Angelina's "unequivocal victory," Janet tried to mix up some Jack and cokes. Her hands shook and flailed. She knocked one glass into the sink.

I know this, Angelina thought. *I know the moments after. I can be useful.*

"You know what's weird? I haven't even drawn on my own cast yet," Angelina said. "I mean, I'm an artist, right? Isn't that what I'm supposed to do?"

"No, I think your friends are supposed to do that for you," Janet said. "When my friend Maxine broke her ankle, we drew flowers and pasties all over her cast. She's a burlesque dancer, so we figured we'd draw all the stuff she was missing while she was cooped up."

"I would like that," Angelina said. "I mean, I would like for you to draw on me. My cast, that is."

Janet pulled a Sharpie out of a kitchen drawer and told Angelina to sit on the couch.

As Angelina offered her left arm to Janet, it sizzled with the kind of pain she would've clenched her fist against, if she could. Janet told her to focus on her breath: deeply in, slowly out. The rhythm of pressure and release in the center of her chest lulled her. She wasn't aware of any pain, only Janet moving the cast into her lap.

"What are you going to draw?"

Janet didn't answer. She glided the marker over plaster, rendered a crude broom. Angelina laughed. The broom would be a little in-joke. Nobody else would get it. Then Janet gave a theatrical "Ha!" and drew a stick figure witch with a triangle hat sitting on the broom, shaking her tiny fists.

CHAPTER SEVEN

JACK LEFT THE JOB FOR lunch. He drove to the sub shop with his driver's side window open and his Sirius XM radio queued to the Johnny Cash station. The guys he'd grown up with used to rib him for his Cash eight-tracks: "What kind of self-respecting Wop listens to country?" Still, they couldn't help but nod along to "Get Rhythm." More than one of them laughed his ass off at "A Boy Named Sue." That voice filled the drives past gated storefronts and Black girls playing hopscotch under the skeletons of impending skyscrapers, through strip malls the length of football fields.

He'd planned to let the song play out before setting up at one of the benches outside of the market with his sub, Italian cold cut with extra hots, and his chips. When she was a kid, Angie used to beg Marie to let her order "Daddy's sandwich." Marie insisted it was "too severe for a ten-year-old." But when Marie wasn't looking, he'd sneak a pinch of the hots onto Angelina's bland spaghetti.

Then "Street Fighting Man" came on, and he figured that was as good a time as any to dial up the insurance rep, Hunter. Who sounded like a kid named Hunter: a boy forced into too many team sports.

Jack wasn't one for hellos. Especially when all this kid could offer him was a measly $5K.

"So where are we, Hunter?" Jack absently rapped his knuckles along the window. He exhaled slowly. His heartbeat synching with the steady drum of bone against glass. "Tell me we were able to rattle Geico into giving us something more appropriate."

"Well, here's the thing, Jack," he said. "They're feeling like their driver, yes, she made a mistake—"

"Several mistakes," Jack said. "Speeding. Running a stop sign. Texting. That's a hat trick of bad driving, my friend."

An Orthodox family, a pretty young mother and her little girl, walked into the grocery store. The mother pushed a stroller in front of her. She took quick steps that made the hem of her black skirt float over her ankles.

He'd watch Marie breastfeed in the days after Angie was born. Marie didn't try to cover up. She sat on their bed, smoothing her fingers over the base of Angie's bald skull. She was still his wife, the woman who laughed and laughed when, slippery-drunk on rail whiskey, he blew raspberries on her nipples. After the delivery, her physical being was charged with contradiction. She was more vulnerable, her breasts swollen and hurting. The veins under her skin were so thick, so brightly blue that they seemed hot. Like sizzles of electricity, like they'd singe his hand if he touched her. She'd been ripped apart and here she was, smiling and singing softly. She was primal.

Angie had never been so perfect as she was when he could cover her whole face with his hand. Sometimes she'd move her lips and suckle against his palm. Sometimes she'd yawn into the gaps between his fingers.

"Well, the thing is, we can't prove she was texting. There's only your daughter's word versus the other driver's, and the other driver says she wasn't texting."

"Did they read the police report? Did you? That cop, Banzini, he would have put it in."

"He didn't mention texting specifically. I mean, again, if he didn't see it himself, I don't think he can put it in the report *per se*. He did cite the other driver for speeding and failure to yield—"

"I'm going to get another copy of that report," Jack said. "I specifically heard my daughter tell Banzini that the other girl was texting. They probably only faxed you part of it."

"They scanned it and emailed it to me. The whole thing. There's no mention of texting."

"I'm going to take another look," Jack said. "And even if there's no mention of texting—which there should be—we have a drawing in the back of her pad. Some lady drew an image of where the cars where, and who hit who. She even left her phone number. Have you even talked to her?"

"The witness? Yes, Jack, I've spoken to her."

"Well, then, isn't the other girl's fault self-evident?"

"In all honesty, Jack, I'm not thinking this will really boil down to who's at fault. It's more about what's reasonable to expect in terms of compensation."

"My daughter needs to be compensated for her pain and suffering and lost earnings."

"I didn't see anything about a job," Hunter said. "Didn't she just graduate?"

Jack could imagine Hunter leaning back in his chair, mouthing, "This guy again" or "SOS" every time some pretty coworker walked by.

"She worked while she was in college. She worked as a barista. Won some competition for latte art."

Jack had seen a feel-good story about regional barista championships on the morning news. The girl who won made little sculptures out of the foam: pirate ships and Chinese dragons and cartoon cats.

"I'm not trying to argue with you, Jack. I'm just trying to tell you what the other driver's insurance company would—"

"I'm trying to tell you what you need to tell them. She's a working artist. Now she only has one hand."

A trio of teenagers, two boys and a girl, wandered into the parking lot. The girl and the taller of two boys wore a grocery store's uniforms: black polos, black pants, and black visors. Nametags. The smaller boy wore jeans that he had to keep hitching up his ass and a T-shirt he was fairly drowning in.

Hunter said he'd tell Geico that the offer was "insufficient." Yes, he'd fax his copy of the accident report to Jack's office right away. Of course, he just had to mention that he "honestly wasn't sure" they could get anything over seven thousand.

"I'm not low-balling my child's pain and suffering," Jack said.

On his way out of the sub shop, he saw the Jewish mother again. She crossed into the parking lot, wrangling her stroller one-handed. Her little girl gripped her free arm. The girl's dark curls sprang out from the sides of her pink kerchief. She kicked her sneakers feet in the air, and in a tiny, tinny voice, she sang, "She certainly can, can-can."

They approached a Subaru Legacy with one of those stick-figure families on the back windshield. A dad with an oversized tie and briefcase, a mother with a baby on her hip, and a girl in a ballerina tutu. The mother struggled to set her basket down. There were eggs and milk inside, and the pavement was hot. People simply walked by her—all perfectly able-bodied assholes. They could've stopped their carts and held the basket for her for just five minutes. Jack offered to take the basket for her while she dug out her keys. She looked at him as if he'd thrown cold water in his face. He knew her people were a little hinky about touching the opposite sex. She could've at least smiled when she mouthed *No, thank you.*

The little girl looked up at Jack. There was something sly and mocking in her eyes as she smiled. Jack was never at ease around younger kids—they could do or say anything, at any time. He just waved with the tips of his fingers. The girl started laughing. Not a mean laugh, but a loud one. It drew the eyes of everyone in the lot. Jack felt his whole face turn into a Halloween pumpkin.

As he walked away, the little girl sang out a single word: "No."

Before he drove back to the site, he piloted his Pathfinder to the light rail stop. Just to make sure his daughter's rental car was still there, not to mention intact. Some jerk in a silver Cobalt must've flunked kindergarten. He couldn't stay inside the lines. He'd parked dangerously close to Angelina—she might even have to climb in through the passenger's side. It wasn't like he was boxed in, had no other choice. He'd had plenty of room to back out and then edge in straight.

Jack parked in a restaurant lot about two blocks away. He snapped on his tool belt, empty save for a single hammer. He walked toward the

Cobalt, scanning the light rail lot. Tons of cars but no people around, and no cameras.

Leaning with his back against the Cobalt's driver's side door, Jack palmed the hammer. He counted to ten. With a single swing, he drove the hammer into the door. His weight against the car muffled the crunch of metal. He counted to ten again. Swung again. Again. Again. Swung until it looked like the hand of God had slammed a basketball into this douchebag's car door.

Jack slipped the hammer, head down, into his tool belt. He'd wipe it clean of metallic bits when he was back in his car. In the meantime, he'd just walk into one of the cafés. Order a coffee to go. If anyone even dimly remembered a guy in a tool belt, he'd only be that guy who ordered a black coffee and flirted dumbly with the girl behind the counter by saying lots of sugar, sugar. He could let himself be laughed at, gently, just this once.

Angelina was in her basement bedroom, drawing, when her father came downstairs to give her an update about the settlement. The only news was that there was no news. The offer, he said, was "insultingly low."

He bent his knees as if to sit, and the joints popped in a rapid crackle. Angelina had never imagined him old enough to have fireworks in his bones, though his hair was silver at the temples. She was born in his "Jesus year," as he'd told her more than once, "And you've been my great test of character ever since."

Valentina greeted him in a burst of wagging tail and joyful tongue; she lowered her head to let him rub her ears from top to bottom and back again. He said, "Okay, okay, Valentina bambina," but she butted her head against his forearm, and he massaged circles down her neck. He crooned that tuneless little ditty—"Val-en-tina, baaaaaaaaaamb-i-i-i-i-n-a"—and Angelina wondered why she hadn't been allowed to sing her own made-up songs in her room. He always had a headache whenever she wanted to have fun.

When she called Valentina over, the dog stalled, continuing to lick his forearms, his wrists, happily resting her head between his hands. Angelina snapped her fingers. Finally, Valentina came. She put the dog in a sit beside her, moving her knuckle vigorously over one of her sweet spots, right between the eyes. He looked at her with a muddle of admiration and resentment; said that she was doing such a good job training the dog, maybe now she could appreciate all the hard work of parenting.

Yes, but I would never hurt her, Angelina thought.

She was a grown woman now; he couldn't—or, she wouldn't let him—make her feel like a dumb child anymore.

"Just tell me the number, please," she said.

"I told you, it's too low. You're going to screw yourself out of some real money."

"Why don't you let me be the judge of that?"

He grabbed her jaw so quickly, so roughly, that she bit her lip. The skin wasn't broken, but she still tasted blood. Valentina was up and snarling. Her eyes pinned back, her tail an arrow, she lunged between Angelina and her father. She barked loud enough to make him wince. When his eyes were closed, even for a moment, Angelina could catch him in the belly with a straight jab or slam her cast into his groin.

"You think it's your *right*, huh?" he said. "That I'm *obligated* to help you?"

Her eyes would have to answer for her.

"Jackie, why is the dog upset? I can't hear my show."

Mother must've been standing midway down the stairs. He hated when she yelled across the room, or really, when she just raised her voice—"You were an actress, Marie, you project too much." Distracted, he loosened his hold on her face.

Angelina could let her body go pliant with apology. Or she could clench up, make him earn it.

"Jackie?"

Mother must've been damn near the bottom step. If she cared to look around the banister, she'd see him—not having changed, not even a little bit.

The stair creaked, let out a thin whimper. She must be shifting her feet, deciding whether to turn around or come down.

"I told you, not now."

With one last cymbal crash of a bark, Valentina nipped at his knee. Startled, he jerked backward. Angelina felt the scrape of calluses as she jerked free.

She met her mother on the stairs. Mother's mouth was a mussel that wouldn't yield its pearl. Her blond hair was swept up in an azure scarf, arranged with an artful carelessness. Angelina recognized the scarf, a Christmas gift to her from Mother that she'd "forgotten" before heading back to Takoma.

"Angie."

Mother's tone wavered between apology and excuse. Angelina didn't know which would piss her off more.

"Dessert is ready. Come help me set the table?"

Angelina's vision fuzzed a hot white. She could only see negative space, the patches around her mother's shape.

"Angie?"

Her anger melted Mother's face into a fleshy smear. Angelina had never wanted to hit something so badly, to obliterate it with her hand. She struck the wall instead. There was only hurt. No satisfaction.

She lit off toward the front door—still in her slippers—as her father yelled something behind her. She caught the tail end of a *damn it*. Then she was gone.

Valentina would not come near him until after Marie left to look for Angie. The dog followed Marie, as if this other, taller woman who had Angelina's nose could somehow make Angelina come back. He sat in the living room holding a dog biscuit. Marie paced the kitchen, asking him—in that voice that came so close, too close, to calling him an asshole without saying the words—what had happened down there. Couldn't the two of them just be nice to each other for a few days, at least? There were other words, words he should've gotten pissed at.

There was the sound of her purse rustling and her keys jangling; there was the front door, closing hard (but not slamming—slamming really would piss him off). There were many things that came to him: flashes of his little girl as she aped his boxing stance, yelling, "Show me!" But, really, there was only one thing: Valentina's eyes. They weren't just sad dog eyes. They were damp and soft with what, in a human woman, would have been anger dulled into disappointment. Which was always more damning.

The dog sniffed his fingers and drew back. He whistled for her softly.

"Come on, baby."

She approached him again, lapping once, twice at the biscuit on his flattened palm before she grazed his skin with her warm snout. Crumbs fell into the creases of his hand, and when he shook it clean, Valentina flinched away.

"No, no, I'm sorry. Look—"

He had nothing to else to say. He just let his hand dangle, limp like a hanged man, so she could smell his knuckles. She did, eventually. Dogs did not have long memories.

CHAPTER EIGHT

MARIE SEARCHED FOR ANGELINA, DRIVING to three different twenty-four-hour diners before she spotted the rental car in the parking lot of the Nautilus. As soon as Angelina could drive, at sixteen, she would run off and hide in diners just like this one, like the ones Marie used to work in when she wasn't much older than her daughter was now. She didn't understand how Angelina found comfort in these dull, dingy places. Marie knew that other women would be grateful for a daughter who didn't hide out in bars. But she always wished Angelina would escape to someplace where she could meet people, where she was running to something, not just away.

Back when Marie used to work the diners, she'd change in the bathroom at the end of her shift, smoothing on her cat's eyeliner, reapplying lipstick, and spritzing herself with a Chanel sampler one of her roommates had stolen from her retail gig. Then, with her tip money, she'd take a cab to meet her friends at some new club. Dreadlocked artists, construction workers, and junior executives took her from the front, from behind; they grabbed her roughly, like something they'd seen work for Al Pacino in a movie, or else slid their hands over her hips and belly with a sloppy, boyish enthusiasm magnified by their drunkenness.

She had first met Jack in a diner not unlike the one where Angelina sat now. A greasy spoon on West Fifty-Fourth Street, at the tail end of the theater district. She'd been wearing her white rubber sneakers and starched white uniform, complete with an apron that wouldn't yield its mustard stains, and still, he called her over (even though she wasn't his server) and told her she was too pretty for dishpan hands.

"I don't wash dishes," she'd said, looking over her shoulder. She'd pivoted her hip ever so slightly, the bodily equivalent of a hair flip (something she'd seen Ashe do, with great success). Imperceptible, she hoped, to everyone but him. "I serve food."

"You're too pretty to do that, too," he'd said.

She conjured him ("thought of" was too banal a term) in her fundamentals of body movement workshop (she'd attended the same one for four years because it was the only one she could afford). *Think of an animal.* The instructor spoke with a breathy reverence. *Think of how an animal inhabits space, and how its movements express its intentions. To hunt. To fuck. To burrow, to nest.* Marie closed her eyes and willed Jack into being: shrugging off his jacket, pointing and thrusting with his forefinger until the man across from him set his coffee down and really listened.

The instructor said that she'd mastered her predators.

The night he asked her out, Jack came in alone. Ordered his usual: the milkshake with bacon cheeseburger, only he'd swapped the onion rings for French fries, which first alerted her to his intentions. He offered her his straw, and when she said no, pleading other customers and a watchful boss, he slapped his money clip on the table.

"Sure you can," he said, wryly enough to keep his conviction from feeling cheesy. The money clip was so thick with twenties.

"What is this, *Goodfellas*?" She sat down and took a sip. Her mother's voice flicked at the back of her brain with the precision of a snake's tongue: "If you can't be in the movies, you can at least live like you're in one."

Marie entered the Nautilus Diner. She didn't even have to scan the room; she went straight for Angelina's back booth.

Angelina was hunched over a sketchpad, surrounded by shavings and gobbed-off bits of gum eraser. A half-eaten cherry pie sat perilously close to her elbow, and she was still in her long-sleeved work blouse—

the olive green one with the built-in cream-colored camisole that Marie had bought her to celebrate her new job.

"Is Valentina okay?" Angelina asked in a thick voice. She did not look up from her drawing.

"She's fine, honey. You know how much he loves that dog."

Angelina stared at Marie with eyes that were reddened, rubbed raw, not with tears, not yet—though Marie could see (to her surprise) the fine sheen of water. Angelina had not cried since she was a little girl. Marie rued that knowledge: crying, after all, had been her art (well, part of it), and there was some purity of release, even in a minor scene. She supposed, though, that Jack was right: "The crybabies will never inherit the earth."

"I shouldn't have left her," Angelina said.

"It'll be fine. She'll be really happy to see you when you get home."

"Why are you even here? I thought you had dessert already," Angelina said. "Sara Lee pound cake not filling you up?"

Marie sat down, took a sip from Angelina's half-full glass of water. *Keep calm. Above all else, stay grounded.* "All the calories are in the packaging."

Marie strove for a tone as smooth and neutral as the ice chips slipping toward her throat. She asked Angelina for a bite of her cherry pie, since she was torn between that and the coconut cream cake. Angelina nudged the plate over.

"You're torn, huh? Like unsure of the validity of a two-state solution torn?"

Angelina was just like Marie's own mother that way, hawkish and sharp.

"You know, if I'd taken that tone with my own mother, she'd have eaten the rest of the pie just to spite me."

"Go ahead. It's cold anyway."

"I'm not saying I want it. I was just asking to see if I'd even like it."

"You can tell him I'm not sorry. Actually, no, don't even tell him anything. I shouldn't even say the word 'sorry' in any context when it comes to him. Unless, of course, I'm talking about what a sorry excuse for a Tony fucking Soprano wannabe Neanderthal he is."

Marie realized that, as she stood on the stairs, she'd been waiting for the sound of a slap, a shove. Something worse. She wondered what the dog's presence might have prevented. "I can't say anything unless you tell me what I'm supposed to talk about," she finally said.

"Why don't you talk about who was on the Ellen DeGeneres show this afternoon? Or what the top-selling nail polish was this week?"

When Angelina was born, Marie's bones went hollow. As if her marrow, her core, bled out of her in that final push. Marie could still feel this essence in the new body pressed against hers, but it was like a goldfish skittering through a clear pond, glimpsed in flashes, too quick to catch. Marie would only feel it again when Angelina cried—it re-entered her body like a homecoming.

"Maybe I'll tell you about Chekhov instead."

"Don't try to tell me that he's tired or stressed at work or whatever. I know that Eleanor works twice as hard as he does."

"And for less pay, I'm sure," Marie said sympathetically.

She'd periodically Googled Angelina, just to check for a Facebook page. Until recently, she'd found nothing but a few college papers on topics like "the hidden violence of line thickness," with titles like "I Spit on Your Canvas: Artemisia Gentileschi as Foremother of the Exploitation Genre," posted on some of her professors' websites as examples of student work.

Marie had been searching for a foothold, however tenuous; some random picture or Tweet that would betray (no, not betray, but *reveal*) a snippet of information she could use to start a conversation. She'd always been adept at improv: letting her simple objective—to get a phone number, to steal a bicycle—propel the mechanics of human connection. Just in the past week or so, she'd found a Facebook account for "Angie M." with a picture of a skeletal hand as the profile picture. The wrist bone was cracked, and bits of broken bone floated in a black background like tiny stars.

She'd found a few pictures of Angelina and Janet, mostly those sweet, goofy pictures girls took together, cheek pressed to cheek, camera held overhead.

The rest of Angelina's Facebook page was filled with articles about women's rights—female circumcisions in Africa (Marie didn't know how that would work on a woman, but she didn't want to click and find out), laws against abortion in the Midwest, and the wage gap—along with a few of Janet's essays about makeup and "slut shaming."

One of Marie's old roommates, a Greek girl named Tina, had been very political. Tina and her friends marched for abortion rights and the environment. They drank vodka and ouzo secreted out of the restaurants they worked for. They sat for hours at the kitchen table, debating whether Bill Clinton could "mouth-fuck his intern and still be good for women." Marie was often too wired from her last shift to go to sleep, so she hung out at the table with them and listened in. Tina asked her what she thought, and Marie said that she admired and respected Hillary Clinton, she really did, but there was still something to be said for "embracing beauty." Tina—who wore her white server's blouse unbuttoned to the bust line, left her black tie loosened—asked, drolly, what exactly that something was.

"Look at you," Angelina said. "Women's Lib 101."

"I watch the news, you know," Marie said. "I'm not a complete philistine."

The server who approached their table seemed like one of those brassily maternal women who'd always warned the younger girls about which GMs they really didn't want to be alone with for too long and which guys were simply lonely. Of course, those women still took advantage of their "old crow" status to cozy up to the creepers and snag all the Friday dinner rushes.

"I've got a soft spot for coconut crème pie, but I don't see any up there," Marie said. "What's the next best thing?"

"You can just have the rest of mine," Angelina said. "I was finishing up, anyway."

She nudged the plate over with her cast, smearing a thin ring of cherry filling on the plaster. Marie's hands moved without thought; she dunked a napkin's edge in the water glass, dabbed it along the cast.

Angelina wrenched her arm away so fast that a spittle of water caught Marie in the face.

Angelina dipped her fingers into the glass and ran them over the cast, spreading the cherry paste around without removing it. Marie saw that marker had bled into the plaster's weave, but she couldn't decipher the drawing.

"What is that?"

"It's a witch on a broom. Janet drew it for me."

Marie hadn't heard that kind of bashfulness in her daughter's voice since Angelina was a child, asking for a second piece of birthday cake.

"You and Janet are getting close?"

"You can go back to all my grade school teachers and tell them that I'm finally making friends."

Angelina was trying to come across as brittle and wry, but the subtle dimpling of her chin gave her away. Her narrowed eyes and the haughty tilt of her head were electrified fence posts; Marie could wave her hand in front of them and sense the rippling of the current. Perhaps that's why she said—after she said what she was supposed to say, which was that she was glad Angelina had someone she could talk to—"I wish I had a friend." The words just sparked out of her.

"Why don't you ever try those theater classes at the community college? They're cheap, you know."

Marie pictured all the pamphlets about summer acting workshops and the postcards for fall selections at the theater department, their Web addresses written on the back, that teenage Angelina used to leave on the kitchen table or clip to the fridge. The postcards featured Marilyn Monroe and Marlon Brando. Marie kept every one of them at the bottom of her top drawer, under her slips. It seemed to matter so much to Angelina (at least back then) that Marie take up acting again. Even now, her daughter looked at her with such concentrated tenderness.

"Oh, well, you know."

This was all Marie could say.

Angelina filled in the rest, tartly: "He wouldn't like it."

Her face assumed a milder version of the look that had emerged in her early teens, when she'd started blaming Marie (in part, at least) for what Jack did.

There was a night, not long after Angelina's sixteenth birthday, when he'd gone too far. Marie knew he had a temper—had *known* his temper—but she'd never thought him capable of *that*. Marie had taken to bed with a headache; she woke up to a thump, a soft knock of flesh on the floor. Her baby. She ran down the stairs, past Jack, who spoke without looking at her: "Don't let her sleep."

Angelina was in the kitchen, flat on her back, a pool of green water leaking from the back of her head. She was like a beached mermaid, eyes open, unblinking, her breaths sharp and shallow. Marie was only dimly, peripherally aware of her actions: sitting Angie up, smoothing damp hair away from a cheek that was already red and bruising. Angelina could hardly walk the few feet to the living room sofa; her body slumped drunkenly against Marie's. Angelina wept into the folds of Marie's robe. All Marie could do was murmur assurances, and then turn the volume up on the talk show laugh track every time Angie started to drift off.

Angelina would never believe her, but she'd hated him then. Hated him so much, she'd wondered what her life would look like on her own, with her baby. She'd burned with the kind of heat that can only come from freezing.

"You don't have any experience dealing with insurance companies," Marie said before taking a bite of Angelina's cherry pie. "They'll screw you over any way they can."

"Well, now, isn't that just vintage *Daddy*?"

They drove back to the house in separate cars.

Angelina arrived first. Marie couldn't see much, just the silhouettes of Valentina hopping with joy and Angelina bending down to kiss the top of her head. As Marie opened the front door, she heard the door to the basement closing. She walked up to the bedroom, taking each stair on the balls of her feet. *This is mild*, she thought. *We can recover from this.*

This was not that night in the kitchen, or the night a week or two later, when she'd come upstairs to find Jack sitting on the foot of the bed. His body was perfectly, neurotically erect. His mouth trembled. When he said her name, that diamond-sharp part of him that could cut through glass with a single look shattered. They blinked at each other through the pale dust.

"She hates me, Marie. She wants me to die. And I can't blame her."

Marie couldn't say that wasn't true. She couldn't blame Angelina, either. She also knew she couldn't leave. Angelina would, perhaps for good. Marie would suffer for that, and, at times, she'd hate him—maybe to the point of death. But the pale dust would settle, and without her hand to steady him, to pilot him through that debris as if he were a blind man lost in a blast site, he'd be lost to the cold suck of the void.

She wanted to tell Angie that once upon a time, it hadn't been scary to wake him.

Once he'd been fun, even sweet. Then they'd loaded his clothes and all her furniture into a U-Haul. She remembered the sunrise yawning across the windshield; how she'd thought the nip of fall air, cool and cleansing, could be a sign. "It's too fucking early," he'd said, rolling up both windows and cranking the heat. Angelina only knew that Jack, the man who'd come home from his first day of "schnook work" and punched the wall.

Marie had known the man who'd laughed as she'd iced his knuckles: "Well, that bastard will think twice, won't he?" Often, she didn't love what he did; sometimes, she didn't even love him, not like she used to. Always, though, she would love the man who heard her sigh in the passenger seat and knew to roll down the windows again.

CHAPTER NINE

ANGELINA SHIFTED HER HIP TO reposition the sketchbook balanced on her knees. The free fingers of her plastered hand grazed Janet's bare thigh. The feeling was a long, slim needle that frayed apart the straw doll of her body.

They were seated on the wooden planks of the stage where, in two days, Janet and some of her friends would perform in a queer cabaret: burlesque, spoken word, and a film screening. The night before, Janet had invited her, via text, to come down to the "creative living space" (which was really just a warehouse that had been divvied into dorm-like studios, still over $700 dollars a month) to help with the set decoration. When she arrived at the performance area—rows of fold-up chairs in front of a twenty-by-sixty-foot stage; cement walls, painted black—Janet greeted her with a hug just snug enough to give her hope.

Janet wore a shirt made from two tank tops sewn together, black under pink, and artfully frayed the edges. She'd stitched a design in the center of the chest, a horse skull with a unicorn horn. Silver thread with some glued glitter. Angelina chuckled, shyly pinched the fray along Janet's hip and twisted it between her fingers. Janet said she'd thought Angelina might like it, "what with the bones and all."

Angelina thought to ask about an exchange, a drawing for a T-shirt. But when she looked up on stage, she could see Janet had already given T-shirts to two of her friends. Not skulls and bones, but similarly unique: a bunny with butterfly wings and a cat with antlers. The girl in the bunny shirt was Maxine, a burlesque dancer with a sweet, shirt-stretching little belly and Bettie Page bangs. The girl in the cat shirt was one of the poets, Frankie.

The three of them had been puzzling over how to paint a pair of set pieces—"steampunk clouds: one a man's face with a monocle made out of the clock gear, and the other one a woman's face with copper wires for eyelashes"—and how they'd get those pieces to come together as the backdrop, then pull apart to sit offstage so a short film could screen on a large piece of blackout cloth nailed to the back wall. Angelina suggested they lay down a track like for a walk-in shower; even at ten feet by twelve, the plywood sheets they'd bought for the clouds were thin enough to be adequately supported.

"I told them you and your dad are two Sicilians working in construction who actually work in construction," Janet explained.

"I don't work for my dad," Angelina said, holding the hair trigger in her tone.

"Whenever my mother tries to give me 'career advice,' she tells me to network," Frankie said. "Anything that takes the brown-nosing out of the occasion is most welcome."

"You just have to brown-nose the director," Janet said. "But at least the director isn't wearing a suit."

"Oh darling, I'm going to *be* the director," Frankie replied.

So, this is a group of friends. Angelina felt like she'd spent the last four, almost five years confined near the windowsill of a tiny, empty room, where she'd only experienced the change of seasons by putting her hand on the glass, marking the heat or chill.

She knelt in front of her sketchbook and told Janet to start painting the plywood a "very light blue—cut it whiter than you're comfortable with, if you have to" while she started on the design. When she shook her right hand to loosen it, Janet took hold of it. She lifted Angelina's fingers, took them between hers, and twisted them gently, as if rolling cigarettes. She gave each one a soft tug. Popped knuckles teased relief before setting in a familiar stiffness.

They worked in tandem putting the basecoat down. Afterward, Janet worked on the costumes and Angelina painted the faces on the wooden planks. Janet sat on the edge of the stage with petticoats she had to let out, a pair of red hoodies that needed sets of black angels' wings sewn along the shoulders, and a bra and hot shorts she was stitching over with metallic sequins. She pulled a thin blue moleskin from her back pocket, set it on the floor, and squinted down at the open pages. Angelina smiled. Janet had sketched tiny skeletons and built her figures around them. The figures weren't quite in proportion; still, they were more solid and accurate than anything Janet had drawn before.

On their third date, hanging out at the Cylburn Arboretum—gardens of bright orange hibiscuses that Janet said looked like "tongues of fire;" so many rows of roses, the delicate white teacup roses, the solemn blue-gray roses, the red roses so hot in color and so thickly clustered that they seemed to throb on the bush; and the peonies, relaxing their obscene plushness in a feathery spread of pink—Angelina showed Janet how to draw figures. They sat on the steps of the old mansion house turned information center, the sketchbook open across Angelina's knees.

"I'm simultaneously jealous of, and aroused by, your talent," Janet said, watching her sketch the first outlines. She leaned into Angelina, the scent of her perfume—an ylang ylang essential oil that was a core element in the Chanel No. 5 she couldn't afford yet—supplanting the flowers and the night air.

"Well, show me what you've got."

Angelina had become accustomed to being the nervous one—the one who had less to offer, and not only knew it, but knew that the girl she was with knew it too. Now, as Janet took the pad from her and babbled about a lack of formal training and studying from magazines and those dummy models from the art store, all the "ums" and "you knows" were like fizzy little bubbles that rolled over Angelina's skin, delectably ticklish. Janet knew exactly what she wanted the clothes to look like, but her figures were skewed, the arms too short and the torsos too long.

"What you need to understand is that the body is in rhythm with itself," she said. At Janet's blank look, Angelina stood up, held her arms straight at her sides. "See, my wrists are flush with my hips and my elbows pretty much align with my waist."

Janet leaned back on the stair, pressing her weight into her elbows. She looked at Angelina in the same way Angelina had looked at many models, lingering yet clinical—then that look at became a look over, a soft leer that held onto her hips, her belly, and her breasts. She waited to hear that siren wail inside her head, urging her to sit down. But Angelina heard only that recent memory of Janet murmuring that she liked these flowers like she liked her women, plush and pretty, as she inhaled the scent from one of the fluffier peonies, as she stroked her fingers through the petals.

On the drive back to Janet's place, Janet brought up the burlesque show and asked Angelina if she'd be interested in helping with the set. Angelina agreed at once to do a giant set of panels as stage decorations. She did not say that she'd never ever attempted anything like that scale before.

Smaller drawings hadn't been so taxing on Angelina's right arm, but working on the larger plane, it became a rusted lock. Still, she watched the female face emerge from swirls and dashes of paint, and the pleasure of putting the light in its eyes, the heat in its cheeks, pushed her through the pain.

"We should find a way to save these when we're done," Janet said.

"I guess I wouldn't mind if they stayed here," Angelina said. "It's nice to have work that will actually be seen. Even if it's just commissioned work."

"Listen to yourself. *Just* commissioned work. You know, Michelangelo did commissioned work."

"I'm not Michelangelo."

"Not yet, but give it time, and someday you'll be yelling at the Pope."

Later that night, they sat on crates backstage, drinking Ruby Redbirds. Janet said Angelina's first foray into the theater was worth "springing for the good beer". Performers bustled out of the dressing rooms in kinetic blurs of fishnets and tassels. Frankie served as MC, cracking jokes about her Marxist feminist dialectic bringing all the boys to the yard, and sharing the story of how a cashier at her co-op with "an allergy to bras" had "unconsciously encouraged" her to start eating more granola—"I may have the clitoral equivalent of blue balls, but my cholesterol has never been lower!"

"Please tell me she doesn't think she has a career in this," Angelina said.

"I don't know. I mean, with time and experience, maybe. She's at least doing something with her passion," Janet said.

Angelina chided herself for *doing that fucking thing again. You always find the worst in other people.*

"Yeah, you know, there's that at least," Angelina said. "You should seriously start your own clothing line, just sell it on your own website. You could write your own marketing copy."

"I've considered it, what with the plentiful array of jobs for English majors who like to sew and my disdain for the time-swallowing world of corporate marketing," Janet said.

"I hear that," Angelina said. "I'm honestly scared I'll end up as somebody's secretary who just shows her drawings in little cafés."

"Oh no, you're too good for that."

"We both are."

"So, what do we do about that?"

"Between the two of us, we find a way to make something that's *ours*," Angelina said. "But you know, also something that other people would want to buy."

"I'm assuming that sex robots are already patented," Janet said. "Although maybe we could do artisanal sex robots."

"What would that even look like?"

"They're programmed to start quoting Neruda as soon as you come, and then afterward, they make you a pour-over coffee. And of course, they'd be painted to look like they were made from varnished oak."

Angelina started to laugh, but under the plaster, her skin ached with an itch; she had a desire, a drive as primal as eating or shitting, to scratch and scratch and scratch until she'd obliterated all feeling in her forearm. She tapped her cast against the crate, hoping the slow, rhythmic banging could distract her from the pain.

Janet reached into her backpack, pulled out a wire hanger, and gently bent the right side into a skinny oval.

"Do you just carry wire hangers around in your bag?" Angelina asked.

"It's a perk of the job."

Janet gave her a look that said *let me.* Angelina didn't pull away when Janet slid the wire oval through the narrow opening of her cast and slowly, with force and precision, soothed that wild itch.

The forwardness of the gesture made Angelina remember her first kiss. It was only two years ago, right after her nineteenth birthday. One of those shy nights in an un-ironic divey dyke bar: an older woman, salt-and-pepper hair, close-cropped, her body soft yet blunt, still in her work scrubs, who'd left the cluster of her friends for the corner of the bar, where Angelina sat drawing on a cocktail napkin. "Oh doll-baby, don't look so lonely," she said. Before Angelina could offer a "no, I'm fine" and a small smile of appeasement, the woman took her face in strong, dry hands and kissed her. The kiss was hard, but without heat. It tasted like whiskey. Angelina would remember it sometimes when she touched herself—the force in that woman's hands. *Here. Now. Mine.*

Angelina tried to conjure that force when she kissed Janet. A sense of infinity came rushing toward her with the loose-muscled elegance of an underwater swimmer. Then Janet pulled back, and that feeling slipped away like a current under a paddling limb.

Jack got up earlier than usual on a work day. He sat at the dining room table, looked through his files. As he chewed on a piece of microwaved bacon, he glanced down at his thigh. In her early days of being at the house, Valentina would've been resting her head there, giving him those *please, just one bite* eyes. His daughter had left, taken the dog (*her* dog, as his wife kept reminding him) with her to stay at a friend's house. Angelina had only been home for four weeks. Now she was gone again.

A bit of grease dripped onto his papers: the prices and mileages of used cars from all the Honda dealerships in Baltimore and the CarMax. He hadn't even plugged in anything ridiculous, just basic sedans from the mid-2000s through the current year. The cheapest option—a 2007 Civic—was still $8,848.09 (and that was the Internet price). Then there were the listings for apartment complexes he'd found online. A second-floor studio in a good neighborhood could easily run $1,000 a month at least; a building with a doorman or any kind of buzzer was in the $1,600s. Jack dabbed the papers dry, swearing *testa di merde* and *vaffanculo*. At least now he could curse out loud, and loudly. There was no Valentina to scare anymore.

He rubbed his eyes with the heels of his hands. He stared out the window behind him—at the deck he'd have to refinish and the rain-stripped wood fence that needed replacing, at the cul-de-sac of newer, larger houses owned by couples who were far younger than he and Marie had been when they bought this house, their first house. Marie came down in her nightgown, one of those slip-like numbers that always pleased him. Her bare feet slapped against the tile floor. All those costume shoes had eroded her arches, and the sound carried louder than she probably would've liked. Marie didn't mutter or curse when she was annoyed. She hummed and sang. Her voice had the metallic delicacy of tinsel. It evoked every frail thing you'd ever used up and tossed out.

"Your daughter could stand to show a bit more gratitude," he said.

She "uh-huh honey"d him without skipping a line in her song. *We are stardust*—uh-huh, honey—*we are golden*. She started fussing at the coffee maker. She always put the water in first, which he never liked. Made the coffee taste stale, somehow. Jack told her she needed to put the coffee in first. She just kept singing—*we've got to get back to the garden*—so he had to get up and reach into the cabinet above her.

"Don't just whistle it away, Marie. I'm down here at all hours trying to figure out her life for her, and she's out there—"

"She's out there trying to live it," Marie said, the song still in her voice.

"She's lucky she has a father who gives a shit about her future."

"I know that. Better than you seem to remember sometimes."

As Marie fiddled with the coffee maker's settings, her ass flushed through her white nightgown. She looked over her shoulder. Her face bloomed in laughter. It was not a mocking laugh. Something in the music of it galled him like a stone in his shoe. She knew this. She bet on it. She hinged forward at the waist, wagged playfully against his crotch. Her warm skin purred through his mesh shorts, coaxed him hard. Marie danced her feet apart, heel toe, heel toe. An awkward little shimmy that—as she bent, hands flat on the counter to square herself, to prepare herself—gently edged her open.

Jack's left hand lifted her gown. He kneaded the small of her back and felt the granular crunch of coiled muscle. He lowered his right hand in a loose fist, swept his knuckles through that dark crescent and parted her at the sweetest spot. Marie couldn't stand to be touched right on her clit, at least, not right away. It was too much, too soon. He pushed, hard, along the underside, worked his way in tight, concentric little motions. When she was just soft enough to shudder, he slowed down. She tried to crane her face to meet him at the eye, but he pinched the back of her neck right where her hair met her skin.

She held her neck in that position with a kind of martial fealty, even after they were finished, a tangle of stiff knees, slapped-red stomachs, and elbows grated raw along the rims of the countertops. His ankles ached. He thrummed with the brute satisfaction of taking a piss at the end of a long car trip.

On one of those ghost hunter shows he'd watched while Marie was at work, the geeky kid who led the team said that ghosts were "malevolent energies" lingering in a place where something terrible had happened. Maybe that was why his hands always hurt when he stood at the kitchen sink. Why he couldn't find anything more than a dry relief in how he and Marie had just come together.

Jack ran the dishrag under the tap, wrung it out once before dabbing the insides of her thighs. Her skin rippled with gooseflesh.

The backs of her knees had gone pale. He rubbed the blood back into them. She asked him to please, if he didn't mind, put that rag on top of the hamper when he went upstairs.

Marie turned around—to kiss him, he thought, but she was staring beyond him, at the constellation of magnets that had held Angelina's drawings until the paper yellowed and tore. When she spoke, her voice was a mournful crackle. She must've been tired. He knew she didn't sleep well when he didn't sleep well.

"Tell her that dinner's at six thirty, if she wants to join us. Tell her she can invite Janet." Marie turned around again to scoop grounds into the paper filler. "Janet is her friend. The girl I know from work."

Jack didn't say anything, only nodded. She knew as well as he did how many plates she'd be setting that night.

Marie pushed the on button, and the coffee maker rumbled wetly to life. Hazelnut smothered the smell of sex and sweat.

"Jackie? Please," she said. "Be nice."

Angelina bobbed on the balls of her feet like a boxer, like she always did in front of an easel when she was alone. She'd gotten used to being off balance; she held her cast up and slightly off to the side, as if she was consoling her left hand with the fiction that it could be called back into action at any moment.

She'd used the scanner at work to print out a page from her anatomy book, along with the study she'd drawn on her lunch break; now, she clipped them to the upper left corner of the canvas. A human back, a landscape of bones: the crags of vertebrae, the wide mesas of shoulders, and the peninsulas of ribs. She wouldn't bother with the base of a skull; she'd start with the C1, the Atlas vertebrae, the very tiptop, and end at the coccyx. Angelina laid the very thin lines down in graphite, fluid strokes that could be tightened and refined, darkened and deepened in a layer of choppier, heavier lines.

She would lose time and space, self and being, to that rasp, that feeling. Her life drawing professor once told her there were two types of artists: those who like making, and those who like having made. "And you, my dear," she'd added, "are definitely a process person." That same professor said that process was about conjuring—choice by choice, movement by movement—something human from the terror of blank space. For Angelina, process was about pushing something human back into that terror: a totem, a talisman. Some raw shape the terror could latch onto and be contained.

This was the void. She offered it the rhythm of the spine, that bob and weave between the slopes of bones. Angelina took charcoal to the hips, used a crescent of shadow to define the sockets. She applied the same stroke to articulate the underside of each rib.

They came to her, even here. Her parents. Mother slathered sunscreen on her back, blew a big wet raspberry between her shoulders. Mother's kiss tasted like coconut, only sour, with a chemical kick. Her father led her to the deep end of the kiddie pool, snuck her to the adult side when Mother wasn't looking; he held her up, the flat of his hand gentle and strong against her belly as her legs kicked vigorously, building momentum. And then he let her go.

Angelina sprayed the canvas with fixative. While it dried, she whittled her graphite into a pinpoint sharpness. She wrote one word inside each of those bones—in a script that looped and flowed like a laugh, a kiss, or else the word cramped up like a scream caught tight in a throat. *Daughter*.

The owner of the artists' space that housed the burlesque show was "ready to propose to" the set pieces Angelina had created. At least that's what Janet told her over dinner. "He was that in love with them."

They were in the corner booth of a diner popular for its rural kitschy décor—the wallpaper strategically snagged and coffee-browned, the chandeliers of Christmas lights strung around dangling hives of deer antlers and taxidermied animal heads. Angelina sat catty-corner to a bison head; she looked up from a menu full of twelve-dollar burgers and into the bison's eyes, which still conveyed the glassy dampness of life.

"That's great. Do you think he'd be interested in a show or anything? I mean, I have some of the bone pieces ready."

The bone pieces—or, sometimes, when she was feeling particularly ambitious, the bone series—would sync up, eventually, as a complete human skeleton. Janet thought the writing inside each section of the skeleton should align. "You know, flow like a story." But that seemed too tidy. The words had to come as intuitively as hunger, or an urge to kiss. She had just finished the back that read *Daughter*; shortly before that, she'd finalized the drawings of the hands that held the names of building materials, with an occasional *HIM* in extra-dark lettering, and that tango of scapula, humerus, radius, and ulna covered in *don't* and *please*. She would walk into work half drunk with exhaustion, but the knowledge of what she'd made beat inside her with the prideful insistence of a pulse.

"I think he wants to talk to you," Janet said.

She took a sip from her gin and tonic, her "old man summer drink." Angelina stuck with water, after having done the mental Jenga of phone bill and co-pays and dog food.

"Talking is good, but I'm a woman of action," Angelina said.

Janet gave a little snort, a gentle, teasing sound, but still, Angelina could detect a subtle sharpness. Their evenings were spent tussling on the bed, which Angelina enjoyed in the safety of darkness; Janet, though, wanted to keep the lights on. Wanted to "feel your extravagant tits up close and personal," and not just under a shirt.

"Just go talk to him. It's a start, right?"

Janet dumped out all the sugar packets and began to reassemble them in a new pattern of white, pink, yellow, and blue. Their server arrived, and Janet ordered a BLT with avocado, a side of tots and Sriracha sauce; Angelina requested a simple side order of fries. Janet interrupted: "Switch that to a burger and fries, my friend."

Angelina protested that it was okay, really, she wasn't that hungry. Janet said it was her treat, a thank you for working so hard on the burlesque show background, and on such short notice.

"A thank you I can accept. Charity is another thing."

"Consider me your patron who pays in upscale diner food," Janet said.

She took the fingers poking out of Angelina's cast and rubbed them, one at a time, as if trying to get a spark from kindling. Already, this had become a familiar gesture between them, a kind of shorthand for "be cool" or "it's okay." A sweet ticklish pain moved from Angelina's hand into her wrist, and from her wrist, down deep into her gut. It scared her; still, she liked it.

Later that evening, when they were back at Janet's apartment, Angelina emailed the owner of the artists' space—or, rather, she asked Janet to write her email to the owner of the artists' space. She really did try, but her hand was clumsy. It didn't craft the image of a mature, business-minded young artist with exciting new work to show; it painted a portrait of a pigeon-toed bumpkin fresh out of art school.

"Dear Mr. Dixon, My name is Angelina Moltisanti and I am the artist who created the set pieces. I have heard that you are interested in purchasing these pieces and I think we should meet to discuss prices that are fair and appropriate to the work. I am also a recent graduate of the Corcoran who has a plethora of new work that builds on my expertise in drawing the human form, while also offering an innovative take on that form through the use of anatomical drawings. While we discuss the pricing, I will show these new pieces to you."

When Janet read this, her face crumpled in that soft, about-to-laugh way; Angelina got up from the sofa and paced, said, "See, damn it, I told you I should have just showed up during office hours or whatever."

"That would not have been well received." Janet rubbed her fingertips over her lips, trying to make a show of wiping away her smile. "I'm sorry, I'm being an asshole. I don't mean to be. You really want this. I get that. Showing up would have shown initiative. Not this milquetoast 'mother may I' shit."

"You mean pitching? Welcome to being a working artist, lady."

Angelina stopped pacing. She stared at Janet; her eyes must've emanated the heat that flushed her neck and face, because Janet glanced down at the computer screen on the coffee table. When Janet looked back up, her expression wasn't, entirely, fearful—it held a cat-tail flicker of bemusement.

"I like a challenge," she said. After a pause long enough to make Angelina feel like she had to conjure a response, she held up one finger—a cue for silence—and got to typing:

"Dear Mr. Dixon, My name is Angelina Moltisanti, and I'm the friend of Janet Henderson's who pitched in and created the set pieces for the burlesque show this month. I'm glad to hear that you want to purchase these pieces, and I'd like to make a time to come in and discuss my commission. I've also got a portfolio of new pieces that I think you'll be interested to see as well. What days and times work well for you?"

Angelina sat down on the sofa, feeling blissfully hollowed with relief. She kissed Janet on the mouth so hard that Janet flinched a little.

That night, Janet slept atop the rumpled sheets wearing only her green boy shorts. Her bare breasts and belly emanated a soft heat that made Angelina think of early autumn air: it invigorated and lulled her, conjured memories of those night skies in her favorite season—plum-dark, streaked with inky blue clouds.

The glow from Angelina's computer screen washed Janet's skin a bright, ghostly white, illuminating a scar along the slope of her breast, near her armpit: a thick bolt of lightning, which, she had said, was a tribute to Aladdin Sane, cut with an Xacto knife she smuggled out of art class when she was only thirteen.

When she first saw it, Angelina asked if Janet had been "one of those girls who cut." Her tone was benign, even curious—she'd considered it herself, when rage turned her whole body into TV static and she needed to get steady again, but she'd decided that one kind of pain was more than enough. It was a tattoo, Janet said, or an attempt at one; she used to color in the raised flesh with a permanent marker every day before school, "Now I can't even get a real tattoo in that spot because of the scar tissue." She didn't want that tattoo—or any other—anywhere else. Only that image, and only there. "I want what I want." Said with a shrug, followed by a kiss.

When the response came that next morning—a simple "Sure. When works for you?"—Angelina asked Janet if "it could really be that easy, for once." Janet, adjusting her bra strap, mused that nothing about making or selling art was easy. "Because if it was, we'd get bored of it and become lion tamers or public defenders, just so we could get that petty rush of masochism and poverty."

The way she smiled as she said this, her mouth in a subtle half-tilt, her eyes hardened by the truth of it, stirred Angelina to take her hand and kiss each knuckle. Janet's eyes widened as if she'd been seen while getting dressed. The spontaneous gallantry of the gesture surprised Angelina. She'd only ever known surprise as a prelude to a scar, a moment when fear calcified into memory. Now surprise was the soft taste of skin salt and a floral lotion.

The next day, she returned to the artists' space with her portfolio. Mr. Dixon's office was on the ground floor near the theater; she could hear a man murmuring through his closed doors— "uh-huh" and "Well, now, we have to see" made audible just above the lock. She should knock. Be bold. Confident. Unless she shouldn't knock. She was fifteen minutes early. Knocking might be rude. She had scuffed her boots on that fine line between bold and rude many times.

The theater doors were open, so she stepped inside and stared at her set pieces, still on the stage, but covered in heavy black drapes. To protect them, she knew. Still, longing and anger, its twin edge on the blade, knifed her in the ribs. She wished her work wasn't veiled, that it could be appreciated—even though she knew she sounded just like those pricks who talked in CliffsNotes Nietzsche and only bought black coffee.

The closed-door murmuring got louder, added a "then there's the budget," so Angelina walked down the narrow hallway, stopping in front of the gallery. A sign above the doors read that the space was closed between exhibitions.

Between exhibitions. Like between jobs. Or between addresses. Only this time, the void winked at her. She swung her portfolio—filled with her bone pieces, and, because there were only three of them, some naturalistic paintings rendered off the nudes in her old life drawing classes, and four of the Kahlo-esque animal portraits—lightly at her side until a man called her name and apologized for making her wait.

Mr. Dixon (who insisted that she call him Elliott) didn't look much older than she was. His features were handsome in that long, vaguely Mediterranean way, though he was red-haired and freckled. When he took her portfolio to set it against his desk, she noticed a tiny tattoo along his wrist: two pairs of initials linked in anchor shape. He noticed her noticing, and said they belonged to his wife and baby daughter. All she could say was, "Oh, wow, cool," feeling as useless as a half-dried lump of clay. Photos of the wife and kid were tacked to the corkboard behind his desk, along with a scrawled-over calendar and a random scattering of Post-its. The office was small and windowless.

"I wanted to thank you, again, for pitching in on such short notice," he said. "You did really stunning work with no real time to do it in."

"Oh, you know, I had help."

"Yeah, Janet is a great girl."

A great girl? And just how did he know that?

"I didn't know you were friends, I mean, good friends," she said.

A tiny smile flittered over his face like a moth gliding along a hot pane of glass. Angelina couldn't decide if this was the kind of smile that came after years of being Janet's friend and recognizing that something sweet was happening for her. Or maybe he was smiling because he knew that sooner rather than later, he wouldn't have to be civil to another fleeting conquest. Did he know that Janet was a pretty girl, a popular girl, a magenta sunset and cobalt sunrise of a girl—and inevitably, there would be someone else to take in all that sky; that soon, black smoke and the heavy scent of burning would blot the horizon.

"She does good work," he said. "We're lucky to have her."

"Yeah, me too," Angelina said. She pulled her portfolio onto her lap, hoping he might notice and offer the mercy of a segue into business. He talked about how excited he was for the next burlesque to include male dancers: "I'm not sure Janet has ever designed for men before, so I'll be eager to see what she does."

"I brought some new work to show you," Angelina said. "Like I mentioned in the email."

"Don't you want to hash out payment for the set piece?"

"Can we do this first?"

"Sure, we can," he laughed. "But I've never met anyone who didn't want to talk money first."

Her heart clipped on in staccato as she tried to hand him her portfolio on the table; it clipped harder still when he said, "Please, let me," and opened it on the floor. He crouched down to squint, study, and "uh-huh" over each piece.

Finally, the judgment: "I can't say these aren't interesting, but I'm not sure they're right for our space."

Her voice came surging, with a missile's heat and speed, from the cragged depths she'd fallen through; she watched him zip up her portfolio from the center of the earth. "How are they not right?"

"Well, they're a bit discordant, for one."

"For one?"

He gave her that *how-do-I-say-this-nicely* smile. Usually, Angelina reacted to these smiles with a look back that said *then fucking don't*. But he wasn't a classmate or some old lady who frequented the coffee shop and felt the need to tell her that she had "such a pretty face" that would be "even prettier if you just gave a smile now and then." She had to force that smile now, and sugar her tone in asking, "I mean, can you elaborate?"

"What I mean is that you don't really have a cohesive show in these pieces. They're all in different styles, like different voices that don't really talk to each other."

"Oh, well, I didn't mean for them to all go together. I meant, like, if you had any particular pieces you liked above others, I would do more of them for a show."

Elliott rose up from his crouch and put his hands on his hips. He stood over the pieces, cracking his neck as he studied the piece open in front of him—one of the bone pieces, the back branded with *Daughter.* The best piece of all, she thought. Surely, he was about to say that these newer pieces had potential.

"I'm working on a whole human skeleton," she said quickly. "I've got the whole thing mapped out, so I imagine if I hustled, I would finish them up within a month or two, tops."

Angelina pictured the headlines for rave reviews in the *City Paper* ("Local artist turns broken wrist into heartbreaking works"), walking into her debut with her arm around Janet—Janet wearing her motorcycle boots and that mauve slip dress she wore on hot days when she wanted to go braless. She'd sell a piece and she'd kiss Janet on the cheek; before she drew her lips away, she'd whisper into Janet's ear, maybe a joke about what a good provider she was. Maybe she'd flex a bicep. Casted arm would be funnier.

"I think sitting with them some more would be very beneficial," he said. "You should really think about what it is exactly that you want them to articulate."

The headlines turned into those back-page ads for Larry Flynt's Hustler Club. Janet slipped back into her long-sleeve, ankle-length cotton nightgown she called "grandma chic."

"I think it's clear what they articulate."

Angelina had never actually considered what the pieces meant—at least not in a way that could be coolly articulated on a gallery wall.

"You know, they're about, like, our bodies as the foundational materials of, um, our beings. And how we carry the things we carry down to our bones. Um, trauma. And, you know, family."

"I'm sorry. I just don't see it."

"Why not?"

The "not" cracked like a brick struck by a hammer. The dust covered her tongue; she tasted powder and grit as her mouth began the blunt, mechanical motions of talking. "I mean, I would be invested in your professional opinion. About how I can improve."

"They're too stylized," he said flatly. "Almost like graphic design in terms of how wed they are to aesthetics alone. Your set pieces also have that strong sense of style, but there's such character in those faces, and in the choices you make with color, that they still have an emotional pull. But, like I said, I don't know what these new pieces are expressing."

If Janet were here, she'd be nudging Angelina's foot with hers or cutting a side-eye that said, *Be quiet, for fuck's sake. This isn't going to make him change his mind.* Angelina knew that "like I said" was code for "I'm done with this"; she knew that his smile was a locked door. Still, she had to have the last word. If she didn't, the heat in her cheeks might rise into her eyes. She wouldn't get teary. Not here. She hadn't even cried when she heard that telltale snap of bone or felt the bruising begin its heavy throb. This pain was both sharper and more lingering.

"Okay. That's your opinion."

"It certainly is," he said. Not entirely kindly. "Now, to the business at hand. The set piece."

She hated the set piece already; it was broiled chicken and broccoli and goddamn it, she'd come here for the steak. *Stop being an idiot. You sell this, you pay your medical bills, and then you tell Janet you're going to pay this month's rent, entirely—and with whatever's left, you take her out to dinner. One of those nice places on Charles Street, where you'll have to wear your work shoes.*

"Six hundred seems fair to me," she blurted.

The war drum of *negotiate, negotiate, negotiate* beat between her ears. Justifications sprang to her lips, and she swallowed them, hard.

"For both?" he asked.

"For each."

She was supposed to know her worth, to be a boss bitch, a baller. But negotiating didn't feel like landing punches. It felt like steering into a skid.

"I wish I could give you that. The work is worth that," he said. "But, sadly, I'm contending with a fixed budget, so I have to make an appalling counteroffer."

He gave a chagrinned little smile as he offered her four hundred and fifty dollars. For both. Angelina exhaled through her teeth.

"Four seventy five."

You give Janet some rent money. And you treat her to takeout from The Helmund. But you do a full four-course meal.

"Four sixty?"

You skip dessert.

She couldn't bring herself to say "sold," so she nodded. He talked 1099s and purchase orders, and all she could understand was that she was going to be taxed.

"So, we're going to be starting a new thing in the gallery, having pieces in there while we're getting ready for the next show. Little in-between exhibitions. I'm calling it the 'Not Really a Show' Show, and I'm definitely planning on including your set pieces, so I hope you come to the first opening. Day after next, so short notice. But it should be fun."

He sat back down at his desk, pulled a contract from his drawer. That was that.

That night, and the night after that, Angelina sat in front of the neck vertebrae and collarbones still in light sketch phase on the canvas; she took long sips of a neat, cheap whiskey and thought of how, within the span of hours, she'd gone from regarding them as elegant to the point of pathos, like a swan's body, whose long, gracious shape only announced its fragility, to seeing only the negative space. It was all a boring blankness—or at least that's what she finally said when Janet—fresh, or not so fresh off a double shift at the mall and on deadline—looked over her laptop, and said, in a clipped way, that if she wanted to be around "constant brooding, I'd watch those nineties teen dramas that Netflix is always recommending for me."

Angelina took a deeper sip of her drink, hoping it might make her sweeter and not meaner. Even her dog didn't want anything to do with her. Valentina was snoring by the kitchen table, under Janet's feet. It was a wet, gross sound, and Angelina snapped at her to stop it. The dog lifted her head with her eyes still half closed.

"Oh, come on, be nice," Janet said. "She can't help it if she snores."

Valentina grunted in agreement and laid her head back down on Janet's foot.

"She's starting to like you better, I think," Angelina said.

"She's thanking me for my tireless advocacy. Also, I might feed her toast in the mornings after you've left for work."

Angelina almost said something about little birdies dressing Janet in the morning before she thought better of it.

Janet could so easily insist on sunniness because everyone adored her—she was a blonde Snow White in an artful slip dress, radiating a buoyant, uncomplicated kindness that made girls, even straight girls, greet her with the most hopeful of smiles, like Janet's physical grace and inner levity could be absorbed, sweet rain into dull soil. *Trust me, girl, that's impossible,* Angelina would think. *I wish upon a star whenever I kiss her.* Janet always had her articles accepted. Janet was designing for two more shows in as many weeks—and she had a lead on a local theater gig that would, she said, pay her twice her hourly rate. Angelina didn't even know what that hourly rate was, or if she herself should have an hourly rate.

Janet even got to do work that tangentially interested her at her damn day job. But she meant well. She did. She was helping, really, when she said, again, that Angelina honestly should consider making all the words "sync up in a story." Maybe then she'd achieve that cohesiveness that Elliott wanted.

"Who's to say that what he wants is right?"

Janet stood up, gently extricating her foot from under Valentina's head. She signed as she arched her arms overhead in a long stretch that lifted her shirt up, just slightly. That wink of belly lulled Angelina into a momentary quietude, an awe—and yes, prickle of envy—at such casual beauty. Being embodied would never be so simple for her.

But there was, at least, the reward of watching Janet, swathed in pale blue fridge light, bend down to get a beer. Janet placed the cold bottle against her temple and closed her eyes. The colors playing over her eyelids must be exquisite: brown glass-shade reflected over that fridge-blue and the bright gold of her eye shadow. Angelina almost got up to look closely. Then Janet started talking:

"I know you're not a writer, so I could do it for you. I'd like to do it for you."

There was warmth in these words—Angelina could recognize that. Still, she put the drink down. She was one sip away from spitting back a barb. She licked her teeth and said thank you. She'd consider it.

"You're not really going to, are you?"

"I said I'd consider it," she said.

"I'm just saying that I think if we unified the images around a story—"

"We? Is this your work, too, now?"

Angelina's mouth flooded with a sweet blood taste, even though a quick sweep with her tongue confirmed that she hadn't bitten her cheek. She liked the taste too much; it went too well with whiskey.

Janet regarded her with a bemused aloofness that made Angelina think of a certain stray cat who hung out in the alley behind the building. Whenever Valentina approached, all hackles and snout, the cat would slink back toward a trash can, though not entirely behind it—he'd bat a paw at the bigger, toothier beast, as if to say that he wasn't stupid, but he wasn't afraid, either.

"Anyway, I'm disappointed in Elliott," Janet said. She sat back down at the kitchen table. "What's wrong with graphic design? Graphic design is beautiful, and it sells. You live in design; it's on your body every damn day."

"Would you seriously have them on your wall? The bone pieces, I mean. As they are."

"I would." Janet started picking at the label on her bottle, tearing it off in ginger little strips. "I'd even wear them on a T-shirt."

"You'd probably get some assholes trying to get all up in your boobs, saying that they're 'just trying to read' your shirt."

Janet's voice lowered in a flirty, ticklish little lilt that made Angelina's skull tingle. "I'd have you to punch them for me."

"But you'd wear them on a shirt?"

"Actually, truly, I would," Janet said. "You put the drawing of the backbones squarely in the center of the shirt—or you put the hands coming around the sides, like they're caressing the ribs. You'd have to tweak them a little bit, but yeah, they'd work. The skull should be really badass."

"I don't know what I'm going to do for the skull yet."

Already, though, Angelina was imagining her images everywhere: being stared at on subways, complemented in grocery stores and classrooms, traveling from Baltimore to Los Angeles and from Los Angeles to—Mexico, yeah, Mexico. Her drawings standing at a bus stop in Mexico City, wandering through a market and soliciting questions from a stranger—someone who'd ask the owner of this artwork (who could be anyone, really, not just somebody who happened to see a flyer for a show or who could afford to spend nearly five hundred dollars) where she bought it, and that owner could give the name of a website—or better yet, pull it up on a smartphone. Janet would have the fashion savvy and the copywriting expertise—but the art would be all Angelina's.

"The 'Not Really a Show' Show" more than lived up to its name. It was a random assemblage of pieces from some residents of the artist space, including a sixty-four-by-eighty-four-inch line drawing entitled *A Portrait of My Taint*, which was exactly that. There was a wall-sized photograph of a rattail disappearing down a sewer splashed in Warhol pink and yellow, and a sculpture of the Natty Boh man rendered in toilet paper papier-mâché standing square in the center of the room. Some drawings and poems were done by the elementary-aged kids who attended an after-school workshop held at the space—lots of stick figure families, rhyming pleas to older siblings to STOP MAKING MOMMA CRY/WHY OH WHY? and signs that read STOP THE VIOLENCE with the lone i dotted in a daisy head. And then, mounted along the very back wall, Angelina's set pieces. Which Elliott had titled *The People of the Clouds*.

At least there weren't many gallery-goers around to see it. Hell, Elliott himself hadn't even shown up—apparently, he'd asked one of the interns to open the space and lock it up again. The intern, whom Angelina and Janet passed in the hallway, didn't bother to stay, either.

Even Janet, who'd threatened a prolonged pout if they didn't "at least make an appearance," clucked her tongue. "*The People of the Clouds*. That sounds like one of those maudlin indie dramas that becomes inexplicably popular because everyone wants to seem so smart and emotional, and then it wins the Academy Award."

"What do you think it's about?" Angelina asked.

This had become one of their familiar riffs—they'd hear a cheesy song title or read an ad tagline or one of those "inspiration porn" article headlines like "You won't believe what this twelve-year-old boy can teach us about gender equality," and Janet would make up an entire movie around it. Right off the top of her head. She was like a knife-thrower, casually hitting bull's-eyes while the sideshow screamed on around her.

They needed a moment of levity. Janet had dashed home from work so they could carpool together and was none too pleased to find Angelina still in her drawing clothes and combat boots, her bare face flushed from walking Valentina. Angelina was none too pleased by all the huffing and puffing.

"Why should I give up even more of the time I barely have to make art to do myself up for a place where we're only going to make an appearance?"

"Appearances matter, though."

"They only matter if people like your appearance. Some of us have to make it by our wits alone," Angelina said.

"Some of us are smart and cute," Janet said. She gave an exaggerated shrug. "Binaries are boring."

Angelina made a show of picking the charcoal out of her nails. The tiny clicking sounds made Janet flinch—but wasn't this exactly what she'd asked for? Clean hands. Angelina even put on lipstick.

The car ride over may have been silent, but at least the car ride back wouldn't be. They'd keep riffing on this imaginary movie until they were washing up for bed:

"*The People of the Clouds* stars some really hot young blonde actor who plays an earnest Mormon missionary living in some East Asian country. Of course, he's gay and tries to be in total denial—"

"Of course."

"He falls in love with a beautiful young male prostitute, who plays him for his money by getting him strung out on sex and heroin, which of course gets him ex-communicated from the church."

"Of course."

"But the beautiful male prostitute has actually fallen in love with the hunky Mormon, and he flees the city, unable to deal with his guilt. So handsome blonde actor man becomes a junkie vagabond on the streets of this foreign city. He even loses an arm to some kind of infection. A crew of drug smugglers are about to recruit him to carry some smack back to the US when—spoiler alert—the beautiful male prostitute returns to save him, nursing him back to health and tearfully begging for forgiveness. And you know, the Mormon forgives him, which means he's found a new way to embrace his faith."

"Where does *The People in the Clouds* come in?"

Angelina leaned her hip against Janet's, and Janet reciprocated in kind.

"It's from a postcard of a mountaintop that the beautiful male prostitute keeps in his hovel; he shows it to the hunky Mormon while they're in bed together and tells him the story of how, as a child who was forced into tricking by his wicked junkie mother, he stole it from one of his first johns. Ever since then, he's dreamed of leaving the horrors of this life and living in the clouds. It humanizes him, even if it's a bit on the nose."

"You're a genius, you know that?"

"I'm good at cocktail parties."

Janet curled her fingers around the free fingers of Angelina's casted hand. She seemed to like this sweetly awkward gesture more than actually holding hands. Angelina liked it better, too. It conjured memories of the more benign, soothe-able aches of her girlhood: her mother smoothing aloe over sunburnt cheeks; the school nurse gently lifting that loose tooth out of her mouth; her father pulling a splinter from her thumb with an exquisite attentiveness, cursing under his breath but not hurting her, not once.

"Angie, honey, is this your piece? It has to be your piece."

Angelina turned around to see her mother walking into the gallery—and her father right behind her. He stopped in front of *A Portrait of my Taint* and made a fart-smelling face before he shook his head and joined them. Her mother embraced her with a startling vigor, the kind of hug Angelina would have expected for a college graduation or an actual solo show. "I'm so excited for you!"

Mother wore a black camisole, matching slacks, and a crisp white linen blazer—the kind of clothes she hadn't worn in years, not since she and Jack stopped having "date nights." The lipstick smear was hot and greasy on Angelina's cheek. She couldn't rub it off, though—not with her father staring at her. He had a jeweler's eye for her faults. His eyes finally flicked over her shoulder to take in the piece on the wall. Still, she didn't wipe the smear away. She stood there, waiting for a reaction to break across his face.

When Mother and Janet hugged, Janet was the one to kiss Mother's cheek. Theirs wasn't a benign, coworker kind of affection, as Angelina believed it to be. Even after they parted from their hug, Janet's hand remained around Mother's forearm. Mother smiled at Janet the way Janet would smile at her friend Frankie, with the brightness of genuine affection.

"I'm so glad you came," Janet said.

The *Kill Bill* sirens began bleating in Angelina's head: a loud crash of horns announcing the presence of an enemy. As the heroine advanced on the bitch or bastard who'd left her for dead, the movie screen always flashed hot red—the same red that filled Angelina's vision now. She watched her mother introduce Janet to her father. She heard Janet describe herself as "Angelina's friend." She heard her father say "Nice to meet you, honey" as they shook hands. His hand far eclipsed Janet's, sun-spotted and amply callused consuming the pale and nimble-fingered. Jack eyed Janet from her pixie cut to her polished toes

in a subtle nod that could've easily passed for a nice-to-meet-you. His
eyes narrowed around Janet's waist and hips. Angelina swore she could
see the corner of his mouth lift in a soft smile of approval. Janet, for
her part, seemed to study his face, searching for similarities, no doubt.

"Do you like the piece, Mr. Moltisanti?"

"You can call me Jack, hon."

Hon. Seriously? Hon.

"I think it's the best piece in the whole show, and it's not just
because I'm biased," Mother said.

There were so few people around that her voice boomed between
the walls, drawing the attention of the three hipsters in front of the
Natty Boh sculpture. Her father looked at the hipsters who'd tortured
their moustaches with hot wax, and then around the room again. He
shook his head with a sort of subdued disgust.

"Well, it's certainly better than anything else in here," he said.

Angelina rubbed her cheek. Like a child, she sucked at her knuckles
to clean the frosted pink of her skin. It didn't taste like candy or fruit. It
was bland and chemical. Her thoughts—*you did this. I can't believe you
did this. You brought them here*—must have emanated off her like smoke
rolling up from the tree line of a forest fire. Janet must have sensed it,
because she offered a tremulous, "I thought it would be a nice surprise?"

"I think it's amazing in its own right," Mother said. "I love all the
colors and the facial expressions. Did you base the faces off anyone you
know?"

She stood up close to the set piece, far closer than she would've
been allowed to get in a proper gallery, and air-traced her fingers over
the faces. Angelina looked at Janet and mouthed *no*.

"Actually, Angelina created the whole thing from scratch," Janet
said. "Then she free-handed it on the boards."

"Isn't that impressive, Jack?" Mother said.

"I don't know what free-handed means. Like I said, it's better than
any of this other stuff in here."

Janet started to explain what free-handed meant. He didn't look at
her. He looked above her, at the piece. Then Angelina noticed that he

was wearing his clean, pressed jeans, the ones he reserved for days when he'd be in the office, and the red polo shirt he saved for meetings. He'd polished his boots. Her heart slipped into that old hiccup, the exhilaration of waiting at the window for his truck to roll up in the driveway, even though he'd snap at her for leaving fingerprints on the glass.

She couldn't stop herself from explaining how she'd directed "my helpers" into setting the pieces up on a sliding track, so they could move on and off the stage as needed. "It was all my idea, so you know, maybe I did learn something from the job."

"That is so clever," Mother clucked. "I bet you could do this more regularly, like as an actual job."

"How much did you get paid?" Father asked.

"He bought the pieces off of me, so—"

"Okay, but did you get paid for the hours you worked?"

"He reimbursed us for the materials and bought us dinner."

Angelina's words were tiny and dumb, like mice scrambling over each other in a pet store pen. Janet inched imperceptibly closer. Angelina should've given her, a "don't you dare" stare, should've conveyed, somehow, that everything that was about to happen was on her. She elected to accept whatever small sympathy she could.

"Sounds like he, whoever he is, got some free labor."

"Mr. Moltisanti. Um, Jack. The way it works is that typically, you just get paid for the piece at hand, after it's done. Labor is usually factored into the price."

Janet spoke so casually, so confidently. He nodded at her, gave her a look that might've passed for approval if not for that loose bemusement in his smile, that princely haughtiness.

"I never got paid per hour when I did my parts, small as they were," Mother said. Mother's oh-so-helpful self: one of those blow-up figures outside of a car dealership, a giant balloon woman with her painted-on smile as her limbs were blown around recklessly by the wind, but she called it dancing.

He ignored her, spoke to Janet. "I don't know if Angelina told you, hon, but I'm working on her accident settlement for her. One of the things I want to use to strengthen our case is that she's been unable to do her art. She wants it to be her primary source of income at some point, no?"

"I made almost five hundredf dollars off of these," Angelina said.

Shut up, shut up, shut the fuck up. Please. God. Let it go. But the gallery space was empty now. She couldn't tell herself that she'd backed down to avoid a scene in public. Janet's breathing quickened, aligning with Mother's.

"Each one?"

"No."

He exhaled slowly. Angelina couldn't tell if this was his way of easing himself away from a fight, or if that heavy breath truly held the brunt of his disappointment. She felt the way she did when he used to snap at her for leaving those finger smudges on the glass—anticipation hadn't diluted the shame at all.

"It's still more money than I make at a full week of my nine-to-five job," she said.

"I know. We'll likely just have to subtract it from the settlement total."

"Oh Jack, how would they even know?" Marie said. "Janet, you'll have to excuse my husband. He's like a dog with a bone when he gets onto something."

"Intensity can be a good thing," Janet said. She patted Angelina on the shoulder, a conciliatory touch. Mother glanced at Janet's hand, and then at Angelina's face. Angelina denied her the sight of any relief or surprise—anything informative.

"Sounds like he got a real deal," her father said. "I don't know anything about art. Seems to me like you should have gotten at least one K for them, total."

"Now that we can agree on," Janet said. "I just wish these venues could afford to price out an artist's work more appropriately." Angelina shrugged Janet's hand off her shoulder.

"Hotels. Whenever we do the specs on a hotel, they always want a hefty budget for art. You ought to get your work in hotels," he said. This was his olive branch, laden with salty black orbs of blunt practicality.

"I'm thinking of going into business for myself," Angelina said. "Putting my art on T-shirts and messenger bags and other kinds of gear."

Perhaps she really had been. Perhaps the concept was like an ink in water, a ghostly tadpole of color and form—and perhaps she'd just tipped that water onto a blank page, waited to see the image that emerged. Janet gave the slow nod of "Well, now, that could work." Mother said she thought that the faces were "certainly pretty enough to wear."

Her father reached out suddenly. Before she could flinch, his hand was on her shoulder, where Janet's had been. He pressed his fingers down hard enough to draw up all the aches in her muscles, as if sucking the venom from a snakebite.

"Well, kiddo, based on what I see here, you certainly have the chops for it."

"Thank you."

"But don't discount what I said. Hotels. I can look up the next few hotel projects we've got coming up when I get back to the office."

Angelina and Janet couldn't even sit in the car and talk it out before they got home. Jack insisted on walking them to the car. "I don't understand why all these art places have to be the worst areas," he said. "It was like that when your mother did her plays, too." Angelina waited until he was a speck in the rearview before she put her weight into her foot, and her foot down on the gas pedal.

"Okay, I'm sorry," Janet said, her voice breaking around the "r." Angelina took too wide a turn onto Saint Paul. Angelina let the blur of road and the hot burst of engine answer for her. She ran a red light. Then a stop sign.

You will not be him. You won't. You aren't. You won't enjoy the sound of how scared she is as she tells you to stop it and talk to her. It's not a victory. It's not.

Janet followed her into the apartment, still pleading. Valentina was asleep near the sofa. She raised her head as soon as the door opened but lowered it again at the clamor. Smart dog.

"I know how disappointed you are in what Elliott did, and your mom is so nice and she just wants to—"

"Do me a favor," Angelina said. She grabbed Valentina's leash and whistled for her to come. Valentina approached with her head down and her tail low and cautious. "Don't tell me what my mother is."

The subject of mothers, in general, was a bear trap for Janet. It latched through to the bone, a blood trail of voicemails left at 4 a.m., teary and fearful about Janet's soul. Angelina found her in the living room after one of these calls. Janet sat lotus style on the floor; her breathing was jagged, and her face was slick with tears. When Janet took her headphones off, Tupac Shakur rhymed "bodies droppin'" with "ain't a-stopping." Janet gave a rueful little grin, cranked the volume. "What can I say? My Om needed some oomph." Angelina said that, as a fellow passenger to Hell, she could vouch that Janet's soul was absolutely, one hundred percent times a billion, going to be fine.

"I said I was sorry. And that he was an asshole. I'm not going to have the rest of the conversation while you're like this."

Don't ask her what she means by "like this." Don't do it. As much as you want to let a bomb burst through your skin—you'll end up back at his house. Hearing about hotels.

The bedroom door was closed when she got back from walking Valentina. Angelina was too vexed to sleep, or even to work. She paced around the sketchpad she'd propped up on her canvas, which held the first unsatisfying strokes of a skull, until she was too spent to do anything except lie on the couch and pet Valentina, letting the slow and repetitive motions of stroking between the dog's ears lull her into a shut-eyed stupor..

Janet was already gone for work when Angelina woke up, but she must not have been gone long, because the coffee she left in the French press was still warm. On the steamer trunk coffee table, she'd left several sheets of paper that had been stapled together. Each sheet bore a drawing, close-up, of a T-shirt, and each T-shirt held one of her bone pieces—the backbones squarely in the center of the shirt, two thigh bones along each side, frontward but just under the armpit, two hands coming around the sides, as if caressing the ribs. The last page included a list of sizing options, and then a list of "other goodies" (messenger bags, water bottles, and pins). At the very bottom, she'd written: "We can do so much better than some stinkin' hotel."

Jack got into the office early to look up forthcoming hotel projects. He'd seen hotel managers spend three or four thousand dollars on paintings that were just blocks of colors. Not even half as good as the piece that Angelina had let some asshole pay her less than one thousand for. Once she was healed, she could make a lot of money. Would never have to take another desk job or get lowballed by douchebags again.

He turned on his computer and saw that Crostini had emailed him—at five thirty in the morning—the specs for the job they'd be starting today: a "fitness center for children ages three through twelve." A kiddie gym. Then, a minute later, there was another email about Hector's promotion. Hector, fucking Hector, had soft-shoed his way to a promotion. Assistant foreman. Just a slight pay raise and some more responsibilities. He'd be watching the guys while Jack was at another site or stuck at the office.

Crostini said that she'd recommended "the expansion of Hector's role" because she'd been "impressed with his leadership, his sense of fair play, and frankly, after knowing his story, by his strength and perseverance." Jack supposed that was the only advantage of being weak the way Hector had been. Once you acted the way you should've acted all along, everyone threw you a parade.

Jack stood at the kitchenette, rocking back gently on his heels to let his Achilles yawn wide.

Women's voices rose over the crunch of gravel. Angie walked with her cast bound in its sling. Crostini carried her high heels in one hand, dangling from the tips of her fingers.

Angie bent her head as if she were staring down at Crostini's shoes. Jack couldn't gauge her expression through the dirty glass. He saw the way she slowly rolled her neck side to side, faking a stretch to get, if not a 360-degree view, then at least a 200-degree view of Crostini's legs. He'd have thought he was mistaken if he hadn't tried the same trick as a kid.

"No, seriously, you should register your business name and design the website," Crostini said. She nodded at Jack, the first tossed-off acknowledgement of his presence.

"We're building a new website?" he asked.

Angelina's cast knocked the box of sugar packets to the counter. She shrugged him off when he tried to help. He watched her assemble his coffee one-handed. Once she recovered from the sugar spill, she moved quickly, with purpose. He remembered her as a chubby kid, standing in the hallway between bedrooms after he'd had some fight with Marie: "I'm mad at you, Daddy. I don't like you at all. I don't like you ever." Hands on hips. Blanket tied around her neck, a crocheted cape dotted with juice stains. He'd laughed at her. What else could he do?

"That thing I told you about at the show yesterday," she said. "That business idea."

"Designing T-shirts?"

"Janet is a costumer. She knows what she's doing."

Janet, right. Pretty girl in an odd dress. He remembered a manicured hand on his daughter's shoulder. It wasn't just a "there, there" kind of touch. He understood, Marie's relief that Angelina had a friend, or a "friend." Even if it was a strange, sad, sort of relief. That hollow, nervous way Marie raved about Janet on the drive back from the show—"Janet is just such a bright girl, you know, always so cheerful and good with people. I really think she can teach Angelina how to be more relaxed"—made him snap, "Well, why don't you start fucking her, Marie?" Marie pouted all through dinner at the Olive Garden. He'd planned to invite the girls, but before he could even offer, the bright and cheerful Janet said something about "another engagement."

"And what do you think you're calling this business?"

"J and A Designs," she said. "Well, that's tentative, until I talk to Janet."

"Why not A and J?"

He looked over her shoulder at one of those laminated posters. A tiny earth sat atop one of those ancient Greek-looking column, over the words "KNOWLEDGE doesn't just CHANGE the WORLD, it IS the WORLD."

"J and A has a better ring to it," she said.

"A comes before J in the alphabet."

She nodded and shrugged. Her usual move to shut him down.

"How is my grand-dog doing?" he asked.

"She seems pretty happy. When Janet's not working, she takes her on walks during the day. Lots of squirrel sightings to report."

"That's nice, that you trust your friend with the dog like that," he said.

Angelina looked at him with minesweepers for eyes. But he hadn't meant that in any kind of way. Just that it must be nice.

"Yeah. Valentina is an easy dog," she said.

"Well, give her some pets for me. Tell her I miss her."

He walked away from the counter and over to his desk, pulled his windbreaker from the back of his chair. It wasn't cold out at all. It was just something to do.

Jack headed out to the site that Hector would be practice-managing— some rec center down in Sandtown, a great tax write-off and good PR. He let Hector drive, since Hector was "more familiar with the area" and willfully oblivious enough to take that as a compliment. Orange shag carpeted Hector's '05 Dodge Stratus. The windows and windshield looked soaped over with smoke. The stink of cigarettes and damp wool coat clung stubbornly to the seats. Hector had slept in this car. Not just one or two nights when he'd been too shitfaced to drive.

He babbled on about how grateful he was for the opportunity "to advance within the organization," and to Jack "for the refresher course in the ropes, so to speak" as the city glided by in a sidelong whir of brickwork and faded awnings, the Day-Glo piping of fast food signs and strip malls anchored by "Supreme Mercados" and "Dollar Values" the length of football fields.

"What does Angie plan to do once she's gotten used to being a graduate?" Hector asked.

Jack told him about A and J Designs. Hector said that name had a real ring to it. Whenever they were at a red light, Hector worked his stubbed, gnawed-nailed fingers over the grooves in the steering wheel as if they were rosary beads. His ma had shared that nervous habit, churning forefinger over thumb. Even as a kid, he'd known that the confessions he'd made up, and the real ones he'd hidden, were just like the space between his mother's fingers: only air.

"I can really see Angie starting her own business," Hector said. "She's very meticulous and driven. Got a good head on her shoulders."

"I always thought she was more like her mother," Jack said. "The creative type."

Marie really had been talented, at least from what he'd seen. She never had a lead part, or even many lines. Still, when he watched her, some mechanical hand in the center of his chest flexed open and fisted shut; he heard the slow groan of rust breaking up, flaking loose every time she opened her mouth.

But then she'd leave cartons of juice around her apartment, letting ants gather as she paced around, reciting lines to parts she didn't even have. Or she'd let the sauce bubble up and splatter on the clean stovetop. Or she'd forget her share of the gas bill and they'd find a nasty note one of her roommates had taped to the fridge. Or she'd leave the baby crying in the highchair as she squinted at some movie on the TV like she was taking notes.

That's why she'd let Angie get away with so much. Sneaking a few sips of his Jack Daniel's into her ginger ale. Staying up too late on school nights. Giggling or, worse, crying, into books that hadn't been assigned in school, books with titles like *Bad Behavior*. *Love Medicine*. *Bastard Out of Carolina*. *Dykes to Watch Out For*.

"Better to have a head for both," Hector said. "My son is gifted with the hair stuff, or at least that's what people say. I mean, I don't know what's 'artistic.' I just know what looks good and what don't. But he has no head for the everyday practical things. I'm glad that Jacob does."

"Is that your other son?" Jack asked.

"No, no, Jacob is Mike's partner. At least that's what they're calling it these days. Partner."

"Angelina has a friend," Jack said. "Pretty girl. She seems nice, too. Real artistic, like she is. They're going to be partners. Partners in a business. Clothes and things, you know, that girls their age will like."

He looked out the window again, at the bus stops with wooden planks lifting from the seats and a row of street trees that had sweaters knitted around the trunks, little sleeveless sweaters. People had been doing that for years, even when Angelina was little. Whenever she saw "a sweater tree," she pointed it out, so very happy. She was *whimsical* like that. He supposed this girl, Janet, she was whimsical, too. She certainly dressed sort of odd. Odd but pretty. He thought of Janet's hand on his daughter's shoulder, how soft and light her touch seemed. How familiar. Wasn't that what you always wanted for your children? To know they wouldn't be alone?

"My son's partner manages one of those big retail chain home good stores. Thank God he knows how to manage money, because Mike certainly didn't learn it from me."

"I taught Angie how to balance a checkbook when she was in middle school," Jack said.

He started to show her, a few times. In the third grade, or maybe fourth, she was given a sample checkbook to help her learn addition and subtraction. He was bone-weary from work and wanting a beer, his dinner, some merciful quiet before he'd nod off to the bad, always bad news, before he'd have to get up and live the same day over again. But he had to sit with his temples ticking and his throat dry, and explain, again and again, carrying over in subtraction. She couldn't understand how you made a zero into a ten. Couldn't get it. There was little kid literal-mindedness. Then there was just acting dumb to get his attention. "How does just putting a one in front of nothing make that nothing worth ten somethings?" Then she'd yawn in his face.

She looked at him like he'd *enjoyed* slapping her. Like he hadn't just wanted to be left alone in the first place.

"I don't know if this girl Janet knows how to handle money. I mean, I don't really know her," Jack said. "She has her own place though, and a job. Works with my wife. My wife says she writes some articles too."

"She sounds like a smart girl," Hector said. "Sounds like they'll have fun working together." He cleared his throat. "The important thing, you know, is that they're happy. It's always about that."

Hector's face softened like putty left out in the sun. His features opened with that half-melted dumbness of an object losing its form. Still, there was a shining hopefulness in his dumbness. That hopefulness made Jack feel cornered in the tiny car, like something unseen would catch him by the throat and never let go.

"The most important thing is whether they have a roof, a car, the skills to make it in the world. That's why I forced the numbers on her. Everything is online, and all the phones have calculators. But the Internet goes down. Phones fall in the toilet."

"That's very true," Hector said. His face cooled back into its proper form. "And they don't teach the basic skills like they should."

"I taught her just about every home repair she could ever need," Jack said. "I didn't want some random workmen in and out of her apartment."

"Well, you know what men are," Hector said.

A Viewmaster of the guys Jack had known clicked through his head.

"I wanted to teach Mike all that, you know. Snaking a drain, fixing a doorframe, unclogging toilets. The lot of it. We got about as far as hanging a picture with a level. A lot of that was me. But some of it was him. No interest."

"Did it ever piss you off?"

"I wouldn't say it pissed me off, but it sure annoyed me. But back then, whenever anything annoyed me, it could be DEFCON one. The thoughts I'd have."

Hector trailed off. The turn signal ticked dully into the silence. They slipped left past a mural of a man's hand holding a dove. The hand was so rain-mottled that Jack thought, for a moment, that it was a boxing glove wringing the bird's neck.

"It's not like there's a manual, or even a Post-It with a to-do list," Jack said.

"You know what I used to hate?" Hector laughed. "Killing spiders. Little bastards just creep me out, always have. Whenever I'm alone, I just toss a shoe at it, or a stack of papers, or what have you. I'm not even ashamed to say that I've gotten up and left the room, just thinking maybe the bastard will be gone when I get back. But when I hear someone else yell 'Spider!'—"

"You're the dad. Instantly, you're the dad."

Jack snapped his fingers on the "instantly." He remembered all the bugs he'd ever killed for Marie. She'd play up her fear for laughs, huddling in corners and jumping on chairs, crying for "Daddy" to come. "Kill it, kill it, kill it."

"Angelina was never scared of bugs," he said. "She'd stare at them in this scientific sort of way, like she could dissect them with her mind."

"You never had to deal with your kid joining the counterculture when it came to frog dissection time."

"No, and I think Marie was actually disappointed by that."

Hector shook his head and smiled.

"Your wife would have been proud of Mike, then. He bought a gallon of that fake blood from the Halloween store and threw it on the walls of the science lab. His poor mother was so livid she nearly sent him to live with me. Now that would've been a real punishment."

"Do you blame it on him just living with his mother? The acting out, I mean."

"No," Hector said. "I blame it on me."

Jack nodded, clucked his tongue along the roof of his mouth. A nice, noncommittal gesture. An appropriate gesture.

"It's good of you to get Angie that settlement," Hector said. "You must like feeling useful to her again."

"What do you mean by that?"

"Oh, I just mean, I know those years, teen years, college years, what have you. You lose them—they're out in the world and they're beyond you."

A woman's voice floated out of the radio, proclaiming its independence from some meeker previous self, and the unseen "you" that had held it down. It likened itself to thunder, to a tiger. It wasn't thunder; it was a bubble. It wasn't a tiger; it was one of those strays he'd find on sites, hissing and swiping, but always slinking out from under the truck for an opened can of tuna. *I'm so mad at you, Daddy. I don't like you at all.*

"Sorry for the singalong," Hector laughed. "That's Mike's new favorite song. He plays all the songs for me whenever we Skype. Makes his old dad a little less uncool."

"So, what's the worst thing you ever did?" Jack asked. "I mean, given all that we were talking about before. What's the worst thing?"

"You know, I wasn't even fucked up when I did the worst thing," Hector said. "I pretended to be, though. Pretended to be passed out on the couch while Mike yelled about some spider."

"Made him stronger, though. Tougher."

Hector sighed and said *you know* in that limp, deflected way people used when, actually, they didn't know and, actually, there was nothing smart to say. Jack steeled himself for the obvious follow-up, Hector asking him about the worst thing he'd ever done. Hector didn't say anything, just turned up the radio.

Jack remembered that night in the kitchen. She'd come home from some friend's house with green hair. Looked like one of those trampy girls from the old neighborhood. Girls who dyed their hair all kinds of unnatural colors and wore shirts that had been cut up around the chest, held together with safety pins. Girls who thought that every day was Halloween. Girls who didn't have to be smart because they were fun. When he told her to wash it out, she looked at him like she was too good to be his child.

If she was going to act like a baby, he'd treat her like one. Wash her head under the faucet. She bucked and twisted in his arms. She fought too hard, which made him fight too hard. He ended up driving the side of her face into the basin. He hadn't meant to, at least not with that degree of force, and certainly not so many times. She just needed to hold still.

After that, every time she looked at him—even, especially, when she'd threatened to kill him—she was that kid with a ratty old blanket for a cape. *It's a bird, it's a plane, it's Supergirl.*

Daddy, I'm so mad at you. I don't like you at all. His little girl. She hated his guts.

CHAPTER TEN

ANGELINA STOOD IN JANET'S KITCHEN, feeling sweet and silly from a mug of Jack Daniel's and ginger ale. She sang to Valentina, who was, as she always was in the kitchen, underfoot: "When I was seventeen, I was a very old dog. When I was seventeen." She had to improvise with the knife she'd stolen from her mother's kitchen, leaning her cast against the handle and pushing down on the dull edge of the blade with her good hand as she chopped basil to sprinkle inside the ground turkey crackling and browning inside a thin pool of olive oil. She'd stir in goat cheese crumbles and dried cranberries once the meat had cooked more thoroughly. Then she'd add it all to the nude pasta boiling on the back burner.

Angelina had taken to cooking dinner most nights. She joked about "earning her keep," a pong of sonar to detect any hint of annoyance, any feeling of imposition, in Janet's response. At first, Janet cracked wise right back, her voice a playful elbow to the rib: "Oh, you already earn your keep." She'd wink and nod back toward the bedroom. They'd discovered each other in the talk that followed, nipping at breasts and bellies, kissing and kneading the insides of their legs and touching, tonguing the bittersweet saltiness between those thighs.

Valentina stretched her snout toward the stovetop, sniffing avidly. "I'm sorry, baby, but this is not for dogs," Angelina said. Then she reached up into the cabinet bearing the big jar of peanut butter with BAMBINA written on it in black marker. "But this is." She held the jar against her chest with her cast and unscrewed the lid with her free hand; bending down, she offered the open jar to Valentina's tongue, giving the dog a few vigorous licks before it was time to serve the kibble. Angelina even caught herself crooning, "Time to serve the kibble," the way her father had when he'd made a show of feeding the dog.

Their evenings were spent on the living room sofa, consisting mostly of Netflix and work. Valentina lay beneath them, since Janet had taken to running her feet along the dog's hips: slow, tight circular motions giving way to broader, harder strokes. Sometimes, Angelina would watch Valentina for a flinch or a whine, a sign of too-fast, too-hard, too-much. Other times, she would just stare at the long arch of Janet's legs. She drew and Janet sketched designs or notes for an article, their shared silence broken occasionally by Janet's *hmm* or an *uh*, a tacit ask for feedback.

Angelina was sending more slides out to galleries. This time, at least, she could funnel that jittery sense of doom that came with every rejection by looking up similar businesses on Etsy to get a sense of how to price things. She told Janet she wanted a fall launch. Janet said not to worry about that, just focus on the work. Janet was supposed to identify vendors for the T-shirts and messenger bags, as well as a silk screener who could cut them a fair break. She said she hadn't found anyone she liked yet—although Angelina wondered how hard it had to be. Janet sure did talk a lot about her deadlines for articles, and what a dick the director of the latest show she was outfitting was.

Still, Angelina was trying to relax more. Sometimes she would be chopping vegetables or standing in the shower, and then Janet was behind her: hands resting on her hips, and then her waist, her ribcage and her clavicle, the hollows of her elbows. Janet would glide her fingertips between the thin bones of Angelina's right hand, or she'd lather shampoo into Angelina's scalp, rubbing her hair and the back of her neck. "I'm just studying my anatomy and proportions," Janet whispered.

Most nights they fucked with such vigor that Valentina, locked out of the bedroom, would whine and paw the door. Once, when Angelina came with an intensity that made her think she'd peed herself, the dog threw herself against the doorframe. Janet had to calm Valentina and Angelina, who was returning back into her body from some hot white cloud staring at the sheets with horror. Cradling her face, Janet said, "Oh no, honey, that's normal. That's actually really good, like *really* good. That means I did something right." Janet laughed and slapped her bicep, and Angelina's heart slowed.

Janet said she kept the framed poster of Brigitte Bardot as biker femme astride a motorcycle above her bed as "inspiration." Janet's movements were deft and muscular, their power magnified by the delicacy of her build. Her touch opened an infinite hallway of iron doors somewhere deep inside Angelina, burst them wide one by one, though the hinges had long rusted shut.

She was trying to lift the pot and dump its contents into the strainer when Janet's key turned in the door. The two left fingers that were un-plastered were simply too weak to grip the pot handle, and the pot was too heavy to be held by one hand alone.

"You're going to drop that thing, and then I'll have to rush you to the E.R. with a broken foot."

Janet hip-checked Angelina out of the kitchen and emptied the pot over the strainer. Valentina's nails clicked briskly across the hardwood floor as she rushed toward Janet. "I love it when she leans on you," Janet said. "It's so sweet. It's like, 'here, you're mine, and you can't go until I have properly loved you.'"

"Don't forget to run the faucet," Angelina said. "Cold water."

"So, Mr. Doodiecakes," Janet said, kissing Angelina on the cheek. "How was your big board meeting about the Hellmouth construction project?"

"I think Hades Corp is interested in partnering with us. I did have to decapitate Jenkins for missing a semicolon in the RFP."

"Well, I hope you were able to take his head off in one clean blow."

They'd taken to calling each other Mister and Missus Doodiecakes after mutually admitting that their lust for women was discovered, or at least confirmed, by surreptitious YouTube viewings of a TV movie about a doomed supermodel. The lead actress' features were so hyper-feminine that they bordered on caricature—especially the thick petals of her lips, which evoked all things that flush and swell. The model meets the love of her life, a straight-laced makeup artist, on a job; the makeup artist succumbs to the model's charms, a Brando-esque sensitivity both feral and kittenish, as the model succumbs to heroin addiction.

But, for a charming moment, while the model is enrolled in a methadone treatment plan, they live together in a tiny apartment; the model, who stays at home, calls herself "Mrs. Doodiecakes" and the makeup artist, who goes to work, "Mr. Doodiecakes." The model serves takeout hamburgers on paper plates. "I could be a fucking housewife," she says. "I could be very happy." She straddles the makeup artist, who sits at the head of the table, while lifting her shirt and laughing that dinner is served. The model relapses, and the makeup artist forces her to choose: love or drugs. The model ends up desiccated on skid row, dying of AIDS.

When they'd watched the movie together, spooning on the sofa, Angelina's laptop perched on Janet's knees, Janet cried over the model's death. All that the model had really wanted, in the end, was the love and acceptance of her mother, who'd regarded her like some rare and expensive collectable to be admired by company but never touched. Angelina had less sympathy for the model. She'd had the makeup artist. She'd had love. What did it matter if it didn't come from her parents?

Between mouthfuls, Janet spoke of a Web designer friend of Frankie's who was willing to cut them a deal on a site. "I wish you'd come out with Frankie and me to talk about it, but I'm having her leave a sample of the guy's portfolio."

Angelina had already purchased their domain name and found an artists' co-op with a silk screener they could use; she'd also walked out of a Target with packs of white undershirts (for men and women) in her backpack. Janet was to order the tote and messenger bags and whatever other fashion supplies she thought she'd need. Then she'd draft the copy.

"It's better for me to hang out here and make the art we'll be selling, my beloved Mrs. Doodiecakes," Angelina said.

Janet started laughing as she pulled a strand of Angelina's hair, black and wavy, out of her mouth. "Oh, Mr. Doodiecakes," she chuckled. "I'm so glad you didn't opt out and become a house husband after all."

My life never gets to feel this good, Angelina thought. No matter who she cared for, no matter how much she loved them, she was, and would always be, the girl who'd threatened to kill her own father. When she'd said those words, her molecules became planets, shifting their orbits to create a darker, colder universe.

She would tell Janet that Valentina had to go outside. She would tell Janet that she needed to get half and half at the twenty-four-hour grocery store on Forty-First Street. She would wait until Janet was deeply asleep and could only murmur "Okay" or "Get me some Skittles, please" in response. Then she would leash up Valentina and get in the rental car and go, go, go—a long drive through the city, the nightscape over her windshield like a wash of silver and plum.

As she drove, she told Valentina all about her Baltimore, the girl she'd been here, which felt somehow more intimate that telling Janet about those battles with her dad. Mostly, she supposed, she didn't want Janet to feel sorry for her, or for who she'd been on those long-ago nights: a girl alone.

She led Valentina through Hampden and Remington and swathes of Mt. Vernon. The dog would sit up, perfectly erect, perfectly alert, and look out the window; her face was mirrored in the glass, and streetlights glided through her eyes. Her mouth dropped in a heavy pant, as if she wanted to take in everything. Angelina talked about going to art shows and burlesque shows and shitty garage band shows and surprisingly good garage band shows in the concrete basements and plant-choked back patios of row houses turned into galleries and record stores and comic book shops that still had nicks along the wall where the old owners had marked years of growth spurts. Even the bathrooms smelled of boot leather and musk.

Angelina would walk out to her car, her heart ticking with bass and color and form, the slow swivel of hips. The wink of streetlight over chain link would turn dirty fences into weaves of diamonds. She should've had her keys between her knuckles. These were *those* kinds of neighborhoods: scrawny people wilting on their feet; bored men drinking on porches, whistling low and long as she passed them; cackling women with mottled faces spilling out of 7-11s, slapping cigarette cartons on their palms. Still, she felt at ease there. Nobody pretended to be kind.

"What do you think, girl?" Angelina said. "Did you like rock shows when you were a stray? Did you beg for scraps outside of the Black Cat Club?"

Sometimes, Angelina wondered if Valentina ever considered herself *her* dog, or if she was just some bipedal rest stop before a new life on the road. She would come home (and she guessed it was home now, wasn't it?) to find that Janet had left the door ajar, or flat-out open if she was hauling in groceries, and feel panic drive through her skull like a hot blade. Just before that panic could twist into anger, she'd see Valentina curled up near the column, contentedly chewing on her bone. *This is what I want out of life, too. An urge to stay put.*

Yet, coasting through the city, remembering her own stray days, she felt a full-body bang of nostalgia. Back then, her loneliness had revolved, inch by inch, in the center of her chest. Now that she was becoming familiar with someone else's breath on her back, someone else's fingers coaxing her out of herself, someone who would hold her face and tell her she was okay, she remembered that loneliness differently, like it was the rainy-day pain she'd know when her wrist fully healed, a dull, insistent sort of pressure that could almost feel good.

Angelina moved through her day job like a sleepwalker. She took notes and made coffee, transferred the phone lines and scheduled meetings without thought or purpose. She didn't realize how far gone she was until she looked up from what she'd doodled on the stationery or the calendar page: a set of foot bones, male-sized, running up through the ankles, mid-fib, and tibula. Those longer leg bones faded into plumes of smoke. Child-sized vertebrae were scattered around the feet, each bone perfectly intact but orphaned from its spine. She didn't fill each bone with a word; she let that word dance from bone to bone, leading the eye up to the smoke or down to the shadows under the tiny vertebrae, the long toes. That word: Love.

She imagined the larger version of this piece: She'd put this on canvas, could even burn some paper and have actual smoke marks. She could use bits of twine dipped in ink around the outlines of the bones to give them heft and menace. No, not this piece. Another one. Maybe an arm or a wrist bone. Let this one call attention to the smoke and all the delicate oblivion it conveyed.

Her father was at his desk, studying some plans, absently rubbing under his eyes, along the bridge of his nose. When he felt that no one was watching, he'd take the cartilage and gently twist until it cracked. She watched him do this at the dinner table, in the car; nobody else seemed to notice. She hoarded those moments of his odd, unthinking fealty to his body's demands like a prisoner secreting sugar packets from the mess hall; they wouldn't help her tunnel through the walls, but they were hers, and nobody could take them back.

The sudden ping of incoming email startled her out of her reverie. Ms. Crostini, who was offsite, thanked her for cleaning up some proposal via InDesign and asked if they could meet to discuss some "irregularities I've noticed in the August invoice report."

And this is where she figures out what an idiot I am.

Her father asked her if she was okay. She mumbled sure, apparently unconvincingly, because there he was, standing right behind her, reading the email over her shoulder. She flattened her good arm over the calendar page she'd drawn on. Her breaths were sharp and tight.

"This isn't anything," he said. "Could be someone on the other end messed up, forgot to round a decimal point or something. Happened to me a few times."

His tone was surprisingly solicitous, and the hand he put on her shoulder wasn't proprietary, but in consolation. That consolation had a campfire's warmth that crackled; it filled the grubby little office with the magnified brightness of flames.

"I don't know what to tell her," she said. "I couldn't make the numbers fit."

"Well, you're not a numbers person," he said. "Besides, you're not even going to be here that long anyway."

"The settlement is coming soon?"

He lifted his hand off her shoulder after giving one final, affirming squeeze. Now that he was older, his hands were thinner and blunter, ribbed with vein.

"They always want you to take less than you're worth. You just have to fight them."

She imagined her father, ant-sized in a subterranean pit, wielding his fists against a gang of humanoid bat monsters with men's legs, barefoot with ripped jeans and large muscular wings. A perfect pulp novel cover: garish flesh tones, blue bat fur, and hot lava red beating through the black stone. She laughed. He must've taken that laugh as an invitation because his eyes darted down to the drawing on the calendar. She flattened her arm into a barricade, even though it just made her look guilty.

Her father nudged her arm away with a soft hand. He hadn't touched her so gently since she was a child.

"I like this. I don't get it, but I like it," he said. "Or maybe like isn't even the word."

"You feel something?"

"Yeah, I do. I can't really put my finger on it, though."

"That's what I intended."

"You couldn't really show that at a hotel," he laughed. "But they show all kinds of stuff in a museum. I bet it would be a big hit."

"Yeah, I'll focus on the Baltimore Museum of Art once I can get a small gallery to actually take a piece."

"You had a piece in that one place."

"That doesn't count. It was a hole in the wall, and he didn't want the piece I wanted him to want."

"Whoever he is, he's a goddamn idiot."

This was the longest conversation they'd ever had about her work. When she was a child, he'd sit in his recliner, nurse a beer, and watch her between innings. His silent attention was like some bubble that floated over her, emanating a silky static that warmed and tickled her before it broke against her skin. She was aware of that bubble now, and the titillation of waiting for it to break.

"Are you going to put this in your online shop?"

She looked down at the drawing when she laughed. Laughing, however benignly, to his face, would break the bubble too early.

"Who are you and what have you done with my father?"

For a moment, they could have been, if not a sitcom family, then perhaps a father and daughter in a car commercial.

"I never said I didn't want you to do your art. I'm trying to help you get a head start with some money, so you don't have to job hop your whole life."

"I guess I thought all that hopping was just paying my dues," she said.

"I don't want you to end up like me, at the same place for so many years."

The guys were outside waiting for him to drive them to a job; she heard their voices—a laughed "don't be fucking dumb, man," a mumbled-but-affable retort, and some impression of the mumbler done as a dull slur—over the thrum of the AC.

She'd see them out there all the time, talking to girlfriends and mothers on their cell phones; they'd shift foot to foot even if they were leaning against the trailer or scratch at their necks with an absentminded vigor. She was moved by the inchoate delicacy of their gestures. They tried to smother that delicacy with a thuggishness that only amplified how sweet and unformed they really were.

Her father had been one of them once.

"So, anyway," he said. "How's my grand-dog?"

"She's okay. She's happy."

"She's going to be a wealthy doggie soon."

He started to cuff her, playfully, on the shoulder, and then stopped. He must've noticed her arm instinctively rising to block. Then he flattened his hand, patted her between her shoulders. She felt a quick cold stab of grief when he moved his hand away.

"Oh, and hey, don't worry about that thing with Crostini—she can be a busybody. Just her personality, I guess. Email her back and tell her that you're going to go over the numbers again, and she'll forget about it."

"And then get back to her about it?"

"No, you let her forget about it. I promise you, it's not that important."

"Sounds good to me," she said. "Anything to get me out of trouble."

He crossed over to the door, paused before he opened it. "The whole world is trouble. There's no getting out of it. That's all I wanted you to know."

Later that night, after she repeated his words to Janet, she said he was dragging out the settlement to punish her. They were in bed, with Angelina big-spooning. Janet's drowsing body as soft with heat.

"I don't know," Janet murmured. "I think this is his chance to finally be your dad."

"It's not like I asked him to start being my dad or whatever."

"Or whatever," Janet said. She kissed Angelina on the temple and eased off to sleep.

"I've never really needed him. Like once I wasn't just some kid, you know. Once I started paying my own way. I'm fine. I've *been* fine."

She was answered with light snoring.

Angelina could remember loving him. Her love for him was wild and whole enough to consume anyone else she might've ever loved; it coated them in amber, held them fixed in a cold space, apart and alone.

CHAPTER ELEVEN

MARIE HADN'T SEEN JANET FOR a while, not even at work. They seemed to be on different schedules. She knew she shouldn't think too much of it. Still, she wondered if, after spending all that time with Angelina, Janet had formed certain impressions about her. She was too old for these feelings, and certainly too old to get attached to a girl Janet's age who wasn't even family. She just missed her friend, even if that friend had only been a work friend.

Marie was more excited to see Janet in the break room than she had any right to be. The break room was small and gray, filled mostly with overstock, a microwave, and a fridge. It smelled of baby powder, burnt leftovers (pot roasts and carrots prepared by mothers, chicken tenders brought home from the bar), and body sprays in lemon and vanilla.

"Fancy seeing you here, stranger," Marie said.

"Oh yeah, I've been getting odd shifts lately," Janet said. "Either opening or closing."

Janet pulled a Tupperware container out of a canvas bag. Marie knew that most of the girls who worked until close ate their dinners before clocking in. She had never worked until close herself. Jack didn't want to come home without knowing what, and when, dinner would be. When Janet heated up her Tupperware, the scent of goat cheese and oregano filled the room. Janet shyly explained that Angelina (well, she'd said "she," but Marie knew exactly who "she" was) was

experimenting with black bean burgers, and there was an extra patty
for Marie. "Although, of course, in my haste of just waking up when I
have to leave the house, I forgot the buns."

Marie wondered then if Janet's sudden distance had more to do
with the awkward familiarity of that "she": the "she" who cooked for
her, who shared her apartment and probably didn't sleep on the couch.
Marie had wanted this for Angie—for someone bright and fun to make
her happy, and for her to make that someone happy in return. Still, she
felt a tiny pain in her chest.

"I certainly won't turn that down," she said. "Smells good. She
certainly didn't get her ability to season from my side of the family."

Janet set the Tupperware in front of them. Marie was surprised to
see two fat patties resting on paper towels. She supposed she'd thought
there would only be one, which Janet, out of pity, would split. Angelina
was content enough, now, not to hold grudges.

"Cooking is all part of being creative as a whole," Janet said. She
started talking about the online shop. "She is—well, I mean, we are, I
guess, starting a business. Which is going to be a lot."

"You girls are so enterprising," Marie said.

A nice, flat Mom thing to say. What else could she say?

"It's a little intimidating, I guess. But she's very gung-ho, so I'm
sure it'll all turn out well."

There was a pause between "gung-ho" and "so" that welcomed
Marie to say something like, "Oh, Angelina has always been that way
when she takes on something new, but she mellows out eventually."
She didn't, though. Angelina would stay up all hours on a school
night, drawing under her covers with a flashlight under her chin. Jack
would ask, with varying degrees of annoyance, why she'd come to the
breakfast table "yawning and droopy." But Marie would never open
the bedroom door and tell her "lights out." Nobody would ever have
to give Angelina permission to practice her art.

"Maybe it just feels weird to be thinking of life outside of the
college cocoon, where my biggest threat is my crazy neighbor," Janet
said.

Janet wore minimal makeup, a coat of mascara and pale gloss. She looked like a little girl, with tiny roses along her headband and her face still faintly swollen from freshly waking.

"I haven't seen much of you, but you haven't mentioned Mr. Paulson lately."

Janet flushed, shrugged, gave one of those *well, what can I say* smiles.

"I can see where she wouldn't stand for that," Marie said. "She's like her father in that way."

Janet took a large bite of her patty. She pressed her lips together—to seem like she was savoring that final taste, but really, to not seem so stricken when she asked: "In what way?"

"Just very Sicilian. About some things. When she was in middle school, I got a call from the principal. He said that some of the jocks in her science class had been threatening one of the gay boys. Angelina, apparently, told them that if they wanted to beat someone up for being feminine, they could take her outside and get on with it. The boys were so stunned, and, I think, so honest-to-God scared of her, that they reported everything, including their roles in it, to the teacher."

"I'm not sure that's Sicilian, just brave," Janet said.

"I certainly wouldn't be capable of it," Marie said. Then she put the lid back on the Tupperware with a satisfying little snap.

After her latest "thanks but no thanks" from a gallery that (per its website) "focused on the various intersections of the graphic arts," Angelina began to worry that maybe the bone pieces just plain didn't work. That Janet was really saying something without saying something when she "forgot," again, to email the T-shirt vendor and the silk screener. Angelina sent slides of the new work to her old life drawing professor. She didn't expect the professor to respond back to her within a day—or, honestly, even at all—and she certainly didn't expect the response she got: "I'm sorry you had to break a bone to get this work, but the pain is worth it. These pieces feel dark and urgent."

The professor listed a few contacts at some DC galleries and told Angelina to drop her name.

"Dark and urgent," Janet said in a singsong, I-told-you-so tone.

"I don't know why you think I'll get anywhere this time."

Angelina couldn't muster any excitement, only a benign resignation to try again—a full-body shrug, a great big whatever.

"Because once upon a time, young lady, I had to send out ten pitches before I had an editor bite. But an editor did indeed bite. And then I walked barefoot in the snow to deliver that essay. Uphill. Both ways."

A few days later, she let Janet do her makeup, purple cat's eye and plum lips, before she put on her black dress and dress flats. Portfolio in tow, she boarded a MARC train for DC with Janet and Maxine and Frankie, who'd come along, on Janet's invite, to "show support."

Her father had called her en route—she dismissed the background rattling as a bad connection in Janet's apartment—to tell her he was still "working those insurance fucks to a number I can tolerate."

"But it's what I can tolerate," she whisper-hissed. "It's my injury. My money."

Mercifully, Frankie and Maxine were engrossed in the sketchbook open in Janet's lap. Janet was guiding them through concepts for an apocalypse-themed burlesque: zombie rags with Velcro for easy tearing-off; machete-wielding hunter-babes in elbow pads and thigh-highs—and not much else. Maxine wondered if Janet could add heels to the boots. Janet said she'd considered that, but who would wear heels for the end of the world? Angelina's father clucked his tongue into the receiver.

"You really don't get that it's what's best for you."

The train lurched. Angelina flattened her right hand against the window.

"I know what's best for you," he said. "You want to try this business? Be your own boss?"

"Of course, I do."

"Then you've got to follow me on this."

She leaned her forehead into the windowpane and let the glass rattle through her skull. "Do you really think this business is, like, viable?" *Why do I care if you think it's viable?*

He answered her with a firm yes. No pause. No hesitation. Yes.

Janet mouthed, "Are you okay?" Angelina nodded, gave a "just nervous."

They filed off at the Dupont metro stop and walked several blocks to the gallery, which was called The Gallery at Seventeenth, even though it had moved to Fourteenth Street. The air was thick enough to swim in. Sweat gelled at the backs of Angelina's knees. Before they approached the gallery doors, Maxine wished her good luck and Frankie told her she looked hot: "Janet did an awesome job on you."

"I'm her huckleberry and her Frankenstein," Angelina said.

Janet said that being her huckleberry sounded "kinky and sorta gross." Her goodbye kiss wasn't full-lipped; her lips just grazed the corner of Angelina's mouth, enough to leave a trace of gloss, an unexpected taste of candied melon.

Angelina had expected the curator to be a chic-suited type with severe-looking glasses. The woman who shook her right hand, while murmuring sympathetically at her left hand, and lead her into a small, cluttered room in the back of the gallery wore a man's suit jacket and the kind of fisherman's sandals Janet had called, in one of her articles, "tissue boxes for the feet." Just above the doorway was a woman's head in papier-mâché, trophy-mounted like a deer. The woman's eyes were pure white with tiny, pupil-less specks of blue in the centers, her mouth made of red paper bunched up to look puckered.

As she watched the curator wordlessly flip through her portfolio, Angelina clenched up like she had waiting for the ER tech to snap her wrist back in place—anticipating a great pain, even though she'd been prepped and numbed. On the walk over, Janet told her, "Consider what the Buddhists would say. You're not losing anything if they don't take you, since you were never in the gallery anyway."

"You did these one-handed?" the curator asked without looking up.

Angelina nodded. The curator didn't say anything, not even an "uh huh."

"I mean, I can redo them, if you want, once my hand is healed."

"Don't you dare redo them. The roughness is vital here. And this one—" She opened to the piece called *Daughter*, that word tattooed inside the backbone, and made a soft *oofing* sound, like some physical pain had finally abated.

"This one is deep. I'd love to include this one."

"So, you want, like, a show?"

"I want to start with that piece, and the sets of hands," the curator said. "We'll go from there."

Go from there wasn't a dazzling debut, but it was, at least, a start. In a tumble of words, Angelina told the curator about J and A designs, asked about using the images on different kinds of merchandise. The curator didn't give her one of those *sure, sweetie*, smiles; she looked at Angelina with a wryly benign expression, as if to say, *You don't know what you're in for, but it's so worth it.* And sure enough, she asked if Angelina had funding for the site domain and design, enough to cover shipping costs. When Angelina said she thought you were supposed to charge for shipping, the curator laughed and said that when—not *if*, but *when*—something was lost or damaged, she'd have to eat the cost of a free replacement item and the shipping. "I'm assuming you want business from people who aren't just one zip code over."

There was also marketing—and promoting on a Facebook page or having a Twitter account didn't cover it. "You'll need banner ads on high-trafficked sites," she said.

Angelina had looked at some of the sites she—no, *they*, her and Janet; she needed to remember that—needed to advertise on. The rates weren't cheap, especially considering that she'd want an initial blitzkrieg and then staggered advertising on a regular basis. Then there were the bloggers and print magazines she wanted to review, or at least feature, the merchandise. So that was hundreds in shipping right there—plus the costs of designing and producing a special media kit. And that was marketing. Not even manufacturing.

"I'm expecting a settlement soon, for this," she said, nodding at her cast.

"Good. Not *good*, I mean, but better to have money coming in that's *yours*. No small business loans."

"Oh, I have loans," Angelina said. "Just not small business loans. Not yet."

"Sallie Mae owns my soul too. Well, her, or whoever she sold it to. That bitch."

The curator asked Angelina how old she was, and when Angelina told her, she laughed and said, "You have your shit way more together than I did at your age." Angelina had heard that before, in different variations, from teachers who exclaimed, "What a little grown-up you are!" to the girls who'd never taken Angelina past the living room sofa because she was just so *intimidating*."

"So, you believe in these pieces?" Angelina asked. She needed to hear the curator say it, directly, needed something she could write down, could tattoo over her heart.

"Yes, I do. I believe in this work."

The curator grabbed a file folder from the desk behind her. Her office was filled with files and papers spread open in bloom, erected seemingly in opposition to Ms. Crostini's tidy, manicured-looking desk. The white bookshelves against the walls sagged with the weight of textbooks and magazines, bobbleheads of green-skinned witches and the heroines from *Game of Thrones*, lady knights and blond women with dragons on their shoulders. Angelina wondered what the curator's home looked like. If she made enough for a sixteenth-floor condo with bamboo stalks potted on the windowsill. Or maybe she had a house with a mudroom that was piled with children's coats and wet boots. Two pairs of kiddie boots and two pairs of momma-sized boots.

"I want you to read this carefully and ask any questions. You'll fill in the name of the pieces here, here, and here."

The curator slid a contract in front of Angelina. Her nails looked gnawed down, not like Eleanor's, which were nude, but smooth. Or like her mother's, which were always some shade of lavender or pink.

"I hope you do get that line off the ground," the curator said. "I'd order a T-shirt. I bet my daughter would love a messenger bag."

————

When Angelina reached the park, Janet and her friends were shoeless and sunning themselves. Maxine lay on her stomach, reading, lazily swinging her calves and offering the soles of her naked feet to the sun. Light winked over Frankie's sunglasses. Janet balanced a book on her knees, absently pulling French fries from a greasy white bag. She looked up as Angelina approached, and her face so sweet and hopeful.

Janet mouthed, "Yes?"

Angelina nodded; she hadn't even set her portfolio down before Janet tackled her to the ground. The girls squealed their congratulations, even though Angelina just had a few pieces on show.

Janet kissed her on the forehead. Then she licked the edge of her thumb and smoothed the gloss off Angelina's skin. Angelina recounted the curator's suggestions for J and A, and Janet popped her thumb in her mouth quickly to skim it clean.

"You are going to seriously be those two bitches who make me feel hopelessly inadequate every time I go on Facebook," Frankie said.

"I may have to unfriend you," Maxine laughed.

"*Angelina* is the badass bitch who's going to make us all feel inadequate," Janet said.

This is what it should really feel like when someone is proud of you, Angelina thought. Janet patted her lap, and Angelina lay down. Her hair spread along Janet's bare thigh, and she could feel the ridge of femur under the subtle plush of Janet's skin.

Angelina closed her eyes. She was dimly aware of Frankie and Maxine laughing, of Janet's breath, calm and steady. She rolled her face toward the sun. The last time she sprawled out in the grass like this had been years ago, when she was sixteen and Mother kept her out of school because she had the kind of black eye that couldn't be explained away by a fall. Whenever he'd hit her before, the bruise would fade, the pain would wane after a few nights of sleeping on her side, knowing that accidentally rolling on her back or belly would turn her nerves into a hiss of broken fuses.

Her father's hands were shaking when he finally let go of her. He held her against the sink, tried to force her head under the faucet. Green hair made her look like a retard, a slut. She needed to stop fucking fighting. He knew better than she did. But she didn't stop fucking fighting. She'd felt his strength in staccato bursts of punches and cracks of the belt, but she'd never known the full torrent of him before. When she reared her back against his stomach, they became a singular beast, dark and snarling.

He smothered the side of her face with his palm, slammed her head against the sink. Again. And. Again. Until she went limp. She lay on the tile floor, a clammy slickness seeping from her head. Not blood, only water. The blood was in her mouth.

She was out of school for a week, but she felt too sore and glazed to read or draw or even watch TV. The pain was a fist inside her skull, knocking against her sockets and the side of her jaw. When Mother left to pick up carryout dinner—Fridays were still pizza nights, even if Angelina had to mash hers so she could bear to chew it— Angelina snuck out to the backyard. She sat in the grass, hoping the sun's warmth might ease her. Fingers of heat teased her face, circled her eye; the heat tapped gently against her swollen skin, but it didn't soothe her. That was what finally made her cry, and the crying did make her hurt worse. That was the one thing he'd been right about.

Years ago, she'd begged him for a dog. Her mother thought she should try and prove to him that she could take care of it, so she drew a picture book called "The Life of a Moltisanti Dog." Each page showed her feeding and walking and hugging a floppy-eared Golden Retriever-looking dog. She and her mother had even performed the book for him, Mother arching back on all fours, barking and shaking her head in a pantomime of canine bliss. He sat in his brown leather recliner, rubbing his temples. He said he'd consider it.

Days later, there was a stuffed floppy-eared Golden Retriever on Angelina's pillow. The dog had a red ribbon leash around its neck, and pinned to that ribbon, there was a paper tag with DOGO written in a large, coarse hand that wasn't her mother's. She wasn't even disappointed, or, if she was, it was a droplet of a feeling lost to the swell of giddiness—a present from her dad! The dog's fur held his smell: the earthy sweetness of tobacco and the clean, spicy tang of his cologne. She slept with Dogo every night; he had his own pillow on her twin bed, though she often burrowed with him under her purple bedspread.

Whenever Dogo's ribbon got ratty or torn, Angelina would beg her mother to replace it with a new one. And each time he got a new ribbon, she drew a new picture book about him: Dogo the Space Dog; Dogo Becomes President; Dogo, the Dog with Super Powers. Whenever she drew a new book, her father would sit in the white rocking chair in front of her window and take her into his lap. He loved it when Dogo farted on the aliens, made the Secret Service find his bones, and used his laser eyes to free all the animals in the pound. His chest quaked with laughter. Angelina felt like she was sitting on a fault line.

She'd have taken Dogo to school with her if Mother allowed it— and mother almost allowed it, but her father said she'd look like "a sniveling baby" and "the other kids would kick her ass over it." Over time, the oils of her fingers stained his fur; he lost his glass eye and the stitching in his tail. In time—around the same time she swapped out her blue plastic easel for a real wooden one and the Fisher-Price vanity dresser for a sturdy burgundy number—Dogo was relegated to that white rocking chair, the only piece she couldn't quite give up when she went from her little girl room to her big girl room.

The morning she left for college, she found Dogo hanged from the ceiling fan. His limp body circled the room, casting shadows over her father's face. Her father sat in the rocking chair, legs spread, slowly pushing up on his heels.

"It's a bird, it's a plane, its Dogo the Super Dog!"

He took a long sip from the mug she'd gotten him for some ancient Father's Day: a blue cartoon crab with a speech bubble in block letters over its head, DON'T BE CRABBY, HON. Angelina couldn't remember if she'd used her allowance to buy it from one of those mall kiosks way back when shopping with Mommy was something she looked forward to, or if she'd snapped it up at the gas station near the part-time job where she'd worked full-time hours and given it to him with the receipt still in the bag. The mug had been washed until it faded: only the crab's claws and the HON remained.

"I wanted to name him Dago," he said. "Your mother wouldn't let me."

He leaned forward, held the mug out toward her. She had come up for the easel; she should have just taken it and left. But she sat down on the bed and took too deep a drink of neat whiskey.

"It's okay to cough," he said.

She wouldn't, though. Her belly was a hot stone and her eyes were leaking. Still, she smiled back at him. His mouth sagged in a gentle, nondescript way that felt sadder, more contemplative than an ordinary frown. Finally, she cleared her throat, told him that she had to go.

"I shouldn't have done that to him," he said. "I was just fucking around, being dumb. He was your dog and you loved him." He tried to stand up, but his socked feet slipped on the carpet. His face was almost rapturous with surprise, like he was a little kid who'd just discovered the thrill of falling. Angelina caught herself darting forward as if to catch him. As if she could.

"Whoa, partner," he laughed. "Whoooooooa, Silver."

"I thought it was 'High Ho Silver, away.'"

"How do you even know that? That was way before your time. My time, even."

"Well, then how do you know it?" she asked. "Everyone knows it."

His eyes followed the fan; with each rotation, they slipped further into a foggy distance. "You should take him with you."

"No. I don't think so. The other kids would kick my ass over it."

Sunshine sifted through the window sheers; fingers of light swept the room. Except for him. He was backlit, his face haloed. She could only see the whites of his eyes. Shimmering. Wet, she'd have sworn. But he didn't cry. Hated crying. Crying always made it worse.

She stood up and he rose to meet her; he nearly slipped again as he pulled her against his chest. "Hey kiddo, you show them all what some Dago girl from Baltimore can do."

He hadn't hugged her in years. She hadn't wanted him to. But here, now—the warm crush of his arms; his hand, not stroking her hair, just resting tenderly at the back of her head like there was all the time in the world; that Old Spice smell that may have belonged to so many other dads, but would always be uniquely his.

She wanted the dog so badly, back then. She desperately wanted a friend. And he wouldn't give it to her. She did everything he asked. She did more than what he asked. She showed him how talented she was, how smart and creative. She showed him that he should have been proud of her. All that work, all that dreaming and drawing, all that pleading and putting on shows. All for him. All so he could see that she deserved the sweet orbit of his affection. So he could see how good she was—and she was *so* good. She was never good enough. Nothing was, or would be.

But she had her dog now, didn't she? Here she was, lying in the warm grass with girls who didn't make her feel like a stranger, with *her* girl, who gave her a bed and a home; who believed in her, so much so that she was going to fuse her name with Angelina's and share the twinned beauty of their work. All of this, it was hers. She hadn't asked him for permission. She didn't need to.

"I think I'm going to call the insurance guy," Angelina murmured. "Just to see what they're offering. I mean, I'm getting the cast off in a week. It's time to be done."

"Won't your dad lose his meatballs if he doesn't get to play big man?"

"Lose his meatballs. That's funny. I'm going to remember that when he's disowning me."

Janet said sorry, she couldn't help herself; she'd always found machismo funny. "It's a comedy of futility, like watching tiny dogs trying to hump fence posts." Then she asked if Angelina was serious, if he really would disown her.

"He'll definitely lose his meatballs. This will be it for a while."

It for a while. She'd anticipated, even longed for, "it for a while." She'd had spells of "it for a while." But he was always there: ghost fists and the hand on her back, an occasional "attagirl" and the metallic taste flooding her mouth whenever someone drove too fast or too slow. This, though, could be different. This would be scorched earth. When she closed her eyes, she imagined putting her lips to the ground, and trying to hum new life into all that had burned. A whole ecosystem whirling up from the ashes—trees laden with fruits that yielded mouthfuls of sweet water on the first bite; rows and rows of tall rose bushes with blooms so thick and deep that bees got drunk inside them; tendrils of mint blanketing the earth, spreading that lush, clean scent.

"Well, we need to draw something on your cast to mark this auspicious moment."

Janet pulled her Sharpie packet out of her purse, uncapped the brown one. She ran the tip over plaster in a loose round squiggle with thin marks coming off the top.

"What is this, a piece of crap?" Angelina asked with playful indignation.

"No, it's a meatball! See, these are the steam marks, because—" and here she assumed a cartoon Italian accent—"it's a steaming meat-a-ball. Piping a' hot."

"Piping hot, indeed."

"But you're sure you want to?" Janet asked in a low voice. Frankie and Maxine were huddled together, looking at some page in Maxine's book. Janet shifted her hips, and the motion made Angelina feel like she was floating, bobbed and buoyed by tiny waves. Soft, slow rock of sea. Smell of grass, scent of Janet's sweat, sweetened by powder.

"Seriously, are you sure?" Janet asked.

Angelina's father hadn't hit her since she was seventeen. That night at the sink had been the last time. A week or two later, she told him that if he ever lifted a hand to her again, she would kill him. She spoke calmly. She was at the counter, smearing peanut butter over her toast with a steak knife. He was standing right behind her to get coffee from the overhead cabinet. She snapped when he told her to watch her head.

One of the prized specimens in the menagerie of his pet peeves was using the steak knives for anything but steak. He hadn't grown up with good knives—or good anything. He'd tell her to "use your common sense" or "stop being so lazy" and take one of the "right knives" from the dishwasher and wash it. She knew he was looking down at the knife in her hands. In a moment, he'd thunder and bitch at her.

She turned on the heels of her stocking feet, the knife still in her hand. He looked at her as if she was a child landing her tiny punches in the palms of his hands. Then his eyes settled on her cheek. He cleared his throat, the closest he'd ever come to an apology.

"If you ever lift a hand to me again," she said. "I will kill you."

As she spoke, she knew that she could do it, even if it undid her. And it would undo her. He must've known that too. He communicated with her in nods and sighs until she finally left for college. Still, sometimes, she wondered if he ever missed her.

Angelina curled the free fingers of her casted hand toward her palm, rapped them against the plaster.

"Yes, I'm sure," she said. "It's time."

CHAPTER TWELVE

ANGELINA WAITED UNTIL HER FATHER had gone offsite to call Hunter, the insurance guy. Once her father's car cleared the lot, she used her master key to take the insurance files from his desk drawer. Eleanor was away. Still, she locked herself in the bathroom and dialed Hunter's office with her heart knocking against her teeth. He sounded surprised—and pleased, or, more likely, relieved—to hear from her. He asked her if her father knew she was calling. She told him that it was *her* broken bone, her money. Her pain and suffering. She thought of Eleanor on the phone with clients and contractors, firm and cool. No bluster. Confidence.

She accidentally hit the toilet's flush valve with her cast, so he had to repeat the offer. The "if you want any higher, they'll see you in court" offer: $13,400. Angelina could live on that for a while. The down payment on a very used car would strip her down to $8,500, give or take, but the cast was coming off, so she'd have more options for another day job. She could put that money toward a car payment and plead poverty for the student loans until she made a few big sales. Invest the lion's share of the settlement in the business. If—no, *when*; she wasn't going to be negative anymore—she sold the drawings, that would be a nice little nest egg; she could pull out the twigs for groceries, her half of the utilities.

She accepted.

Eleanor was at the fax machine when the paperwork came in. She must've accidentally read some of it, since her expression asked, "So?"

as Angelina rushed up. Angelina told her about her afternoon at the gallery, and then the call with the insurance rep, and how she was ready to get on with her work, her *real* work. "No offense or anything. I mean, you've been really cool." Eleanor said maybe they ought to sit down and talk and led Angelina over to her desk. After taking a sip of the coffee cooling near her keyboard, Eleanor asked Angelina if her father knew about her sudden initiative.

"I should have done this from the jump. I'm sick of waiting for him to deliver my life to me."

Eleanor smiled, and then silently pushed the mug toward Angelina, who took her cue to heat it up in the microwave.

"I know you know this, but I know how I was when I was your age, so I'm just going to say it anyway. So, forgive me, even though I can't forgive myself for actually saying 'when I was your age' and meaning it," Eleanor said. "That's a decent amount of money, but it'll go quicker than you think. Use it to get your business off the ground, but make sure you still have a steady income and health care, obviously."

Angelina looked at the skein of clay-pale cream atop Eleanor's coffee. She teased Eleanor that twice-nuked coffee was just barely caffeinated milk. Eleanor joked back that she'd read too much caffeine caused wrinkles, and she preferred to age prematurely due to overwork, thank you. Angelina could see the subtle strain in Eleanor's face: neutral brown liner that had been smudged in a moment of eye-rubbing exhaustion and wiped smooth with a finger of spit. There was something else, though, something Angelina hadn't noticed before: contentment. She'd always thought that only people who made things the way she and Janet did ever felt satisfied with their work, and even then, only fleetingly. Then again, Eleanor made things, too.

"Is this your way of saying that you'd miss me?"

"It might be."

"I would stay, you know," Angelina said. "But I think it's going to get awkward around here, once I fax the paperwork back and he knows everything. That's not fair to you."

Angelina pulled a red Sharpie from Eleanor's pen holder.

"That's very kind of you. But I happen to know the woman who runs this place, and she's not too easily intimidated."

"Does she happen to have some Hulk-Buster armor in her closet?"

"I don't know what that is, but I'm thinking it doesn't match my shoes."

Angelina laughed. She found a blank space on her cast and moved the pen in half-loops, a heart shape. Very lightly, though. As if it had already faded.

"Your dad reminds me of my dad," Eleanor said. "He's either very *disappointed* or very *proud* of me."

"You have degrees and a staff of men who report to you. That's a peacock feather in any dad's cap."

"You know, I think he's more disappointed that I'm not married than my mother is."

"Your mom is native Eye-talian, then?"

"Oh yes, but she was also the first woman in her family to go to law school."

"I'm the first woman in my family to go to college," Angelina said.

She almost mentioned her mother's acting lessons, but those didn't count—and the truth of them not counting made her suddenly, inexplicably sad.

"You're probably the first to start her own business, too," Eleanor said. She opened her very bottom desk drawer, pulled out a stack of paper cups.

"I guess there's still a lot to figure out."

"I'll help you however I can. I'm that nerd who does her own taxes," Eleanor said. She poured some of her coffee into the paper cup and handed it to Angelina. "Because I don't have champagne."

"What do we toast to?"

"How about new beginnings," Eleanor said. "And disappointing our fathers."

Angelina had always felt the presence of some dull machinery grinding away inside her; like the gears of a tank tread, it moved her forward, but not up. This, she supposed, was survival. She felt something

different now: the slow whirl of a propeller stirring a breeze somewhere
deep in her chest.

Marie was in the mall parking lot, sitting in the car with the key in the
ignition, listening to the radio and daydreaming about the women in
the songs. Stevie Nicks was crooning for the poet of her heart to never
change when Angelina called.

"I took off today," Angelina said. "I actually need to stop by the
house." She mumbled something, of which Marie could only discern:
"So this thing happened."

"What thing happened?" She couldn't help but search for that old
urgency in Angelina's voice, like some dazed, drunken bird banging
around inside its cage.

"I got pieces in this gallery. Like, art pieces."

"Oh honey, that's wonderful. Where?"

Angelina seemed genuinely pleased when she gave the name of the
gallery. Then she said, "Look, Mom, can we please just maybe keep this
to ourselves for now?"

*She hasn't called me Mom in—well, in forever. She's always just
addressed me, somehow.* Marie figured she'd keep the goodwill flowing
by explaining that she understood, of course, if Angelina wouldn't
want her father to know until after the cast came off—which was so
soon, she must be so excited, or maybe relieved was the better word.
Angelina laughed, said excited and relieved were both good words. So
Marie shyly suggested that, maybe sometime, they could all go out to
dinner to celebrate—"And of course, that includes Janet."

A tiny cough, a clearing of the throat.

"I actually wanted to know if I could come over now to get the last
of my things."

"Are you going to bring the dog? Your father would love to see the
dog, that is, if you don't mind staying a while."

"No, Mom, I don't think I can."

Marie said yes, of course, and her words were tiny boxes, painted
prettily; still, her disappointment smoked past the jeweled hinges.

Don't be that way. This is what you wanted for her. And if she's happy, she might even visit. Sometimes.

"Come when you want. Bring Janet whenever you want, too. We should all carpool to your show."

"It's not a show. The curator didn't take all of the pieces."

"Oh honey, be proud of yourself. This is really something. When I was your age, I hadn't even made it to an acting showcase yet."

"But you'd been in catalogs. Lots of people don't even get that far."

"That's nothing, really. People were just looking at the clothes, they weren't looking at me."

One of the first photographers that shot Marie, some twerp who thought he was the first guy to wear coke-bottle glasses, had laughed at her earnestness. Looked around his tripod and fixed his face in an imitation of hers. She saw the unmistakable scorn in his *I hate you, now fuck me* eyes and his absurd, over-plumped mouth. All for J.C. Penney's snow gear.

After a bit of "coaching," the pictures turned out fairly well—well, Marie looked pretty in them. She managed an arresting blankness that she thought made her seem poised and receptive, and she assumed the same face for her headshots. For Christmas that year, she'd given her mother a photo album full of her headshots, catalog pages, and Playbill mentions (she was only listed as "Woman in Crowd," but her name was in print). She'd paid one of her roommates, an illustrator, to draw drama masks and write, in her most elegant calligraphy, the words "The Show Must Go On…" on a sheet that she'd put in front of the album's blank pages. When she'd reached that sheet, her mother's smile was a match that wouldn't spark.

"Don't you think that's a bit presumptuous? New York is such a *hard* city, Marie."

Marie didn't know why she told Angelina that story. She hadn't thought of it in years.

"That's terrible, Mom," Angelina said. "What did you say to her?"

"I don't think I said anything. I took an early bus back to the city. I did steal the bottle of rum she'd used to make the eggnog."

"Did you drink it in a paper bag on the bus?"

"Actually no, I wrapped it in my scarf. And I pretended to have a wicked cold so the other people would leave me alone, let me have a seat to myself."

The heat of the rum made her feel liquid, like the boundaries of her body were slowly dissolving. She could be someone better than a girl her mother could be proud of. She could be boundless. Her mistake came in believing a promise she made to herself when she was spicy with drink.

Angelina must've heard that girl—the girl who'd forced a deep wet cough whenever some sad-eyed businessman approached her and walked away from the bus terminal on Forty-Second Street loudly performing her vocal exercises (and shouted "What? I'm playing Ophelia at the Old Vic next month!" at the winos who whistled at her)—in Marie's voice. Her "wow" was a response to that girl: a held-out hand. A *come out to play, wherever you are.*

"Who did you always want to play, Mom? If you could've had any part."

The engine's idle was a long sigh. *Take me somewhere.*

"Oh, I don't know. It was a long time ago."

"You didn't have a favorite character?"

"Well, I better leave if I'm going to meet you at home."

"I mean, don't feel obligated."

So, she really was moving in with Janet. For good.

"Just let me know when you want me to make a reservation, for us all to go celebrate."

Angelina mumbled an okay, and that held-out hand closed its fingers.

CHAPTER THIRTEEN

JACK WAS AT THE SUB shop near the office. He was waiting in a cheap booth when he found out that his daughter had played him for a fucking fool. He was picking up an early dinner—he thought he'd surprise Marie with her favorite, broiled crab cakes and French fries with extra oil and vinegar. While he had the time, he'd called Hunter to see where they were.

"Oh, you didn't know?" Hunter wouldn't even tell him how much Angelina had sold herself out for. "Since your daughter signed the processing paperwork, I'm not allowed to disclose that information. You'll have to discuss it with her."

No wonder the little bitch had called out sick. And to think, he'd made a special point of stopping at the grocery store on his way back from that morning's site visit, just so she could have ginger ale available when she returned tomorrow.

He stood up so fast that he banged his hip on the corner of the table, had to half hop outside to his car. There'd be a bruise. The flesh was already ripe and achy; it throbbed like a heart as he hustled past the Jewish mothers and their duckling children walking all in a row and sing-songing *hold hands, hold hands.* The guy from the sub shop followed him, waving a bag of greasy carryout, calling "Mister, hey mister!"

Jack didn't even turn around when he yelled for the guy to go fuck himself.

One woman, not much older than Angelina, pulled her girl close, out of his path. The girl wore a wolf's-head hoodie: felt ears and yellow button eyes, little fabric teeth. She stared at him even though her mother tugged her arm; her eyes were wide, but not with fear. With something like laughter. He stared back through his windshield. She reared her head back and howled.

Angelina thought she'd have more time. She even let her mother start making some coffee and talk about how she'd been looking up some restaurants in Washington, so they—her and Jack, Angelina and Janet—could go out and celebrate Angelina's show. Angelina couldn't bear to remind her that it wasn't a solo show, just a few pieces. For a moment, she wanted to live in the vision of a family seated in a back booth at the Capital Grille, debating whether they wanted an appetizer or a dessert until someone said, "Why not both? It's a celebration!" Once Angelina heard his key turn in the door, she knew it was too late.

The thunder of his boots. The way he said her name. He knew.

She was in the kitchen; there wouldn't be much room to maneuver. If she ran, he could catch her with a blow between the shoulders or to the back of her head. Better to hold steady, bend her knees and keep a low center of gravity.

"It was taking too long and Hunter said that—"

He rounded the corner with his arm extended, cracked her hard across the face. His face was a purpled blur. His hand, a white knife. Before her mind returned to her, she was aware only of a ringing in her head and the taste of blood and snot. She dropped the dish that, only a minute ago, her mother insisted—almost argued—that she take: a glass platter gifted at her wedding, since "we never have company, anyway."

Mother edged between them. She seemed like she could barely breathe; still, she smiled, said something insipid and cheery like "that's okay" or "I'll get that." Angelina bent low slowly, her eyes still on her father's hands, which weren't in fists yet, but taut and clawed, primed to grab hair. Her hands shook as she picked up a shard of glass. Her left hand ached inside its cast. All the blood in her body rushed to her most tender places, anywhere she'd ever been hurt.

"So, you're a real badass, now? You're going to take me out, right? Isn't that what you said?"

His voice was flint-struck, sharp and mocking. He flicked his fingers against her chest.

After this moment, her life could be over.

"I am smarter than you," she said. Her lips were already bruising. "I've always been smarter than you."

He pushed her with the flat of his hand until her back struck the sink counter. She looked at his face and saw a wounded bird in a paper bag, thrashing in fear.

"Mom, get the phone. Call 911."

She threw the plaster's weight against his belly as his right fist connected with her jaw. She could fall now. Could let him grab her hair. Could let it be over and done with. Angelina slid her legs apart, turned her knees inward. Her right calf pushed against his right calf, held him at a distance for the time it took to angle her left hip, get her knee in position for a perfect crotch shot.

His breath coated her face, filled her mouth, her nostrils, until she was breathing it back out again. She felt the presence of everyone he'd ever forced her to be—the little girl with a never-ending stomachache, the teenager who could never really fall asleep without hearing her head hit the tile, the grown woman who still believed that she was always one mistake away from never being loved—felt each of them hold her breath, waiting to see who she'd become.

She was aware, suddenly, of blood on her hand. She'd held the shard of wedding platter tight enough to bite through skin.

Mother tried to get between them. He pushed her back with a single shove. That shove, that moment between blows, was all Angelina needed. She kneed him square in the groin. He crashed to his knees, roaring. His head thrown back, baring his throat. The flesh there was surprisingly pale. Blue veins taunted her with their transparency.

Angelina held the shard at his throat. One swipe. She'd say she had feared for her life. Didn't she fear for her life? It would be so easy.

She searched his face for that familiar fury, but it had been blunted by pain. And something that was deeper and softer than pain.

Then she remembered being small enough that driving with him to pick up Friday's pizza had been a real occasion. He could've gone straight after work, but he'd stopped for her. On summer evenings, he'd roll the window down, let his wrist roll with the breeze. They'd sing to his cassettes, and the one he listened to most was a Bob Dylan song about some old gangster. She'd asked him to explain the song, and he said it was about a man who gets caught and goes to jail because he doesn't kill a group of hostages: "He does the good thing, but he suffers for it." They'd sing along together, "King of the streets, child of clay" and "We are not those kind of men."

Her mother would not call 911. All the color was broiled out of her face. She could only hold the phone toward Angelina, who could only tilt her head sideways, let Mother tuck it under her chin. Angelina walked backward toward the door that let out onto the deck. A breeze chilled the back of her neck, tickled her sweating palms. She managed to rush the lone lawn chair against the door, blocking him inside the house.

His face emerged in the glass like a ghost floating through smoke. He mouthed the word "open," slapped his hand against the pane. She felt the vibrations down to her bones, imagined shockwaves shattering the fragile strip of wrist that was slowly weaving back together. Angelina looked her father in the eye, and she dialed.

CHAPTER FOURTEEN

THE KIDS HE'D COME UP with got parties after their first arrests. Even the numbers guys, who never really left the offices, came down to the bar, shared a scotch or a beer— the man of honor's drink of choice. They cracked jokes about popping cherries. Guys who'd be going away for a while, four years at least, had special events, catered and everything, to mark their "going to college" upstate. Jack was one of the few who'd remained a virgin, and he'd been ribbed about this. Even though, really, it just made him smarter. After all, he never got caught. How those guys would have laughed at him now, called him a late bloomer: fifty years old and getting fingerprinted for the first time.

His hands were beginning to bruise. The black and blue started to surface under the fluorescent lights of the intake area. He'd been expecting a giant cell: rat-gray walls and iron bars, the sweetish vinegar of drunks' sweat. Instead, he sat in a room straight out of the DMV: rows of hard plastic chairs facing two TV monitors fixed to the wall, each monitor flashing the names of inmates—or not inmates, not yet—who were called up for processing. There was the dull murmur of people sobering up, the barking of guards' orders.

He didn't know what he thought the guys in jail would look like. He didn't think, though, that most of them would look like him—as he was now. He saw Marie's face through the windshield as she'd followed the police cruiser. He couldn't conjure his daughter's face. He saw the whites of her eyes, a flash of teeth, as her head fell back. That white became a feeling, a center-of-the-sun kind of heat he knew as anger. Only this time, the feeling didn't burn through his whole body; it shot through his spine, combusted at the back of his skull. This, he supposed, was fear.

The man sitting next to Jack—only four seats over—was in his stocking feet. His knees bounced, and Jack could hear the rattling of the man's waist shackle. Jack used to watch this reality show about jail on weekend nights when he'd been too anxious to sleep. He knew that the waist shackles were for rowdy inmates who'd calmed down enough to be processed with everyone else, but still posed some kind of risk. Jack started to stand up, move to another seat, when a guard approached. A young guy, built thick, he got so close he damn near stood on Jack's feet. "You do not move, you hear me?"

There'd be no asking for ice. Even when she wasn't feeling loving enough to put the ice packs on his knuckles, Marie at least left them in the freezer for him. His hands vibrated with pain. By the morning, he wouldn't be able to make a fist.

When he was in his twenties, Jack used to partner up with this kid Mike Volpe. He was a tiny guy, had more hair than height. The guys used to call him Mike Scimpanze. Mike might've been an accountant or some kind of tax lawyer if he'd been born in a different neighborhood. Jack once described Mike to Marie as "the grandfather I never had, sucking on hard candies and saving his receipts." As they grew up, Mike's fussiness ripened into an awkward, if brotherly, affection. He started writing "get dry ice packs" on his to-do lists, would bicker with Jack to put them on his knuckles.

The last time he'd seen Mike Volpe had been at some funeral. They scooped manicotti on paper plates and caught up. Mike had bought his parents' house but he had an apartment on the Lower East Side to be closer to his girlfriend, an ER nurse at St. Vincent's. He worked for a construction group, too, but his title was vice president of community development. Jack had just gotten a two percent raise, a cost of living increase, really. Angelina made honor roll in the first grade.

"Here it is," Mike had laughed, toasting with a paper cup of rail vodka. "The American dream."

Jack grew up with a tongue of clay and muscles ribboned in iron. He'd been valued for those things, paid to use them—but with caution. Not to do anything permanent, of course. Knuckles that sang like a struck bell, and the word, the cry, the spit-blood garble of *please, please, please* ringing in his dreams.

The isolation rooms must've been beyond the doorway beneath the TV monitors. He wondered if that was where the rest of the cells were, too. Concrete couldn't smother the screaming. A man's voice screaming a woman's name.

Angelina drove away from her parents' house for the last time. Truly, for the last time—there would be no more reluctant Thanksgivings. When she got back to Janet's, she slept on the couch, still sitting up. She wanted a little bit of time before Janet saw her, before she'd have to speak or move; she wanted to sit and become acquainted with the pain. It would be with her for a while. Valentina sat with her, head on her lap, in a silent vigil that gave way to the occasional whine. The gentle heft of the dog's head was consoling, the only thing she could feel through the obliterating haze.

Valentina seemed to understand this: she didn't move all night. Angelina was grateful that she didn't even have the choice to stand up. If she undressed or lay down in a proper bed, then she really would wake up to a new day, the day after she had her father arrested, the day she'd have to start deciding how, as one of the cops put it, she "wanted to proceed."

When Janet emerged from the bedroom, Angelina begged her not to turn on the light. Janet flicked the light switch, taking the air and the darkness out of the room with a torrent of "Oh my God, oh my God, oh my God." Angelina told Janet to go back to bed, "since once of us should get to feel like a real person." Janet insisted on sitting with her instead. Angelina described everything that happened using the metallic chips of words gifted to her by the two officers who'd taken her statement at the hospital, then escorted her to pick up her rental car like they were mild acquaintances. Words like "struck" and "at which point," words that dripped turpentine off a flat brush. She'd swept that brush over the image of her father led away in handcuffs. But odd streaks of color—like his face drained white or the faded blue of his jeans against the dark, crisp blue of the cop's uniform, or a very particular shape, the tilt of his shoulder as he flexed and strained against the tight cuffs—still bled through.

When Angelina, dry-eyed, slid her free hand under Valentina's chin, smoothed her thumb up the dog's muzzle, Janet stirred, murmured: "So, I guess this is an awkward time to tell you that I was going to have a surprise party to celebrate you getting off your cast. Everyone was going to draw on it, so you'd have a memento."

"We can have a party," Angelina said. There were only two days until she got her cast off. Valentina started licking her palm with a steady rhythm that lulled her. "I can even pretend to be surprised."

Janet lobbed out a wan little laugh. Angelina didn't catch and return it.

"At least you have the control now," Janet said. "You decide whether to press charges. That's something, right?"

Something in Janet's face, the way her eyes betrayed her oh-so-hopeful grin, reminded Angelina of the way her mother would ask if she wanted to draw her own birthday party invitations. Angelina said she supposed that was something. She said that, as far as anyone at the party was concerned, she'd fallen down the stairs while taking out the trash. Janet sniffled and said that was chilling in its specificity—that she understood why Angelina wanted it that way, but goddamn, she didn't like it.

"Good thing it's not up to you to like it," Angelina said.

The afternoon of the party, Angelina sat in the bathtub, letting the shower spray scald her until some new pain relieved the old one ebbing under her skin. She did not have to call Valentina into the bathroom. Valentina followed her everywhere; the dog's presence was constant and assuring, like having your hand held in a dark room. Angelina told Janet that she would not allow the party unless Valentina was there. "Well, where else would she be?" Janet said. "I was thinking maybe she'd hang out in the bedroom."

"No, she's with me. Or I'm not there."

So, hours later, Angelina sat at the kitchen table in a black dress and a dollar-store tiara. She drank neat whiskeys. Many neat whiskeys. Her pain became a slur of random, discordant sensations, like a wire that was sparking and slowing dying. Between deep sips, she explained to the guests—who were all Janet's friends, because she didn't have friends of her own—that the settlement was "done and dusted" and "that bitch did me a favor, since I have, like, thirteen K to start a new life. I mean, where would anybody our age get that kind of money?" When Valentina wasn't at Angelina's side, she was greeting and nuzzling the guests, distracting them from Angelina's black eye and broken smile. Good goddamn girl.

Most of the guests just smiled and wrote "Congratulations" or drew insipid little flowers on the cast. They wouldn't look Angelina right in the face; their eyes flitted over her bruises like tiny moths along a window. Voices rushed the apartment: talk of needing three more credits to graduate but not wanting to take another music theory class, of some office potluck or grant proposal due, of how annoyingly expensive really good, "derby-proof" fishnets were. All that breath turned the room hot and foggy. Angelina was about to ask Janet to open a window when Frankie straddled the kitchen chair, set a red Solo cup down on the table. Frankie rubbed Valentina between the ears with a "who's a good girl."

"She's about to be a wealthy doggie," Angelina said flatly.

"I don't know, I think I'd rather win the lottery or spend one night, like, dressed up in a panda suit to fulfill the fantasy of some eccentric billionaire than break a bone," Frankie said.

"I believe in suffering for my art," Angelina replied. She lifted her cup to her mouth, but it was empty. She breathed in the scent of whiskey sweet from the bottom. Maybe she could delude herself into thinking this counted as a drink. She snapped her fingers and Valentina came to her side, head on her thigh.

Frankie drew a small black oval on the last free patch of Angelina's cast.

"What are you drawing on me?" Angelina said. "Are you drawing some kind of weird sex panda? Because I won't have that. I will not. "

Frankie giggled, lifted her cup, and the little bit that sloshed out smelled honeyed and sharp.

"I'd love a little of that," Angelina said. "Whatever it is."

"It's the Jack Daniel's Tennessee Honey blend," Frankie said. "I can get you some. I like it with ginger ale."

"Ginger ale is for pussies," Angelina said.

She was loud enough to summon Janet in from the living room, where she'd been ranting about her editor at some beauty blog, who wanted her to pull the feminist history of corsetry out of an article about Victorian-inspired looks for the summer. Janet was trying to act *normal*. Like this was a *normal* party. For a *normal* kind of happy occasion.

"Well, they're both delicious," Janet said. She crossed over to the fridge and opened a can of ginger ale. Took the cup out of Angelina's hand and poured the ginger ale inside; her hands were shaking slightly, and the foam fizzed up over the lip of the cup.

"I wasn't done. I was gonna get me some Tennessee honey."

"Nobody's saying you're done," Janet said. "Consider this a palate cleanser."

When she talked, Janet's face assumed a bright blankness, like unpainted porcelain, something Angelina could break with one good throw.

Janet sat in Angelina's lap; she wore denim cut-off shorts, and her bare skin emitted an intense, opaque heat that made Angelina remember when her father taught her to grill: a face full of steam and the scent of rich, oily meat. Angelina sighed. She mouthed "okay" and drank the ginger ale.

"I'm sorry, Frankie," she said. "I didn't mean to accuse you of drawing a sex panda on my cast. You could if you wanted to. Doesn't really matter anyway, doesn't it? Nothing really does."

"You have a right to hate the whole world right now." Frankie circled her finger around her eye and made an exaggerated "ugh."

"What do you mean by that?"

"Just that, you know, you fell right before you were supposed to get your cast off. That's all." Janet kissed Angelina on temple. A flutter of a kiss—a kiss that didn't want to intrude, to cause more pain; a kiss that tried to float over her sore spot. But she was all sore spot. There was nothing left that didn't hurt.

"Well, you should see the other guy," Angelina said.

She could do this. Banter. Be light.

"I hope you kicked that stair's ass."

Frankie lifted her fist and Angelina bumped it with hers. Pretending was sculpting with air, shifting molecules until she made a three-dimensional image of herself mid-fall, just another clumsy, normal girl—an image she could breathe in and hold inside her cells.

Janet maneuvered Angelina's forearm on its side; the cast bore its white throat. There was a lone bald patch near the base, where the padding frayed gray and loose.

"I'm stealing the last word," Janet said, motioning for Frankie to give her the marker.

She slid her foot out of her cork-soled sandal. Her heel grazed Angelina's calf with the soft rasp of callus. Janet drew a rectangle with a face: X's for eyes and an open mouth with a lolling tongue. Two stick-figure arms with circles for fists reared up from the sides, and a word bubble floated out from the front: "Watch out for Mr. Stair!"

Angelina didn't know whether to take this as Janet "playing pretend" along with her, or Janet calling her out.

The next day, she drove to the orthopedist's to get her cast removed alone, by request. The orthopedist greeted Angelina with a cheery, "So, today is the day. I bet you've been looking forward to this." Then she looked up from her clipboard.

Angelina knew what she looked like four days after getting hit. Though she'd avoided all mirrors or any reflective surfaces, eating dry cereal with her bare hands and looking down when the steel doors of the elevator closed, she knew exactly where her face fell in spectrums of purple, yellow, and green.

She had been bracing for this, prepared two responses—the dirty limerick of "I fell off the curb" and the quick, clipped truth—knowing that, in the end, she'd toss a coin inside her mind. Janet told her that "being brutal with your truth" and "no longer covering for him" would be "cathartic and maybe even empowering." Janet wanted to cry, to talk. The constant expending of breath would somehow suck the venom out. But Janet just had to look at Angelina's face. She didn't have to live with it.

The fluorescent lighting in the orthopedist's office coaxed up every flaw in the plaster: the patches that had yellowed under sunlight and water stain, smudges where marker had bled too deeply into the weave, and a red-brown mark that trailed down her wrist like a comet. She tried to conjure her father's face through the glass door: was his nose bleeding? But the image was blurred and wan, as if she'd been squinting at it for too long.

The orthopedist said she was required by the health care reform law to ask Angelina if her injury was "domestic violence-related." Angelina looked down at Mr. Stair. The X eyes were meant to make him look dead and vanquished, yet they somehow made him seem even angrier.

"Yes."

She didn't say the word. She mouthed it. Coughed once to summon her voice. Yes, she had a safe place to stay. She was "out of the situation." She would be okay. The orthopedist said she understood; she was "mandated, though, to offer you some literature that can provide you with resources."

The orthopedist left, and her physician's assistant entered the room. He plugged a white plastic wand with a long cord into the wall, and as he approached Angelina, she noticed the saw blades winking out from the sides.

"This bad boy looks scary, but you won't feel anything but a tickle," he said. "I promise."

Something in that jocular, conspiratorial note of "I promise" genuinely put Angelina at ease. She was somebody's buddy.

He asked her to hold out her arm, to close her eyes if she liked, but please don't move. Angelina joked that she'd lived through much scarier shit. Yet she reared back at the muffled roar of blade through plaster, the stink of burning. The physician assistant kept repeating "Almost there" in a velveteen murmur. There was a small popping sound, and, when Angelina opened her eyes, the shell of cast had been halved; only the spiderweb of soiled padding held the cast along her arm. Then the physician's assistant snipped the padding away. Angelina's arm was bare—not bruised, only swollen, excruciatingly tender.

The orthopedist walked back into the room with some pamphlets that Angelina could "review in private." Three of the pamphlets were about the cycle of domestic violence, the resources available at a women's shelter, and "what to expect once you've left an abusive partner." The fourth pamphlet was about physical therapy for broken wrists.

"I don't think I'm going to have health insurance after this visit," Angelina said. "I guess maybe he'll kick me off." She cleared her throat. "It's not my partner. It's my dad."

She knew she'd have to get her own coverage, and soon. But she couldn't afford the full cost of physical therapy sessions on her own, and she couldn't wait to be reimbursed. Her father's voice, thick with doom, filled her head with portents of rainy-day pains turning into debilitating arthritis. She remembered him thundering to her mother: *She deserves all the money I can get her, Marie. She's an artist with a ruined hand.* His emphasis on artist caught her between the ribs.

The orthopedist nodded. The physical therapy pamphlet had information about exercises she could do for strength and dexterity. "The first thing to do is to make a fist. Do it so often that you're not even conscious of it. Start loose, and then increase the pressure until it's nice and tight."

Angelina willed her fingers to bend. Every fiber of her skin stretched wide, greedy for air and light. The pain was taut and rhythmic, like a heartbeat or a beating womb just before climax. Somewhere inside that throbbing, there was a tiny grief. That cast had cradled her broken parts, given them a warm space to heal—and if that warmth had been, at times, smothering, it had also been safe.

CHAPTER FIFTEEN

HER VOICEMAIL WAS LOADED WITH messages from Eleanor. She was fired, she knew that much. Eleanor never said so overtly; her irritation was a static crackling through the smooth jazz of her concern: "Angie, where are you?" She'd never really been Angie at work—only to her father. "Angie, please call me back and let me know that you're okay. Your dad says he hasn't talked to you in almost two weeks." Angelina almost did call back, just so she could scream into the receiver, "Have you asked him why?"

Surely, he'd told Eleanor how vicious she'd been as a kid, how she'd rejected his attempts at helping her, guiding her, or whatever the fuck it was that real fathers did. No doubt he swore that he was sorry, really, so goddamn sorry, for bringing her aboard, he just thought that she could make a little extra money, maybe benefit from the structure and discipline. The only apology he'd ever relish, because it would allow him to be magnanimous—more than magnanimous, something far more satisfying. A victim.

"You really should call Eleanor," Janet said, more than once. "She's always been nice to you, right? She'll understand. Maybe she'll even fire him over it, and you can go back full time."

Whenever Janet would say something that breathlessly naive, Angelina squeezed a hard rubber ball: *resistance builds strength.*

"Nothing is going to come of pressing charges, you know that, right?" Angelina said. "He'll go to some AA kind of group for pissed-off assholes and he'll be oddly grateful for it because it gives him one more thing to be mad at."

"Who cares about him? You do it for you."

Janet offered to request some time off so she could join Angelina at the police station whenever Angelina was ready—though they both knew that "whenever" meant "before the bruises heal."

Janet had taken on extra shifts at the mall, since Angelina's mother had, apparently, cut her hours. Angelina only saw her in the late evenings or an occasional early morning. Even then, only for enough time to watch four half-hour comedies or two network dramas. Their how-was-your-day was a tug-of-war between the logistics of J and A designs and Janet's feelings.

Angelina had purchased the domain name. Now she was looking at Web designers to build the site once the settlement cleared her account: "Since I guess you never heard anything from that friend of Frankie's." She found some cheap classes in coding at the community college: "So we don't get nickled and dimed on the maintenance." She also started an Excel sheet of possible vendors for the T-shirts, sweatshirts, tote and messenger bags, and buttons: "So I'm the rare breed who actually picked up a useful skill at my summer job." She had some design comps for Janet's feedback.

Janet said she was wrung out by those extra shifts: "But I guess someone needs to be actively bringing in money right now." That tone of hers. Like Angelina didn't know what she was trying to say. She said she was so anxious about her last year of college: "I grew up in the real world, I've had enough of the real world. I want to stay in Never-Never-Land." Angelina would think, *well who doesn't?*

"It's like I've told you. I'll already have the business going. I'm doing it full tilt now, so you'll get to graduate and jump into something you love," Angelina said.

"I know that, but it's just, like, I need health insurance. I need stability."

"You can still work at the beauty shop and do your articles."

Angelina knew she should've honeyed her tone. She should have remembered her life before the promise of a settlement. But Janet wasn't going to lose the apartment. Angelina had placed work in a gallery. The curator emailed to say that, within a week of the pieces being hung, she'd gotten "a few almosts" in terms of buyers. She'd make, and place, more pieces. She'd sell them. She'd build a business and turn their art into something that could sustain them. When Janet graduated, she could step into a life she actually wanted; she didn't have to wade down into the work-a-day muck.

"Thanks. Good to know that I have permission."

"No, no, you know what I mean. The more you get your name out there, the better it is in terms of brand recognition. Maybe you could even start your author bio with something like, 'Janet Henderson is the J in J and A Designs.'"

"So that's what I am?"

"I think that's actually rather kind of me, given that I've done all the fucking work for this and you've just shrugged it all off."

Janet would suddenly need to shower before work, or she'd conjure a deadline if Angelina didn't make amends. She cycled through the old soft-shoe of "I've just been through so much shit." Offer a line about how this work, her work, their work, *real* work, was keeping her from wallowing. Just so Janet could say that maybe she *should* wallow to "someone who's trained to, like, let you do that productively." Then she'd offer her left wrist, still swollen and stinking, to Janet's kneading fingers. Janet rubbed heavy gobs of scented lotions—lavender, coconut, and sweet pea, which didn't have any discernible smell—from Angelina's elbow to her fingertips. Janet used the hard, clinical motions she'd likely seen in those lymphatic drainage massage tutorials she watched online. Angelina hoped for the kind of touch that would coax a soft pleasure from the ache.

CHAPTER SIXTEEN

Alone, Angelina blazed on sketchbooks, did study after study. She'd stripped the words away, started fusing the bones with metal. Ribs as a cage; finger bones, phalanges, as the planks of a bridge; vertebrae as a staircase spiraling down a gradating darkness. Then there was the skull: the right side would be clean bone, the left side made of iron. Thin strands of smoke would billow through the right eye socket. Angelina knew how to use watercolor and charcoal to give the iron its heft and sheen. The smoke took some trial and error at the kitchen sink. She held a lighter over some tissue paper, never letting the fire kiss it; the heat alone turned it black and gray.

Working on the final piece was harder than she'd expected. Her left hand, freed of its cast, strove to be useful, but it was still weak, especially after she'd drawn the skull full scale. She'd managed the study-sized strips of tissue paper easily enough; the larger strips were more unwieldy, and she'd either drop them, or the lighter, in the sink. A few times, the pieces caught on fire, and the air thickened with smoke after each effort. Then, finally, success: she held onto the lighter and the pieces. The heat clicked its teeth at her skin, stung some pain, some life, back into her hand. Angelina was so close, *so* close, to the perfect shade of haze that she ignored the wrathful bleating of the smoke alarm.

The door throbbed on its hinges. Above the banging, Angelina could hear a voice, muffled and yelling. Suddenly, Valentina's barking came to her clearly, as if her head had just cleared water. She set the strips down on the countertop—only when she was done—and opened the door.

"Make that goddamn dog stop. I need to sleep."

Mr. Paulson stood there, at half past one in the afternoon, wearing flannel pajamas.

"You don't mess with my dog."

As soon as she said the words, Angelina was buoyed up by a high wave; it crashed down in the center of her chest, and the shock of such force invigorated her. *If I could feel like this enough times, I'd be invincible.*

"You don't get to say that to me. I've been nice. I've left you alone. Ever since you *threatened* me. Just shut that dog up."

"Don't you fuck with my dog."

Angelina must've taken a step into the hallway, because she blinked, and Mr. Paulson's back was against the railing. Angelina still outweighed him. Now both hands were free. She saw his lips move, heard an aural mash of words. Angelina's left hand darted out, pushed his shoulder. He snatched at Angelina's wrist. The sudden pain made Angelina swing her right hand toward his face. Her own name, cried out, startled her. Her open palm skidded to a stop on Mr. Paulson's cheek. She lost her momentum and the slap fell limp into a caress.

Mr. Paulson's skin was soft, pleasingly wrinkled like careworn leather: the cover of her first high-quality sketchbook, a gift from her father after she placed first in the junior high art show, or that set of "biker gloves" Mother bought her when she was thirteen, after they'd watched *The Wild One.*

Janet ran up the stairs holding a greasy paper bag. She was yelling, though Angelina couldn't clearly hear the words. A name, but not her name. It became sharp and clear as soon as Janet's hand was on her shoulder, pulling her back.

"Mr. Paulson, I'm so sorry. I don't know what happened."

"I don't know what happened either," Mr. Paulson said, in his most affected whine. "I thought something was burning, and I came over and she just attacked me."

"I was concentrating on my work, and you started—"

"Angie, go turn off the alarm." Then Janet looked at Valentina, who stood at the column, still barking. "And *you*, be quiet."

Janet's voice had held clouds before, had threatened rain, but never thunder. Angelina didn't move. She watched Janet *apologize* to Mr. Paulson and murmur sympathetically while he groaned on about some new medication that helped with his moods but made him so tired all day.

Janet ushered Mr. Paulson back to his apartment.

"You're a nice girl, Janet," he said. "You really are. You can do better than this one."

"Were you calling her a nice girl while you were terrorizing her?"

Angelina wasn't even aware that Janet had walked past her into the apartment until the alarm stopped. Janet asked her to come inside, to tell her what had happened, what had *really* happened. Angelina didn't turn around.

"Angie, please, I'm not mad. I just want to talk."

"You *are* mad."

"Okay, I *am* mad. I'm mad now, but I wasn't mad when I bought this funnel cake, and I wasn't mad when I drove it home so we could share it. And I really wasn't mad when I was thinking the surprise it might cheer you up."

Angelina didn't speak. She stood in the empty hallway, looking at Mr. Paulson's door.

Janet must've been clearing out the kitchen; there was cursing and clanging, and a "What is this?"

"It would cheer me up," Angelina said, so quietly that she seemed to be mouthing the words. Her skin got thinner and thinner, the meat of her being pushed out into the hot air. The only part of her body she could really feel now, with any sort of clarity, was her left hand, locked in a fist.

Angelina got obsessive with her new bones. Two large canvases, ribcage and skull, rested against the wall between the living room and kitchen.

She'd gone through half a pack of watercolor paper, hands and pelvis and more skulls. The skulls, she decided, would look best on the merchandise. She varied the designs on the iron sides: some looked as if flowers had been etched in the metal, some had blooming tendrils snaking between the teeth, and others had bright pink daisy heads in lieu of eye sockets.

Janet, looking up from her sewing (one of Maxine's costumes, nothing for J and A): "Shit, this is, like, amazing. I'd wear this shirt now."

Janet, padding from bedroom to living room in her bra and panties: "Don't you want to come to bed?" Thrusting her hip out and giving her best Marilyn: "I'm too tired to sleep."

Janet, standing in the hallway between bedroom and living room, rubbing her eyes: "It's seriously three in the morning. You're going to get sick if you don't sleep."

Janet, returning from work: "My kitchen is going to grow back its hymen if you don't start cooking again."

Angelina would smile, say "thank you" or "Honey, I want to, so much, but I've hit a sweet spot and I need to keep going." She alternated between "I'll sleep when I'm dead or when I get my next concussion, whichever comes first" and "You could keep your kitchen well-lubricated with some recipes online" and "You could practice your figures, you know."

"I work, you know."

"I do too."

"Yeah, but you don't have to put on underwear or deodorant."

They knew it was a lame joke, but they both laughed because laughing let them feel like they were together. Like Janet's feet hadn't been cut up on the edges of eggshells, like Angelina could bear to be touched.

That feeling—the hope for it, the sense of it bumping against their fingertips like some fish nosing its way into the clear water—inspired them to have a night out. Well, it inspired Janet to ask Angelina to join her and her friends at the bar, and Angelina to accept the invitation, even though it was karaoke night and she'd spend the whole time tense with second-hand embarrassment. She wanted to stay home and work. The bar's prices didn't match its artful dinginess: moose heads mounted above velvet paintings of saints and Elvises, Christmas lights in the shapes of stars and chili peppers snaking around the walls. Angelina nursed a single Jack and ginger, quipped aloud that every time someone missed the high note on "Purple Rain," an angel got its wings. But Janet wasn't listening. Janet and Maxine were talking about how cute the studio spaces-slash-apartments above the theater were, and Maxine was ruing the fact that she'd never be able to rent one herself.

"You can't make over a certain amount, or I guess you're too boring and straight-laced to qualify for an artists' space. Once I start teaching full time, I'll have too much money, but only on paper. Especially after that cunt Sallie Mae gets her hands on me," Maxine said.

"You know, at some point, we could consider moving into one of those spaces," Angelina said, gently laying the flat of her hand between Janet's shoulder blades. She felt the warmth of Janet's skin through the thin cotton T-shirt. Not a calm, reassuring warmth; the subtle blaze of a rising fever. "We could get a loft bed and have even more space."

"I thought we were going to make a million dollars in our first year and be on the cover of *Oprah* magazine," Janet said. Not unkindly. But not too kindly.

"Only Oprah appears on the cover of *Oprah* magazine. For us, though, I bet they'd make an exception." *I don't want to fight. I don't want to fight. I don't want to fight.*

Angelina looked at the giant screen that had been set up behind the karaoke singers. It didn't play images from music videos or song lyrics, just an incongruous film, silent, with Asian subtitles. It was about a teenage pop star and an elderly cigarette kiosk owner. Each morning, the pop star snuck out of the recording studio run by her father—who forced her to eat only white-colored foods and drink only hot water with lemon—to purchase a single cigarette. The elderly man never forced her to buy a pack; he never said a word. All she saw of him through his bulletproof partition was his hand when he gave her the cigarette, and his eyes, a fierce red-black like the center of a struck match. They were impassive as she lit up, but as she remembered them throughout her day—between grueling dance practices and costume fittings—they narrowed with a protective indignation that might've been love.

When Janet and Maxine excused themselves to use the restroom, Frankie tapped Angelina on the shoulder.

"So, listen, Angelina. I know you and I haven't ever really talked, like one on one, but, you know, Janet is a really good friend of mine."

Oh God, she's had a thing for Janet. She's always had a thing for Janet. That's the conversation we're going to have now.

"She told me what happened to your eye. What *really* happened, I mean. She came to me because I intern at the women's law center."

Frankie put on her best "I'm here for you, I'm really here for you" face. Still, she smiled that unconscious, embarrassed smile. That faint broadening of the mouth that people thought somehow insulated them from the awkwardness they'd wrought.

"So that means you know that lady in the red power suit who's always on the news whenever some football player beats up his wife? And she's going to take me on? Make me whole?"

Angelina imagined Janet and Frankie at this bar, huddled at one of the high tops, talking earnestly, urgently, about their friend with the *problem.*

"They have legal aid, and we work with victims' services. They have counselors there. There's an Italian guy I think you'd like."

"My legal aid, if I do choose to do anything—and it is my choice, whether it gets your girl power rocks off or not—is going to be a county prosecutor."

Angelina was looking into filing charges. She just wanted to know what it entailed. What the process looked like. That was all.

When Frankie picked up her drink, Angelina noticed her nails, painted just like Janet's: iridescent blue. Frankie said something about the counselors using a sliding scale, how she'd seen them really help a lot of women.

"Besides, I don't need a free shrink," Angelina said. "I have money now."

"I understand. Look, Janet didn't put me up to this. She cares about you so much, and I care about her. And I'm sorry for saying anything. And I'm really sorry about what happened to you. It's fucked up."

Angelina almost asked if that was her cue to cry now, like that handsome math genius juvenile delinquent whose shrink keeps repeating, "It's not your fault" until he finally breaks down, and— Presto! Bingo!—he weeps away his pain. Finds himself healed. Whole. But Janet came back to the table. She put her hand on Angelina's shoulder and asked, with a feigned nonchalance, what was going on. She knew, though. Angelina could see that in her face.

Janet tried chatting companionably—and constantly—about maybe researching holiday craft fairs where they could set up booths that winter. She said "our business" as if the words were chunks of bone in her chicken salad, held cautiously in the front of her mouth to prevent accidental swallowing. Angelina ordered another Jack and ginger. Then she swiveled in her chair to face the screen.

The teenage pop star was about to leave for a world tour, and she ran, in the rain, to the cigarette kiosk. As the old man gave the pop star her final cigarette, she clutched his hand. The kiosk shook from the force of her frustration. She mouthed "please," and he just blinked. Then he shoved her hand back as if it were a tissue he'd blown into.

Angelina did not tell Janet she was leaving. She just walked toward the car. She was not even aware that Janet had followed her out until she saw Janet standing behind her, a reflection streaking the car door.

"Are you sure you're okay to drive?" Janet asked.

"Are you going to ask if I'm okay to do everything? 'Are you okay to drive? Are you okay to take a shower? To take a shit? Are you okay to be okay?'"

"I didn't mean it like that."

"What other way is there to mean it? But hey, since I'm so broken and crazy and out of control, I surely shouldn't be trusted with operating a motor vehicle."

Angelina stepped away with the driver's side door with a theatrical sweep of her arms, a curt *after you, m'lady*. Janet did not move. Still,

Angelina could sense the sweat and bristle of Janet's body, and this sensation was the crank in Angelina's back, drawing her in tighter and up higher. Janet's fear was a soft organ pulsing under her skin. A sudden blood-coppery sweetness filled Angelina's mouth, though she hadn't bitten her tongue.

The air held a muzzling heat. Angelina took her breaths in short huffs. Her left wrist started to throb, as if the heavy dampness in the air had whipped around her whole arm and started to squeeze. She stood with her back to the car and flattened her left palm against the windowpane. Hot air beat through the glass, into her achy joints. Janet started talking about how frustrated and scared she felt, how much she cared about Angelina. She didn't say loved.

"I know I shouldn't have said anything to anyone, but I just felt like I had to do something."

"And I told you, and I've been fucking telling you, that there is nothing for anyone to do."

"You made that very clear. I just don't believe it's true."

"You're not the first person who thinks they know what's best for me," Angelina said.

Janet's friends and a few random club-goers crossed to the parking lot. Frankie moved with the briskness of fear.

Faces under the streetlights became a watery smear of varied flesh tones. There was a crunch of gravel. Voices and grating bass music from inside the bar as the door swung open and shut again. Angelina wiped her right wrist over her eyes. The faces became clearer. No, she couldn't cry. She wasn't going to cry. Crying made it worse. The half-circle of people gathered, gawking, behind Janet was like a cord around her neck. Angelina imagined herself as some dull animal pulled low to the ground, kicking and moaning in piteous protest.

"Come on, sweet pea," Angelina said. "If we're going to have this fight, we might as well have it in the car."

Angelina threw the car keys at Janet. Janet tried to catch them, but she ended up swatting them to the ground. Janet's hands trembled as she picked up the keys and put them in the driver's side door.

"Why you so scared?" Angelina said, her voice thick with a delighted viciousness. "Who do you think I am right now? I thought I was the *victim*. I thought I needed *help*."

A pert odor of citrus spray and Janet's own heat-slicked body filled the space between them. Janet's mascara bled out ever so slightly, and her eyes shone through a diamond-bright blue. She put her hand on Angelina's shoulder; there was no warmth or heft of familiarity in her touch, just skittishness, a premonition of burning.

"This isn't you," Janet said.

"Of course it's me."

"Janet, let's go back inside," Frankie said.

Angelina took one wide step away from the car, eyes fixed on Frankie. Her fist cut the air as she drove it down into her palm. "No, let's make the most of being outside," Angelina said. This was likely Frankie's first fight of any kind. Her face cycled through the seven stages of grief, stopping short of acceptance.

A ripple passed through the crowd. Angelina caught a few isolated "oh mans" or "whoas" and a whooped "girl fight!"

"You're going to let that man ruin everything good in your life," Janet said. "Everything good about you."

Angelina turned around. Janet flattened herself against the car door, as if she knew, before Angelina even did, what Angelina would do. Angelina's fist struck the glass behind Janet's head. Not her open palm. Her fist.

Janet's face was paler than bone. She sucked in a long breath, and then the torrent burst. That sound should've cored Angelina, scattered the rinds and seeds of her. But she felt eerily calm, like everything that had ever been breathless and jagged inside of her was slowing down, becoming still.

CHAPTER SEVENTEEN

As Marie reached for her cell phone on the bedside table, her hand grazed Jack's glass of water. She could hear her heart in her temples until his snoring assured her that he was still asleep. He'd needed a sleep aid every night since the arrest. The first words he'd said to her, back in the car, were, "Go to fucking Walgreen's. I'm going to need some goddamn Tylenol PM." He didn't even get out of the car, just sat there rubbing his wrists. He snapped at her for picking up half-and-half, even though the dairy section was right near the medicines, even though he'd tear her head off if he didn't have cream for his coffee in the morning.

The text was from Janet: "Please come get her. Now." This was the first time Marie had heard from her since that night of what Marie had been calling "the fight" (though merely thinking the word conjured the image of Angelina's red skin, Jack's eyes shocked wide). That night, Janet had texted, "She's here. Sleeping." Marie had checked that message dozens of times, sometimes within an hour, as if it had been written in smoke and would waft away in a breeze.

Jack grumped and snorted in his sleep. Marie had always hated other people's snoring. It reminded her of Daddy passed out on the couch with his mouth open, or Mother flopped on her bed, still in her work apron and pantyhose, more sounds that never should've traveled through walls. This, though, was a comfort: the gentle indignities of being human would tick on, even when their house had become a funeral.

Jack had been so silent, speaking only to ask her to pass the salt (for food he hardly ate) or to call his office and say he was too sick to come in. When that boss woman said, with real concern in her voice, that she hoped he felt better, but to please let him know that, if he took another consecutive day off, she'd have to start Family Medical Leave paperwork, Marie indulged in a brief fantasy: Jack was actually sick—maybe with cancer, or one of those other telethon diseases, anything that would strip and shrivel him. Angelina might come see him in the final days; she'd definitely come to the wake (if only to assure herself that he really was gone). Marie could have her back then.

When the boss asked about Angelina, Marie pleaded off in singsong: "Ah, the patient awakes."

She left a note for Jack: Our daughter is in trouble. I will handle it. Took your GPS. Do not call.

Weaving through the zip code for Charles Village, Marie remembered how she'd wanted to live there, "the bohemian part of town," when she and Jack first returned. Even then, people had begun to paint their row houses in funky colors, hang peace flags over their stoops; every time she'd drive through, she'd see people—and not just kids, but people her age (and at thirty, she still had no idea how old "people her age" could really get)—with canvases and backpacks, women who spoke with actressy flourishes of the wrist. She'd have been closer to the local theater. More importantly, she and Jack could've had fun: slipping home drunk on cheap red wine on Friday and Saturdays (with an occasional just-because Wednesday), a sweeter life than either of them had ever known in New York. But Jack insisted they move straight to the suburbs.

Angelina should have had a wonderful time here, being young and in love. Instead, she was standing on a cracked-up parking pad behind a row house that looked more dingy than funky; she held Valentina on a leash, and the dog was panting with a neurotic intensity. The last time Marie had seen her, she was out on the deck, looking through the glass door with her face twitching between fear and fury. This was the face that met Marie now. Angelina paced the parking pad in tight little circles; she hugged herself, her left hand, now out of plaster, tucked under her right armpit. Valentina followed her, tail swinging low.

At her feet, two suitcases, a giant portfolio case, and that duffel bag Jack bought her when she'd taken up softball for one season. Only one of those suitcases would be full of clothes. The rest would be art supplies and books.

She mouthed "back door," and Marie popped the lock. Before she could even get out of the car, Angelina was hustling the dog in the backseat. Valentina whimpered and pawed at the door. Marie started to console her with an "It's okay," but how could the dog understand that—how could Marie understand. A sudden thump on the trunk startled her (and the dog, who barked once before recommencing her whine). Angelina mouthed "open" and "now." Marie slipped out of the driver's seat to unlock the trunk.

"What happened?" she asked.

Angelina didn't speak; she just put her bags in the trunk and stood there, shifting them so the portfolio could lie flat. Marie tried to move the duffel bag over to the right, but Angelina hip-checked her away from it, snapped for her to "go upstairs and get the rest."

"Are you sure you don't need help?"

"Do I look like I need you to cut my fucking meat for me?"

Angelina held her left fist up, practically under Marie's nose. The skin wasn't bruised, not like her eye. For a moment, Marie actually locked her jaw, steeled herself for a hit.

"Oh, so you think I'm him, too?"

Angelina's anger rearranged itself across her features, drew into a fine, flinty haughtiness. Yet her voice was thick with tears.

"Of course not," Marie said. She should have said more. *You're not him. You're better than him.* Angelina would've called her out for being dumb and cloying. *Was that a line from some after-school special you were in? Are we supposed to hug and cry now?*

"Janet says for you to come upstairs and get the rest of my things," Angelina said.

The stairwell up toward Janet's apartment was narrow enough to be dangerous in a fire; it would go down like a pile of matchsticks under too much weight. Baltimore, New York, these hallways were all the same: doors decorated in long-leftover Christmas wreaths or plastic Easter rabbits, smelling of fried onions and girls' perfume, dank and hopeful in the same few steps. Janet was red-eyed; the sides of her face were smeared with mascara. Her chest heaved in those soft staccatos that Marie knew well: You feel like you'd never regain your breath again. Like you'll die drowning on air.

"I'm so sorry, Janet. I don't know what happened."

Janet padded back into her apartment, an eruption of sweet, pretty things meant to announce that she was more than just a sweet, pretty thing. She had an aesthetic. Marie might gift wrap a few of her old salt and peppershakers as a peace offering. Janet had propped sketchbooks in a row against the back wall, slipped tissue paper between the pages. Janet explained that Angelina—who was already just "she," a memory too painful to be named—had explained that was the best way to keep the images from smudging, even after the fixative had set.

An easel stood in the center of the living room: an image of a giant skull, half metal and half bone. The bone side was drawn in heavy, choppy lines, like ocean waves. Marie had heard, in so many workshops, from so many teachers, that the actor was responsible for breathing the soul into each character. She'd never gotten a chance to exhale. Held everything in her belly. But this, *this* was breath. Heaving lungs. Rich blood. Taut, empty belly.

The metal side was beautifully smooth. However she'd colored it, the metal shone like it could be melted down and worn as jewelry. Then Marie realized that the metal side was the side where Jack had hit her. Unconsciously, she touched that side of her own face; a pink foam curler came loose in her fingers. *You really are so stupid, Marie. There's nothing worth looking pretty for.* Marie let the curler fall to Janet's floor.

"I'm sorry," she said. "I think you two could be okay if you just talked it out. Is the Paper Moon diner still around here? We could all go, get some coffee and some coconut cake."

"No coconut cake, Marie. I'm not like you. I don't let people hurt me like that."

"Did she?"

Janet crossed over to the kitchen, took some whiskey from the freezer, and poured it in a coffee mug. Drank it neat.

"No."

Janet strained to sound hard, but Marie knew that as soon as she left, Janet would start crying again.

"Then whatever it was, it can be fixed, right?"

"There's no fixing it."

Marie wanted to tell Janet that, when she was eight years old, Angelina had insisted—loudly and often—that it was "unfair that Daddy gets to take his shirt off when he eats spaghetti but we don't;" so one Saturday, when Jack had to work, Marie made them a special spaghetti dinner, extra sauce, and they sat at the dinner table—Angie in her undershirt and Marie in her bra—and made a show of slurping the noodles, kissing their fingertips, and exclaiming "Magnifico!" every time. That's who Angelina really was.

"I'm sorry," she said, again. Not to Janet.

"Sounds like you say that a lot," Janet said.

Marie's phone trilled in her purse. Him.

"He's sorry." Marie spoke on instinct. The words tasted different, though.

She came back to the car with a few drawing pads under her arms and plans to pick up the larger canvases tomorrow—although the sky was brightening at the edges, and for all Marie knew it was tomorrow already. Angelina was in the backseat, her face on the dog's neck. Valentina's head rested on Angelina's shoulder. Her jaws opened in a slow, urgent pant that revealed teeth and tongue: a wolf's mouth, a wolf's menace, and yet so placid, so still and tender as her daughter— Marie's daughter, but now, somehow, the wolf's—wept into her fur.

"Is your car around the block?" Marie asked.

"I gave it up. Didn't need it if I'd be working from home. We became a one-car family." Angelina gave a sarcastic little spin to *one-car family*, almost like she was drunk.

"I know it's hard being home all day. You get to feeling a little stale. All you want in the world is for someone to pay attention to you."

Her phone rang again, made her whole purse twitch and hum. Instinct and annoyance wrestled with each other until she dropped her purse on the floor of the backseat.

"I don't know, Marie, it seems like you've had a pretty comfortable little life."

"I deserve that."

The little bell announcing voicemail went off. Then the phone rang again.

"I'm not going back there," Angelina said. She made her fists, rolled her wrist, winced a little at the snap-crackle-pop. When Angelina was a baby, Jack walked through the house, holding her, her tiny pink cheek against his dark chest.

"What happened?"

Marie started the car, figured she could drive down by the Paper Moon. They could talk about it—all of it—over coconut cake and coffee.

"I don't know. I got angry. Got stupid."

The tears broke on stupid. Once, Angelina had been so confident, so valiant. As a kid, she'd spend hours drawing: animals (especially dogs) in people clothes, going to the kinds of people jobs that required hard hats or suits (or, once, on Marie's suggestion, a ballerina tutu); faces she'd seen on TV. She'd chatter for hours about the things she'd do once the president of America bought all her artwork: get a house for Mommy and a house for Daddy, and then a house for all the dogs that needed homes.

Then Marie would lift Angie onto the white stepstool they kept by the kitchen sink and lather their hands until the whole room smelled of oranges or cinnamon or whatever soap had been on sale that week. Angelina would parrot back whatever songs Marie had played—Joni Mitchell, Stevie Nicks, Debbie Harry—in a smart bell of a voice.

"It can be fixed," Marie said. "You give it some time, and then, whatever it was, you apologize. That goes a long way toward making things right."

"Don't you see that only makes it worse?"

Angelina's scream made Marie think of ripped silk. Valentina made a sound that wasn't quite a groan or a mumble—it was low-throated, thick with mood. A sympathetic murmur, an "okay, okay."

Marie turned into the parking lot for the Paper Moon diner, clicked off the ignition. Wordlessly, she opened the rear passenger door and slid in next to Angelina. Angelina looked over her shoulder for a moment; her face was a symphony of micro-expressions, shock sharpening into rage, rage yielding to regret. She turned around in the narrow space and let Marie hold her. The violence of those sobs broke through Marie's body. She waited for the deep drop into calm afterward, but Angelina pushed away while she was still in the hiccupping stage.

"Why didn't you ever choose me? Why did you always let him be right?"

Marie's phone rang; the chime of voicemail. Again. And again.

"He was never right."

"Then why didn't you ever stand up for me?"

Hurt and pride were two live wires that ran through Angelina's voice, never touching. Marie remembered Angelina's first night back in the house after her car accident; she'd gone downstairs for something, probably laundry, and happened upon Angelina in the bathroom. She caught Angelina's silhouette through the shower curtain. Her forehead was pressed against the tile. She held her left arm up, away from the spray. The plastic bag taped loosely around her cast made it look like a torch.

"I'm not as brave as you are," Marie said.

"That is such bullshit. I mean, it's true, but it's bullshit. And you know what really tears me up? I don't just have to hate him. I have to hate you, too."

Marie almost said, *You don't have to hate me. If you must hate me, if that's what you really need, fine. Just be better for it.*

"I saw your art. It's beautiful. Is that what you want to sell in your shop?"

"I guess it really is my shop now."

"I still have all the art you ever gave me," Marie said. "I just wanted you to know that."

The birdcage Angelina sculpted in tenth grade: the cage's frame was shaped and sanded to look like a real house, complete with the French windows Marie openly admired when she saw them on TV (which would make Jack roll his eyes: "Why not have a goddamn neon sign? 'Break in! We don't mind!'"). The bars of the cage, though, were ugly and thick. Jailhouse bars. Angelina had given it to Marie for Mother's Day, wrapped in pink paper, bound with lace; she'd looked at Marie like she had canary feathers sticking from her teeth. Marie knew she was being insulted. But things were already so bad, and her daughter had brought her something beautiful.

"I'm glad you're getting that money," Marie said. "I'm sorry about everything else. But I'm glad you have it, on your own terms."

"Janet said that he'd ruin everything good in me. She wants me to press charges."

"What do you want to do?" Marie asked.

"I don't know," Angelina said. "Sometimes it doesn't feel worth it. And then it feels like the only right thing, even though I know it's not."

Marie remembered following an officer into a windowless room with antiseptic lighting and the musk of coffee and bodies. The cop questioned her with such intensity, as if she were the one who'd been arrested. *What exactly did you see? Have there been prior incidents? And you were aware of them?*

Marie asked the cop where Angie was, and when the cop said he couldn't say, Marie put her head in her hands. Her hair snagged on the diamond in her wedding band. This tiny pain was enough to draw the tears out. She asked what would happen now.

"Depends. Your daughter is over eighteen, so CPS won't be involved. If that's your concern."

"It's your life," Marie said to Angelina. "You do whatever you need to do." She meant it. Her life would be a hell of legal fees and silences more severe than any threat. But she meant it. She was surprised by how much she meant it.

"Thank you." Angelina looked up at the neon sign for the diner. In a small voice, she said, "Mom, I can't."

CPS. They came for kids who were homeless or whose mothers were drug addicts, whose fathers burned them with cigarettes. She and Jack were not those people. They weren't. Or they weren't until siren lights strobed inside their living room and the EMTs came in after the cops. The EMTs knocked on the door leading out to the deck, calling, "Miss, Miss!" Marie yelled, "Her name is Angelina."

"Okay," Marie said. "Where do we go, then?"

"Some hotel where I can take Valentina."

"Honey, I don't know if we can find a place—"

"She goes with me."

"Your father loves her, you know. It could be temporary."

"No. We find a place or I sleep outside with her."

Marie said okay. That was all she could say. She had not stayed in the house after that last fight. She left after the cops came and the EMT knocked on the glass door, called Angelina's name. She followed after Jack. She already knew where she'd be forgiven.

CHAPTER EIGHTEEN

THE DINGINESS OF THE MOTEL room was a kind of palate cleanser after the rococo kitsch of Janet's apartment and the *Italiano craptastico* of Angelina's parents' house. But it was the best Angelina's mother could find. Through a masterful performance that blended charm, almost, but not quite, to the point of flirting and crystalline earnestness, Mother found a motel owner who would let Valentina stay: "Please, my daughter was thrown out of her place and she has nowhere else to go. My husband and I, well, our mortgage is underwater, and we have doctor's bills. He's on dialysis and we just don't know how long he has left. We would take her and the dog in if we could, you understand." Mother was good, very good. Angelina thought she was all cried out, but her throat caught exactly when her mother's did in describing how Medicare wouldn't cover the home care nurses.

For the next few days, Angelina barely left the room, with its hunter-green curtains and mustard-colored walls, beige carpet and an eggshell shower curtain. Everything worked in theory, clashed in application. The only evidence of neighbors was a comforting thrum of TV through the ceiling and laughter through the wall. In the afternoons, it was rough, honking laughter, like someone watching a sitcom alone. Valentina made a haven of the space below the air conditioner; she lay on her side, snuffling and twitching in an unencumbered sleep.

Angelina would be sitting on the bed, balancing a pillow on her knees, and a sketchbook on that pillow, and, for a moment, feel joined in a two-woman commune of people with nowhere else to be at noon on a Wednesday. Then, at night, there'd be a pearl string of laughter— hers, light and pretty, and then his. This sudden presence of a *him* made Angelina feel a prick of betrayal. She'd try and join in, in her own way—even used her left hand, considered it physical therapy—but her hand hurt and she didn't get very wet.

Afterward, she'd sit outside on the curb with Valentina, eating single-serve cartons of vanilla ice cream and making small talk with the smokers. Skinny women in jean short-shorts and high-wedged flip-flops who might have been her mother's age but showed cell phone photos of grandbabies on bicycles with no training wheels. Guys who'd been beat cops and Bethlehem Steel men, who called her *dearie* and *hon* with a casual tenderness that rubbed her like some firm yet gentle animal tongue.

One of the men yelled out, "That dog is like my favorite ex-wife, big and sassy."

The motel was on the industrial side of Pulaski Highway, but just far enough away from anything ever filmed on *The Wire* to let her know that her father was paying for it or at least had okayed the expense. He owed her. He did. No matter when she filed charges. She was forcing herself to switch *if* into *when*, though the most she'd done was call victims' services.

Still, she shouldn't have taken his money. Not when that last assault— that's what it was, or at least Janet's word for it had fully saturated her mind—and all the ones that came before it seized her in her deepest sleep, wrecked her body with the sense of being smothered. She woke in jerks and starts. Then she reached out to the un-rumpled side of the bed, and her hand would graze her thigh. The taut-band tension in her legs and arms, her shoulders, neck and belly made sleep too painful. She let her fingers slowly search out every knot, every granule of muscle that wouldn't let go. She pressed down until the low ache became a sharper pain, and that sharper pain faded like static becoming clean, quiet air.

Morning had slurred into late afternoon when she was awakened by the gallery owner's call.

"Kiddo, you've sold two pieces. I need a mailing address for the check, and I need you to send me more work."

Angelina stammered that she didn't have an address yet; she'd broken up with her girlfriend (a convenient shorthand) and was getting her own place soon. The owner said she surely wouldn't trust a check for eight hundred and fifty dollars after commission with the front desk of some motel. The only address Angelina could think of was Janet's, and she called with her heart in her throat.

"You know I can't," Janet said.

She didn't sound angry, just tired. That exhaustion was the suck of humidity that wouldn't let the front door close completely.

"Has Mr. Paulson been raiding your mail? Stealing coupons?"

"I've been bereft without my Pennysaver."

They joined in a laugh that came easily enough to give Angelina hope. She remembered Janet tipsily humming "the itsy bitsy spider" as she walked her fingers along the inside of her thigh. Janet telling her to open her eyes after she came; Janet smiling like a helpful schoolmate who'd picked up your papers after you'd tripped on your own feet.

Then Janet sighed, and Angelina sensed that she was remembering things, too. Only her memories ended with the sudden thud of knuckles on glass.

"How is Valentina?" Janet asked.

"Oh, you know, she's fine. She adapts."

"She's lucky to have you. You've always been so good to her."

"Yeah, well, it's hard not to be. Good to her, I mean," Angelina said.

"So, you're getting the settlement, soon, yeah? You must be excited."

The settlement would clear Angelina's account in increments, slow increments. No matter how vigorously she argued with the insurance rep—who'd laughed, said that she and her father were "two peas in a pod"—and the bank clerks, she would only get the first amount in a thousand-dollar deposit, and then, a week later, another thousand and five hundred dollars.

"I'm getting a place soon," Angelina said. "I mean, it'll just be a room in a group house or a studio space, or whatever, but maybe you can help me decorate."

"I'd like to see it. See you. But I need time, to know—"

"To know what?"

The answer to her own question stripped the fight out of Angelina's tongue.

"It's okay," Angelina said. "I'll be okay."

Before she left for DC the next morning, Angelina walked Valentina and left her with bowls of food and water. At first, she thought she'd take a cab to the train station; then she decided that, with this seven hundred coming in and the next wave of the settlement forthcoming, she could put a down payment on a used car. She had already done her research online, knew which car she wanted—an '08 Honda Accord with more mileage than she would've liked, but priced fairly, and, anyway, Hondas were the Labrador Retrievers of cars: uncomplicated and reliable. That's what her father said, anyway. Uncomplicated and reliable. The cabbie who drove her to the used car lot—an older guy, straight-up old school Bawlmer, muddled vowels and eyes trained on the corner—asked her if she was meeting up with a father or a brother, or (more shyly, showing his age) a boyfriend. She knew the subtext, and let it steer her tone: "No, just me. I'm enough."

The salesman, who was around her age, spoke with a stilted smarminess. "Listen, I've done my research," she told him. "I can tell you that the price is a bit steep for the mileage, but it is a used car and I'm relieved that I won't have to switch out the timing belt, which really means get a new car, in two years. So, how about this? You treat me like an actual customer, and I'll treat you like a professional." By the end of their exchange, when her monthly car payment had been hammered out—she wasn't ashamed to mention her accident, and how it had made finding work "just too damn hard," so she'd need "something manageable, which means as low as you can go"—he was laughing, asking if she'd negotiate the closing on his condo. "You sure drive a hard bargain." She almost said her father treated negotiation like a blood sport, and she'd learned everything from him. But this was different. The salesman spoke with a genuine respect that made her feel like she'd earned something.

She drove to DC with the window down, moving her left hand with the waves of rushing air. As her wrist bobbed and dipped, muscle and tendon yawned open. It wasn't painful, just tingly. That tingling made her think of everything she'd ever looked forward to. Angelina breathed in slowly, made her belly a moon. Then she exhaled into the wind.

After she collected the check—the curator wasn't in but had left a note for her with the administrative assistant: "Make me a new one now"—she went to the Smithsonian with her sketchbook. When she first moved to DC, Angelina had spent every afternoon at the Hirshhorn; she told herself that she was building a scaffold of influences, preparing for her studies. In truth, it was a just-because thing. She'd sit and draw and marvel that her life could ever be her own. Occasionally, she'd indulge in a vision of her own name on the wall, though the canvas mounted above it was always blank.

Now, someone had made an investment in an original Moltisanti. And someday, that piece—*those pieces*—could be hung here, in the modern wing. Schoolchildren and lonely transplants would walk through rooms full of death masks and ladies' weavings, portraits of royalty and gods in white marble before they came upon her work. The accompanying text might say something like, "The artist was inspired by a gruesome injury." Maybe a chaperone would shake her head, or a tourist might cluck his tongue. But they wouldn't feel sorry for her. They'd know that she turned out okay.

She lingered among the Italian masters. Those sculptures had always unsettled her. Even when their features had been blitzed by time, even when they were mere torsos on pedestals, there was still breath within the stone: in the fine ridges of vein, the gentle creases between stomach muscles. There was life in their cracked faces and broken limbs. In her studies, she left the edges of each fractured part unarticulated, just a series of thin strokes from the edge of her pencil: capillaries licking together, banding outward. Rebuilding.

CHAPTER NINETEEN

He couldn't explain himself to his own kid. The attorney—some woman Marie found online that night he was in jail—told him "not to make any kind of contact with your daughter. No confronting her in public, obviously. No phone calls or texts, no Tweets or direct messages. Certainly, no messages on Facebook or Instagram." As if he had any of that shit anyway. As if he was enough of a dumb animal to hunt his daughter down in public.

The attorney was a stick insect of a woman; tall, and with a sharpness to her features that made everything she said sound meaner than it had to be. Marie thought "It would look better, if you had to go to court, for you to be represented by a woman."

The lawyer's office was drab. She must've inherited it from someone, a father, probably, who thought that furnishing everything in the same dark stain of mahogany made him seem like he was chief justice of the Supreme Court.

"So, what do I do now?"

"We wait and see if your daughter files charges."

"And if she does?" Marie asked.

Marie sat beside him with her hands in her lap. Her left thumb slid up and down her ring finger, carried her wedding band with it.

"We should get that resized," he said.

Marie said, "Huh." That was it. Huh. She'd "uh huh"ed him before, usually in a light, joking way. *Huh* was a jab of a word. It could set up a harder punch or complete a knockout on its lonesome.

"Since this is the first time—"

"First arrest," Marie said

"Right. Well, in the eyes of the law, it's the first time. So, really, Mr. Moltisanti, you'd be looking at some kind of diversion program."

"So, anger management?" Marie asked.

The lawyer may have talked to him like he was her buddy, but she still looked at him like he was the gardener going into the fridge for some lemonade when he rested his hands on her faux-marble desktop. The swirling specks of black and gold and white looked like the Milky Way. He'd been watching shows about outer space on PBS every night until he fell asleep on the sofa, which was just as well, since Marie didn't really want him in their bed anyway. Those were his days now. He went to work and stared at the empty chair that belonged to the daughter he couldn't contact. Even though he was paying for her motel room in a zip code where gunplay wasn't an after-school activity. Crostini asked him what the Hell had happened in a tone that said: *I know it was you*. Hector asked Jack if he was okay, if there was anything he wanted to talk about. Jack said yes, he wanted to talk about the specs for the Thirty-Fourth Street roundabout.

"It's none of my business," Hector said. "But it's just that Angie left us in such a hurry, and that doesn't seem like her."

His daughter's name—especially the sweet little-girl version of it, the name he'd called her when she made him happy and proud, when she made him feel like his shoulders scraped the clouds—was more galling than the lingering sting of the handcuffs that he felt long after the red marks faded.

"She got her money," Jack said. "Why would she stay here?"

Hector glanced down at Jack's hands a little too long; x-ray vision on the bruises ringing his knuckles. He got that look on his face, that oh-brother-I-see-you look.

Then Jack went home to a wife with swollen eyes and a chapped mouth. Marie wouldn't even cry in front of him anymore. Wouldn't give him those broken parts to smooth and fix.

When he and Marie left the lawyer's office, they walked silently to the car to drive, in silence, to lunch at Applebee's, where even the tightness of their corner booth couldn't compel her to speak. He finally tried a joke: "Looks like the Internet is the new 'back of the phone book.'"

Marie gave him most of her fries, as she always did, only this time, instead of shoveling them over with her fork, she tossed them to his plate, one by one, just to magnify each little thunk. Her expression hadn't changed much in the weeks since she'd met him outside the jail: that raw look of crying without end, only slightly sharper, as if her anger was rearranging her from the inside out.

When she finally did let him back in their bed, they slept like tin soldiers under the sheets: stiff armed and straight-backed, never touching. All those other times, she'd let him make it up to her. He knew the rhythm of kiss and touch and suck, knew when he'd gotten her close, so close, by the way she'd slide her heels down his shoulders, his back. She'd push down hard enough to leave bruises: "Just digging my spurs in," she'd say. There'd be a glint of meanness to her voice— she wouldn't want him to think he was forgiven—but it was a bratty, girlish meanness that flicked a whip inside him.

He supposed it would be different now because there would be no more Thanksgivings, no more chances for Marie to pretend that she and Angelina would ever be close. Marie could mourn that, of course. He did, too. He had imagined feeding Valentina a bowl full of turkey and stuffing, how she'd eat so fast, so happily—so much joy from such a small thing. Christmas, of course, he'd have given her a bone, maybe even wrapped it up in tissue paper so she could scrape and paw it open like the dogs in those Internet videos.

"Have you talked to her?" he asked.

"Just a few texts. Just the need-to-know, you know."

"Did she say how Valentina was?"

"I'm sure the dog is fine, Jack."

Her sadness was a glowing ghost that hovered above their bed; it had nowhere else to go, nothing to do but rearrange the air. Jack slid his hand closer to hers, waited for her to meet him halfway, even from force of habit. Marie moved her hand to her thigh, closed it in a loose fist.

"She found a room to rent in some artists' space."

"She's going to live in a commune?"

"No, an *artists' space*," Marie said. "Studios. Places where they live and work."

"She's still going to need some kind of regular job," he said.

"She has some pieces in some gallery in DC, she said."

Jack almost said that some pieces in a gallery weren't a job. Almost. For once, he put a lid on himself—and he was grateful for it. The words just appeared on the chalkboard of his mind. He couldn't recall writing them. He didn't really mean them.

"I guess she's really doing it," he said. "What she always wanted to do."

"She was always going to."

There was nothing he could say to that. Jack eased his hands under the back of his neck, let his fingers search out the stiff spots, and waited for the ache.

Jack had only been to an art museum once, and that was in grade school. He and his buddies hadn't looked at the pictures; they'd hung out in front of that painting of the half-naked Island lady with her thick tits spilling into a platter. A gallery, he supposed, was just a smaller version—at least, that's what he'd seen on TV. He almost told Marie that he was going so he could crack some joke about wondering which wine to pair with which cheese, and so she could tell him what, if anything, he actually had to do or say or not do or not say. There were no wines and cheeses, just a few people, two boys and a girl, milling around with paper cups of coffee.

All of them were so much younger than he was. He supposed they didn't have jobs yet. The girl seemed soft and refined in her sundress, with her long neck and her painted nails. The boys were the beards-and-glasses types, murmuring at some weird sculpture of a woman's head mounted like a deer's head on the wall. The head looked like it had been made with tissue paper that had been glued together and sloppily painted. Angelina could've done better than that even as a child.

Jack looked around for someone who might've told him where her piece was. He almost called out for the owner, but the kids would've snickered at him. He wanted to go one day where he didn't have to be an asshole.

The girl went, "Oh wow," and he followed her voice to the back of the room. He knew he'd find Angelina's work. Sure enough, there were her skeletons, almost life-sized, on the back wall. Backbones. A set of hands.

Her name was on that wall: A. Moltisanti. Beside her name, there was a red dot.

"What does that dot mean?" he asked the girl.

"Oh, that just means it's already sold."

"I don't see the price listed."

The girl shrugged. She turned her attention to her friends, who were standing in front of the hands. He caught whispers about the power of line widths and the personality in each stroke.

"That's my daughter, you know. She did these."

The kids stopped talking for a moment. The boys nodded at him. One of them said he must be proud.

"Yes, I am," he said. "I'm proud."

The girl's eyes widened with excitement. "Please tell her that she's so ridiculously talented."

"I will."

He stared up at the back. The long spine reminded him of the shape of a face: forehead to nose to chin. The ribcage could have been the cheeks. Something in the way she'd drawn it, and he couldn't say how, conveyed all of the feelings he'd ever seen move across her face when he'd lifted her over his head and shouted, "It's a bird, it's a plane, it's Supergirl"; when she raised her fists to meet his, even though there was no point, he would always be stronger; when she looked at him and he could tell he'd gone too far, but there was no saying sorry. Hadn't he made her strong? He remembered her face as the doctor bound her wrist in its cast. The doctor had to manipulate the bones into place, and she closed her eyes.

Jack never told her—and he should have—how much he'd wanted to take that pain on her behalf. Or maybe she knew. When she opened her eyes, she looked at him, for the first time in a long time, like she wanted him in the room.

CHAPTER TWENTY

ANGELINA'S NEW APARTMENT WAS A ground-floor studio in the artist space. It was just snug enough for a Goodwill futon, a leaning bookshelf, and a dresser with a scarred corner, as if someone carrying it had once gotten too careless when turning a corner. The only extravagance was a plush dog bed for Valentina. Once she was settled in, she figured it was okay, or at least that she had a pretext, to text Janet and ask for advice about how to decorate. When Janet responded gamely enough, suggesting glass candles and accent walls, they started up a correspondence. Text messages became phone calls, and the phone calls led to a meet-up in the Starbucks where Angelina worked.

Janet walked in wearing a sensible linen blazer and flats. Her bag, at least, was orange paisley, a yellow scarf tied around the strap—a flicker of the Janet that was familiar to her. She had just finished her second interview for an internship with the Style Section of the *City Paper*. Even though Angelina knew she should be grateful Janet wanted to see her at all, her heart was a tiny wishbone, easily snapped at the knowledge that she was being fit in among the bustle of a busy day. Janet seemed older in the clothes, but not duller—more confident. Angelina knew she was seeing, oh so fleetingly, a vision of a future she wouldn't be a part of: Janet as a college graduate, working her first office job, determining, one day at a time—boring days and bad days, triumphant days and comfortable enough days—whether a nine-to-five was really for her. Eventually, Janet would find another woman to eat dinners with, to watch videos on the couch and dissect the days through conversation. *This is it*, she thought. *We're never going to be grown-ups together.*

"You look like a real working girl," Angelina said as they took a table in the back. She'd given Janet her employee discount, but she resisted the urge to buy Janet's Frappuccino herself.

"You too."

"Oh, well, you know. I mean, I like it well enough," Angelina said. "Leaves me time to do the other work."

"The real work," Janet said. She smiled around her straw. Sighed a little as she took a sip.

"Are you still writing? I haven't seen your byline as much. I've been looking for it. I'm sorry, I hope it's not creepy—"

"Yes and no. I mean, no, it's not creepy. But yes, I am writing—just, not so much now. Mostly I've been sketching. Ideas for shows coming down the way."

"That's good," Angelina said. "When you get the internship, you'll be doing a lot of writing for them, so you might as well do the things you want now, right?"

"You mean *if* I get the internship."

"No, I mean *when*."

Angelina's face flushed. She felt loose and warm all over—a prelude to a kiss, back when she and Janet would have been sitting across from each other at the kitchen table or sprawled beside each other in bed, Janet's feet resting on top of Angelina's, her hand idly rubbing circles between Angelina's bare shoulders, her breath sweet and sleepy and thick along Angelina's neck.

Janet must've been remembering something too, because she cleared her throat. "Hey, you want to see them? My drawings, that is." Angelina nodded.

When she looked at the page, her memory flooded with the clean, sweet smell of those peonies. Janet had really listened to her, had thought about, and practiced, what she'd said. Even if this was the last time they ever saw each other, at least she'd always be the girl who taught Janet how to draw proportions. Elbows aligned at midsections, wrists grazed hips, and the legs didn't overwhelm the torsos. The figures wore white tube dresses; each dress featured a single gold thread running straight along the front or the back, or perpendicular from the shoulder to the hip.

"These are good," Angelina said. "You've figured it out."

"I had a great teacher."

"You've been practicing is all."

"It was the closest thing to having you there," Janet said.

Angelina searched Janet's expression for an echo of her old desire. She found, instead, a kind of soft awe, as if Janet were listening to a piece of music that had reached a sudden high note of glass-cutting beauty and held it for far longer than seemed natural, or even entirely pleasant.

Angelina rubbed her left wrist. "The dresses are really elegant. I like the gold stitch."

Janet folded her hands together around her plastic cup. "I was thinking, you know, about that kind of Japanese pottery—those bowls that are broken, and when they mend them, they put the band of gold where the crack was. It's probably corny."

"Does the white, like, symbolize—"

"I guess I was thinking about bones, yeah," Janet said.

"Well, look at me. I'm a muse."

"You can put that on your website. Angelina Moltisanti: Artist. Designer. Muse."

"Maybe someday, I'll link to your debut Fashion Week collection."

"I hope so," Janet said.

Angelina glanced up at the clock; breaktime ticked down to a precious few minutes. "Hey, listen. I wanted you to know. I have an appointment for therapy. It's at that women's law center. So I guess, when you see Frankie, you can tell her I said thanks. And also, maybe, tell her that I'm sorry for—well, everyone knows, right? What I should be sorry for."

Janet didn't say anything. She only nodded.

"Because I'm sorry."

Angelina folded her left hand into a soft fist, cradled it in her right palm. Her right thumb swept down her still-healing wrist, working little circles between the carpal tunnel. The gesture created a voluptuous sense of pain, one that made her aware of the softness of her physical self. She closed her eyes, waited for that familiar kick of revulsion. Instead, she felt a warmth she could only call gratitude. Through the thickness of the pain, she could still feel her pulse.

"One of the things that I want to think about in therapy is, you know, filing charges. I guess, to sort of parse out what all of that might mean, or how it would work."

"If that's what you want," Janet said. "You know I think it's good. How do you feel?"

"Like Wonder Woman, only bleak and shitty and helpless," Angelina said.

"You're not any of those things. At least not forever."

Janet said she'd be happy to support Angelina if she needed someone to listen or accompany her to court. Angelina asked if Janet wouldn't mind coming with her to the SPCA clinic tomorrow— Valentina was okay, she just needed a check-up and the clinic was cheap. Unfortunately, the clinic was at an intersection about two miles away from her father's office. Tomorrow was a Thursday, and her father would be chained to his desk, most likely. But still, she had to admit, she was a little nervous.

Janet shook her head. "I can't. Being around Valentina, it would just remind me, you know, of our little family of three."

"I get it," Angelina said. She smiled, hoping to hide the heat in her eyes as it threatened to turn liquid.

Janet stood up to leave. She took Angelina's left hand between both of her hands and pressed down, once. The pressure was a hard wave that rolled over the spots that were still tender and sore before gently receding back into the ocean of Angelina's blood.

———

Angelina arrived at the SPCA clinic early, but she'd forgotten to bring in a stool sample. The veterinary assistant handed her a baggie and nodded toward the door.

The summer air was at its thickest. Normally, she hated this heat, rued thighs and under-breasts chafed with sweat. Today, though, she walked on the narrow strip of grass near the bustling roadway, enjoying the contrast of hard black and delicate green. Those colors had marked her body. They were fading now. Her wrist. Her eye. She turned her face up toward the sun, and the sound of Valentina sniffing aligned with the slow throb of heat through her skin.

A loud honk startled her. She looked toward the road and saw her father's Pathfinder, her father's face through the windshield, heading toward the stoplight. He looked surprised. He looked angry. He looked afraid. She had a flash of that night at the kitchen sink when she was sixteen: she heard him tell her to hold fucking still; only his voice splintered around *still*—like he wasn't quite certain he knew what he'd do if she didn't. She'd never considered that he was afraid. Constantly afraid.

He slowed down for a moment, as if he'd pull over near her. She was not frightened. All the blood in her body marshaled toward her heart and held it in a tight, protective fist. She felt her chest expand; her feet spread firmly on the pavement—just as she'd stood on that kitchen tile all those years ago. She shook her head: no. Mouthed the word at him. He sped up, raced through a red light.

Valentina pressed herself against Angelina's side, licked her left hand.

"It'll be okay," Angelina said. "Whatever it is, it'll be okay."

That fist around her heart slowly spread its fingers and let go.

ACKNOWLEDGMENTS

THIS BOOK WOULD NOT EXIST without the support, nurturing, and love of so many people, but I could not start a proper acknowledgments page without expressing my profound and abiding gratitude to my brother, Billy, who has been a true and steadfast rock for the entire family. I also thank my father, who vested me with a spark of emotion that I have turned into a righteous fire. When I was a younger woman, Freda and Charles Levie once gave me a card that read, simply, "You Will Write a Book Someday," and because of their faith in me, I have.

I owe an immeasurable debt to Madison Smartt Bell, my first teacher and mentor, who always believed in this firecracker of a novel.

Thank you to Michelle Dotter and Steve Gillis and the entire team at Dzanc Books, who have given me, and this story, the most lovely and gracious home.

Blessed be to my sister witches: Gina Frangello, Zoe Zolbrod, Amy Monticello, and Sarah Einstein, who championed this book through many ideas and drafts.

Juvy Santos was one of my first friends in life, and she remains one of my first readers.

I'm grateful to Eric Burnstein for his friendship and his wisdom. I thank Allison McCarthy for her unfailing compassion and enthusiasm, for keeping the embers of my hope stoked through some long years.

I owe much to Sarah Hepola, one of my first and formative heroines and teachers. I'm grateful to Tabitha Blankenbiller; Cindy Lamothe;

Michele Filgate; Jen Pastiloff; Lindsey Romain; Matt Zoller Seitz; Sharyn Blum; Jolie Mandelbaum; Shannon Barber; Nairobi Collins; Janice Gary; Matthew Earls; Gloria Shin; Zoe Whiting; Sean Griffith; Danielle Evans; Amber Sparks; Jordan Rosenfeld; Laura Albert; Liz Prato; Chantrese Lester; LaVerne McNeal; Jen Michalski; Melanie Boyer; Jonathan Harper; Melissa Reddish; Erika Salomon; Kim Smith; Trish Broome; Betsy Wexler; Brad Tibbils; Dean Gamble; Victoria Barrett; Jackson Miller; Lisa Borders; and Greg Olear.

I'm so appreciative of my blurbers, who took time away from their own work to offer such kind and generous words about mine.

I am also indebted to Ilana Massad; Rachel Vorona Cote; Briallen Hopper; Emma Copley Eisenberg; Evette Dionne; Kathleen Smith; Lucie Britsch; and Keah Brown—I couldn't think of a finer group to help launch a book. I'm grateful to Karen Stefano, who took me under her wing and offered me advice about how to bring a book into the world.